STORM OVER JERUSALEM

JJ FRINSEL

First published by Den Hertog, Houten, The Netherlands, in Dutch as
Storm over Jeruzalem, translated and published with permission.
Translators: W&A Amoraal
Design and layout: E Visser

Pro Ecclesia Publishers
Armadale, Western Australia

CHAPTER 1

RAPHA BOLTED THE FRONT door of his house and set out to make a thorough inspection of the building, in case an intruder had slipped inside to hide in a dark corner. This daily routine made his heart pound in his chest. He tried to suppress cries of terror when, in his imagination, he saw dark shadows which made him tremble with fear.

With a club in one hand and a smoky oil lamp in the other, he inspected the house room by room, all the while mumbling softly. Whenever he heard a noise, or his near-sighted eyes fooled him into thinking he saw some threatening figure, he would crouch down and wave his club around in self-defence. Breaking out in a cold sweat he would find it hard to gather the courage to come to his senses again.

The house was large and old. And it held a secret…

It had been his parents' house and he had inherited it from them. But well before that it had been a family estate. Rapha would never have bought such a large and expensive house for himself. The thought alone made him feel faint! However, he was glad that his parents had left it to him…

Wait! Was that something moving over there? The bony fingers holding the lamp shook, which made the shadows on the wall dance around like giant bats. Having been through this situation so often before, he was almost sure that it was only his imagination. It was triggered by his fear of the unknown, a premonition that one day there would really be someone there.

The house kept a secret that only he knew.

It had some small rooms below ground, to which the entrance was so well hidden that no one would ever discover them. He was convinced of it. Fully convinced! Well, that is to say... unless someone would actually see him opening the entrance. There was, however, this torturous suspicion that besides his father there might have been someone else who knew the secret. Every time again he tried to push that thought away, but never succeeded. That's why he always felt compelled to make that scary inspection of his house before he could approach the well-hidden entrance. And even then, he would still feel watched. He would never lose that chilling fear of suddenly being found out.

That evening, having made sure that he was alone, Rapha went down again into the underground rooms. Once there, he would indulge in the only joy his miserable heart nurtured - the sight of his earthly goods. Although his parents had certainly not been poor Jews, Rapha had amassed a fortune that even a king would have been proud of. He experienced his daily time in his underground treasure room like a priest in the holy place. This is where his heart was, where he enjoyed the only delight that could satisfy his malnourished soul, where he spent hours in great adoration.

Money... gold and silver... He was convinced that he had gained it by hard work and sensible trading; by being frugal and leading a sober existence. In reality, Rapha was known in Jerusalem as a merciless moneylender, capable of robbing both widow and orphan of their last penny. Woe to the poor soul who, driven by need, fell prey to his greedy hands. He had no mercy. Not people but wealth was his concern. Nothing else kept him awake.

A terrible thunderbolt awoke him from his ecstasy and brought him back to reality. The ground beneath his feet shook and so did Rapha. The fact that the sound of the thunderbolt had even penetrated his underground sanctuary, made him realise that a severe thunderstorm must have started in the city above. Shivering, he carefully hid his treasures and left his hiding place. The night sky of Jerusalem was lit by bright flashes of lightning. A deafening thunder rumbled through the skies.

But even more frightening and scarier than death itself, was the sound he suddenly picked up from among the violent exhibition of nature. It was a man's loud cry of anguish, a voice which proclaimed, 'Woe to Jerusalem!'

Rapha sat down and pressed his hands against his ears. He preferred to believe that he had misheard and tried to calm himself by thinking about all his money.

"There's some heavy weather rolling in," said Shobal, pointing at the sky. "Just look at those clouds. They're hanging over the city like the sins of Israel hanging over the people. Has the donkey been brought in Thomas?"

The son of the potter nodded. "It's in the stable and has plenty of fodder."

"And water?"

"Water as well." Looking up at the skies he added, "And later on he'll have even more."

"Very good. And did old Isaac get the pots he had ordered?"

"I brought them to him just before noon."

"Well, that's it then for today. Let's go inside."

During dinner the storm broke. It could have been foreseen that the humid and unsettled weather would end in a storm, but it arrived so suddenly that the little ones were rather shaken by the first thunderbolt. Miriam, a small toddler, burst into tears as she clung to her mother in fear. Joseph, who was already ten, tried to be very brave. "It's all okay," he said, "but it's certainly impressive."

"Lightning can strike you know," said Thomas.

"Be quiet!" Mother warned.

"This sort of heavy weather always has a message for us," said the potter. "It certainly speaks to me. It makes a human being feel very small. I always have to think of Job, who had so many questions to ask of God. He had to endure terrible suffering in his life, and his friends only made things worse for him. And then the Lord answered him in the thunder."

"And what did the Lord say?" asked Joseph curiously, in between two thunderbolts.

"You ask too many questions," said Mother.

But Shobal answered that a person gains wisdom from asking questions and patiently related how, in one day, Job had lost all his children and all his possessions. He then became involved in an exchange of words with the Almighty. In so far as he had examined himself, Job didn't think he had done anything deserving such heavy punishment. Yet his close friends told him that he was wrong. In their opinion, a truly righteous person would never experience such disasters. In utter despair, Job appealed to God. Then the Lord spoke in the thunder and made Job understand how small and limited his human insights were and how unfathomable his Creator is.

"Was that all?" asked Joseph.

"Careful how you speak!" warned Mother.

"The very fact that the Lord wanted to speak to a human being was already a great miracle," Shobal patiently explained. "In that way Job learned to know the Lord as the only One to Whom we can fully entrust ourselves. Even when things happen which perplex us and which we completely fail to understand."

"That's not easy I reckon," Joseph sighed, being more forthright than pious about it.

Mother shook her head.

Shobal stroked Joseph's curly hair. "Difficult indeed… you are right my boy. But the prophet Nahum said, 'The Lord is good, a refuge in times of trouble. He knows and cares for those who trust in Him.' And so, Job learned to know the Lord better, through thunder… As long as we cling to the knowledge that the Lord is good and intends everything for our good, then we'll never have to despair."

In spite of the rumblings of the thunder, Miriam had fallen asleep on Mother's lap.

"Just look at her," Thomas said tenderly.

"As long as you find the right place to seek shelter, your fear will disappear," instructed Shobal.

For just a moment there was no other noise than that of the pouring rain; water that flooded down into the storm drains via the roof, gutters and downpipes. And of course, the crashing of the thunder bolts.

Lightning will never strike the temple, Joseph thought. Not that he said it aloud because he was not even sure if he was allowed to think it. Perhaps Mother would have another fright. Not Father, he wasn't scared of anything. He was so big and strong…

The temple was the house of the Lord. Lightning was also from the Lord. And you would not let lightning strike your own house, would you? Oops! Now he had even scared himself. Would the others notice that he had these strange thoughts? He looked at his father. He was peacefully sitting there staring ahead, deep in thought.

Suddenly a great terror fell on all of them. It was a voice outside which managed to make itself heard despite the tumult of the elements! Loud crying that seemed a mixture of both anger and pain. A bone-chilling lamentation over Jerusalem.

Mother turned pale. Shobal stood up and went to the door. He could only just make out a lone figure, moving on down the street, faint in the light of a lightning flash. A little later he heard that heart-rending lamentation again from afar.

Deep in thought Shobal came back to his family. The children kept quiet. Their eyes were on him. He shrugged his shoulders.

"Why does anyone go out in this weather?" Mother sighed.

"Did you hear what he was shouting? It sounded rather eerie."

"A voice against Jerusalem and against the Temple…," Thomas said hesitantly. "That is the only thing I could make out."

"I just hope it wasn't a prophet," said Shobal.

They looked up at him in surprise. But on his face they could only see confusion and inner turmoil.

"Well, well, I just made it back in time," Gedor exclaimed. He blew away the rain drops that streamed across his face and onto his lips. Taking off his coat he wrung the water from it. His wife looked at him with some displeasure.

"You call that just in time? If I were in your place, I would have said, 'I just did not make it on time.'"

"Alas you're right once again darling. I thought I could keep ahead of the storm but in the end, I just couldn't make it. Still, I ran as fast as I could!"

"You're getting too old for that."

"Getting too old for what?"

"To be running! It can be dangerous in your old age."

"Old age? I can still jump over the table, would you believe?"

"No, I can't believe it. And if I were you, I wouldn't even try it. You're likely to break your neck if you did and …"

"And what else?"

"Okay then," Tirza laughed, "and you're too precious to me to be doing that."

"It makes me happy to hear it. From now on I'll be more careful and keep a better eye on the weather."

"You even saw that rainstorm coming! But once you men start talking together…ah well, just go and put on some dry clothes now. And give those wet ones to me."

"Tirza you're a darling."

"Yes, I know. If I can be of service to you, you can talk very nicely. Go, hurry up now. Silla is preparing the food and it's just about ready."

"Okay then, if I'm not allowed to tell you how much I love you, I'll think of another way." He dropped the wet coat, took hold of her and pulled her to himself and kissed her. "I'll be back in a minute."

The rain kept pouring down, the thunder rolled around and there was plenty of lightning. "It hasn't been this bad for a long time," said Silla. "I'm glad that the roof of my bedroom was repaired just in time. It leaked quite badly, if you recall?" She smiled warmly at Gedor. He in turn nearly choked on an olive which he had just popped into his mouth. His face turned pink and he stood up, somewhat flustered.

"That's right; I was going to do that wasn't I?" he stammered.

"You even promised to do it!" said Tirza. "Months ago …".

"Yes, I know, that's true. Not sure how I could have forgotten it. Oh, dear child, I'm so very sorry about it! I will quickly go and have a look if we can do something about it. Even if it's a temporary fix."

"Some bowls and pots under the leaks you mean," Tirza said scathingly. "Is that what you mean? Keep in mind that in this weather they fill up very fast!"

"But we must do something! If not, water will run everywhere."

"What you say is true, Gedor. 'We' had to do something about it. If 'we' had not done something about it, Silla and I would not be sitting here so calmly. It's just as well that 'we' asked a carpenter to come and fix it about a week ago. He repaired the roof and didn't even take long to do it. So just relax now, keep eating and don't choke."

"I feel very ashamed," sighed Gedor and sat down at the dinner table again. "If I didn't have you two running the household, our house would be going to ruin."

"Better not promise things anymore," Tirza suggested. "Better not to promise, than to make a promise and not keep it."

Gedor winked at Silla. "What a wise aunt you have, hey? If I hadn't known that the Preacher had said those words, I would pay homage to her."

"You'd better not do that, or I may have to help you stand up again," Tirza teased. "You're not that flexible anymore darling. You should watch out for your back. Besides you've never been that agile anyway."

"In the olden days wives would not dare to speak like that to their husbands," Gedor sighed. "When Israel was still living in tents, the women had their own tent. And I can't really understand why we got rid of that custom."

"Oh, I can tell you why!" his wife replied. "It's because our great-grandmothers were fed up with being called out for every little thing that needed doing. And were they really so subordinate back then? I'm not so sure. Mother Sarah took care of many things and was not shy of telling Abraham what he should and should not be doing."

"But he often disagreed with her," Gedor objected.

"That may be so, but he often gave in anyway."

"I'm not so sure that was very wise of him…" Gedor said doubtfully.

"Doesn't the Torah teach us that Abraham was told to 'do all that Sarah tells you, listen to her voice, because in Isaac your seed shall be named'?" Tirza asked teasingly.

Gedor raised his hands and rolled his eyes, in a dramatic display. "My own wife!" he exclaimed. "She speaks like one of the scribes! No, even better, she speaks like Solomon!" He looked at her and clapped his hands. "Just as well that in our congregation you are not allowed to teach. If you could, I wouldn't dare to go there anymore. I can just about hear them say already, 'Is that your wife over there? How come she married such a dumb husband?' You set a trap for me with all that talk about Mother Sarah. I surrender. But what should Silla make of all this? My authority has all but disappeared. Silla, what do you think? I'm no match for your aunt, but do you at least still need me a little bit? No, the roof has already been repaired… and you can read and write already too. What's left to be done? In what way can I still be useful?"

Silla enjoyed the innocent teasing of her uncle and aunt. The childless couple had taken her in when she was thirteen years old because living at home had become impossible for her. Her faith in Jesus of Nazareth as the Messiah of Israel, had caused tension in the family, because her father and her four brothers considered the Christian faith to be a false doctrine.

She was the youngest and the only daughter, and she had lost her mother early on in her life. Her father who in his heart loved Silla deeply, was a rigid and stubborn man. In his anger over her continued Christian faith, which he experienced as a personal humiliation, he had eventually wanted to expel her from the family. He was supported in this intent by his sons. They were sympathisers with the Zealot movement, a small subgroup of the Pharisees. These Zealots were fanatics who dreamed of an insurrection against the Romans so that their hated yoke could be cast off forever.

Gedor, the brother of her father, had lovingly taken her in. In the given circumstances she couldn't have wished for better. Gedor and Tirza were Christians and with them Silla could confess her faith, something that was not possible in her parental home. In a very painful way, she had experienced how following her Saviour, could cause a break in family relations. Not only was she made to leave her parental home, but she was not even welcome to visit there. The same applied to her uncle and aunt. They were looked upon as outcasts. And yet faith in Jesus Christ was exactly the fulfilment of the promises in the Torah. Through God's Spirit, Silla was convinced both of the truth of the Gospel and of having chosen the right path. However, that didn't take away the pain, and she daily prayed the Lord to work in the hearts of her father and brothers the miracle of conversion which had also made her own life so rich. She was now fifteen years old and an exceptionally pretty girl.

"What was that?" Tirza suddenly asked.

"What?" asked Gedor.

"That noise…"

"I didn't notice it."

"Oh, but I heard something unusual."

"It's bucketing down and there is a thunderstorm going on." Gedor shrugged his shoulders. "The house is full of noises."

"It sounded like someone was yelling. It came from outside, I'm sure of it," Tirza insisted.

"I also thought I heard something," Silla said in support of her aunt.

"Not a soul would be game enough to venture outside in such weather," Gedor replied, "even the dogs manage to find a place to crawl away in or under. Perhaps you heard the howling of one of them."

Then suddenly all three heard it. A call, so loud that it startled them. It was coming from very close by. It was as if someone was standing right in front of their house and shouting out loud. Even before they could understand the words, a certain dread came upon them. It was judgement that was being proclaimed.

"A voice from the East… and a voice from the West… A voice from all four directions… A voice against Jerusalem and the Temple. A voice against the newly-wed men and women… A voice against this entire population…"

The combination of the sound of thunder bolts and pelting rain, together with the woes proclaimed, formed such a powerful message that it made them all tremble. "What could that mean?" Tirza wondered aloud. There was fear in her voice.

"It certainly didn't sound very uplifting," Gedor had to admit.

Silla had gone to the door. Under the shelter of the portico, she tried to discover the messenger. The pouring rain and darkness prevented it.

"In any case, he wasn't looking for shelter," she remarked when she returned to the living room.

"Neither was it the voice of a drunkard," Gedor said. But Tirza voiced what both the others were wondering as well, "Could this be a messenger? A prophet of doom?"

Would the measure be full?

"Woe, woe unto you Jerusalem…"

What did it mean?

Pallu looked questioningly at his brothers.

"Some fool or other," was Nimsi's opinion.

"With the voice of a trumpet," Hassub added.

"And with a message I'm not very keen to hear," Nadab said. "It certainly puts the wind up everyone! Some crazy fellow again, who's come up with some weird idea."

"Well, he certainly chose the right weather to scare people out of their wits. You have to admit that he hasn't made it easy for himself. He's likely to catch a cold or something worse."

"That would probably be best for him, else he might somehow come to a violent end. Such fellows discourage the people, and we can well do without that. It never seems to enter their minds to go and try that out on the Romans."

"They would make a quick end of it."

"I don't blame them."

"A well-aimed stone directed at his head, that will make him shut up."

"And who is going to cast that stone?"

"If it's for a good cause, I wouldn't shy away from it."

"All the same it didn't sound very nice."

"I thought we had agreed on that already."

"But what I mean is… just imagine…"

"I know what you mean, but I won't imagine anything. This is the sort of prophet we can well do without. It doesn't scare the Romans. They only respect the language of the sword."

The message of the doomsday prophet had also reached the ears of Silla's brothers.

"Woe… woe unto Jerusalem… A voice against this entire people."

In the year 62 of the Christian calendar, a man appeared in the temple in Jerusalem during the celebration of the feast of Tabernacles. He caused quite a stir with his doomsday preaching. The Jewish historian, Flavius Josephus, tells us how this man, named Jesus the son of Ananias, would from that time on, speak out day and night, continually traversing all the streets and alleys in Jerusalem.

While people in this busy city were used to a fair bit of excitement, for some of them this doomsday preaching became too much, and the man was arrested and flogged. He took this punishment without complaint and undeterred he resumed his preaching. The government also dealt with him, and he was led before Albinus, who in those days was governor over Judea. Albinus had the prophet beaten with rods till he bled. But to no avail. The man did not shed a tear and never begged for mercy. After every lash he only said, "Woe unto you Jerusalem!"

And when the governor asked him who he was, where he came from and why he preached like that, he did not utter a word.

Albinus eventually regarded him as a halfwit and released him, only to see the prophet resume his work of preaching.

According to Flavius Josephus the man continued this preaching without interruption, for seven years and five months, never complaining or shouting at those who beat him and tried to silence him. Neither did he thank those who, out of compassion, gave him food to eat.

CHAPTER 2

FLAT ON HIS BELLY, his head supported in his hands, Caleb watched the training exercises. Just outside their camp, the Romans performed mock battles. And this was not something for the faint hearted. The small group of soldiers had set up camp on the beach of the Sea of Galilee. The men seemed to be attacking each other so intensely that it could easily be taken for real. While they were very noisy during these fights, Caleb knew that all the slashes were either evaded or fended off with their shields. Yet these fights were not without danger. He had observed once that a soldier was accidentally injured, and blood was shed. It certainly was not a game. For these men this brutal training meant the difference between life and death. In man-to-man combat on the battlefield, it was essential to be in top shape. Not only brute force and agility but also endurance was very important. That's why hardly a day went by without intense training.

Keep in mind that a soldier's life was already very tough. For apart from these mock battles there were the long marches, the building of roads and construction of fortifications that demanded much of their energy. In addition, there was all the work of setting up and breaking down of the encampments.

Caleb counted the horses which were nicely lined up in a row, side by side. Yes, it seemed much better to him to be a horseman. Not only would travelling be more comfortable, but also in battle, the horse was an advantage. High on horseback you had a good overview of the situation. And the cavalry was certainly to be feared.

Suddenly, orders were heard and the soldiers stopped their training. One of the men said something that made the others laugh and look in Caleb's direction. The latter jumped up to make a quick getaway, but the soldiers called out to him that he need not be afraid and motioned him to come closer. Caleb hesitated for a moment. What would they do if he ran away?

A young soldier took a few steps towards him. "Why do you suddenly go all shy?" he asked with a smile. "You've been lying there all along, haven't you?"

Some of the others joined him.

"Do you like fighting?" It was a solidly built soldier who asked him the question, yet he had a kind face. "Did you want to learn the art of fighting?"

"We'd better be careful! You might eventually be chasing us out of the country, hey Jew?"

The men had a good laugh and Caleb half-heartedly laughed along. But he didn't say a word.

"He doesn't understand us."

"Oh, he understands us all right. Jews understand everything, except the things they don't want to hear."

"Hey Jew, be honest, what did you think of that? You came here to have a look at the fighting, didn't you?"

"Do your parents know that you came here?"

"What has that got to do with it? Don't give the boy a hard time."

"That's not the point. But you know how fanatical these Jews are. I bet he wasn't even allowed to come here from his father."

"When you were a lad, did you never do something your father had forbidden?"

"He still does, else he wouldn't have joined the army," sneered another.

"Ah, food is being served," interrupted another soldier. "Would you like to have something to eat with us?" he asked. He noticed how the boy was in two minds.

"Maybe he isn't allowed to do that either," the other soldier started again.

"Lamb's stew? Why wouldn't he be allowed to eat that?"

"I don't know. Perhaps it's unclean in their eyes. They're very particular with food."

"You seem to know a lot about it."

"Once you've been in this country for a while and keep your eyes and ears open, it's amazing the things you pick up."

"But he'll have a piece of bread, won't he? When I was that age, I could always eat some bread."

They took Caleb to their group.

"Did they make you a prisoner of war?" someone quipped.

Caleb didn't know how to respond to that. He felt far from comfortable. All the same, it was very exciting to be among these soldiers. He ate the bread they gave him and listened to their rough conversations. There was a heavy odour of sweat and leather hanging around the men, who sat on the ground as they ate their meal.

They looked out over the water where some small boats were sailing.

When they asked him again where he lived, he replied that he was tending the sheep and travelling around with them. They were surprised that he could so easily neglect the animals and leave them by themselves.

No, no, he was working together with his brother.

Caleb gave as little information as possible.

At home he had been told to be careful when talking to the invaders. There was a deep-seated hatred against the Romans in his family but although he'd grown up in that environment, the soldiers held a certain attraction for him. He actually felt rather guilty that despite his upbringing something about them fascinated him. They were the enemy and yet he admired them. Was that bad?

Observing them from close by, they turned out to be like any other people. He pondered about the recent stories of skirmishes that seemed to happen more frequently between the Romans and the Jewish rebels. A rebellion was brewing. Galileans were trying to free themselves from their enemies. At home Caleb had heard bits and pieces about it, although this was not openly talked about. But sometimes certain men came to their house, who talked with his father for hours on end. He wasn't allowed to be present when that happened.

And now he was here, sitting among the Romans who had captured nearly all the world. Was that treason? All he had done was observe them. But they had spotted him, and he couldn't very well have run off, could he? They were friendly to him, and he most certainly wouldn't tell them any secrets. He couldn't imagine that such men were capable of the horrific violence he had heard about.

They supposedly bashed to death women, children and the elderly when they entered a city. Caleb looked at the men again and could hardly believe those stories.

In the meantime, several fishing boats had come to shore, and the fishermen unloaded their catch.

"Fresh fish," commented one soldier. "I could eat some of that. Makes a good change from the barley stew and lamb's broth."

"I agree," another chipped in, "but I'm not sure they'll want to sell us some."

"Why not? Business is business. Don't you think they'd want to earn some money? They wouldn't go fishing for the sport of it."

"If they wanted to sell us some fish, they would have come ashore a bit closer to us, but I think they're evading us."

"We'll see about that. Who's coming to get us some fish?"

Together with some of his companions he set off to the fishermen.

"Had a good catch?"

There was no answer but from the rigid expression on the faces of the fishermen it was obvious that his companion had judged the situation correctly.

"We would like to buy some fish from you."

The fishermen feigned deafness and that didn't have a good effect on the jovial Roman soldiers.

"Is it asking too much to expect a polite answer at least?"

"This fish has already been sold," one of the older fishermen replied.

"The whole lot? Surely you can spare us enough for a good meal? There isn't much variation in our soldiers' menu. We'll pay well of course."

The soldier had tried hard to speak in a pacifying tone and now rummaged through his uniform and produced some money.

"They've been sold already!"

The soldier looked at the fishermen in disbelief, while his companion who had warned him, said in an irritated manner, "I told you they wouldn't want to sell to us. Come, and let them choke on their fish."

"And make us the laughingstock of these Jews? No way! If they don't like the friendly way, then we'll do it the hard way! We just confiscate a basket of fish. And I'd like to see one of those Jews trying to stop me!"

The soldier grabbed one of the baskets which the fishermen had carried ashore. But even before he could lift it onto his shoulder, one of the fishermen had also taken hold of it. They glared at each other over the basket.

"Let go!" the soldier commanded.

The fisherman did not respond but continued to look straight in his eyes.

"I warn you to let go of the basket."

"Our basket… our fish… We won't be robbed."

"We'll pay you for it!"

"This fish is not for sale. We told you that already! We didn't approach you to sell to you. Try and catch your own."

"I commandeer this fish!" the soldier yelled in a rage and pulled the basket with force toward himself.

The fisherman appeared to have anticipated that move and instead of resisting, he let go of the basket. As a result, the soldier tumbled backward and fell to the ground, covered with the contents of the basket. For a brief moment he lay there in shock amid the slippery fish. Perhaps it would have ended well if some of his companions hadn't burst into laughter. But now the irked man jumped to his feet and before the fisherman could make his getaway, the soldier laid hold of him and punched him on the jaw with such force that he dropped to the ground unconscious.

One of the other fishermen, a younger man, drew his dagger and wanted to attack the Roman, but the others managed just in time, to restrain him. They understood it would only make things worse and they wouldn't stand a chance against the soldiers. Besides, the soldiers had many of their mates close by. They led the hot-headed youngster away and helped their friend, who had in the meantime regained consciousness, to his feet. Under an eerie silence, the fishermen departed with their nets and fish, closely observed by the enraged Romans.

The incident had shocked Caleb. After he re-joined his older brother with the sheep, he told him all about it.

"What was your business there with the Romans? They're our enemies."

"I was just having a look. They were actually rather nice."

"Nice? Father had better not hear you talk like that."

"All they wanted to do was buy some fish, but the fishermen didn't let them. They said the fish had been sold already."

"Good on them; let those Romans catch their own fish."

"Why would you not sell them any fish?" Caleb asked. "They didn't mean any harm. They're just ordinary people."

"Oh really?" His brother looked at him in disdain. "Have you ever wondered what they are doing here? They don't belong here Caleb. You know that, right? They've been here far too long already. It's about time they disappeared."

"They'll never go away."

"Not of their own accord, I agree… How many of them were there in that camp?"

"I didn't count them. I did count the horses; there were ten. But there were more soldiers than horses, I know that much. Maybe about four times as many. It's only a small camp. You would have seen that yourself when we passed by."

"Where are they going?"

"They didn't talk about that. Tonight is their last night here."

Galilee turned out to be a territory that was not very favourable to the Romans' health. During the night, the small camp near the sea was attacked. The sentries were silenced, and the others were killed in their sleep. Armed men appeared out of the darkness, and silently executed their horrific deeds. Quickly they took the soldiers' horses, weapons and anything else that looked useful and vanished into the darkness again. Was this the work of a band of robbers? Or were the guilty men members of the fanatical Zealots?

These sorts of attacks were of course not left unpunished, and the Romans tried hard to find the culprits. Many innocent citizens were killed in the process but that was only advantageous for the cause of the Zealots. Through these deaths, the hatred towards the Romans only grew and as a result more people joined the party of the Zealots or the bands of robbers. Actually, it became increasingly difficult to tell the difference between the two. In cruelty they were equals. And the people suffered both from the terror of their rebellious fellow citizens as well as under the retaliatory expeditions of the Romans. Villages and cities were destroyed. Homes were plundered and burnt with fire. More and more blood was shed in Israel.

The Jewish people became increasingly divided, and rebels put growing pressure on their countrymen. Although many indeed longed for complete national independence, a majority very much doubted that an uprising against the Romans could ever be successful. By no means everyone was prepared to risk money, possessions and life itself for a cause which was predictably doomed to fail. It would take nothing short of a miracle to defeat the Romans. Those who stood to gain from the Roman occupation, naturally disliked the idea of a battle. But there were others, not motivated by short term gain or personal advantage, who considered that the time was not ready for open resistance. However, there were several factors at play which threatened to push them toward a disastrous conclusion. The Roman consul Florus was a tactless man. He wanted to enrich himself by stealing the temple treasures, but by doing so, he brought Jewish blood to a boiling point. And the cruel behaviour of his soldiers, which he had for a while allowed against the population of Jerusalem, made the people's anger boil over.

The Jewish rebels used these conflicts for their own purpose: to keep the spirit of resistance alive and even to stimulate it. At the same time, they continued to terrorise that part of the population that did not want to participate in the resistance. And so, against their expressed will, many were dragged along in an adventure that was doomed to end in a gigantic catastrophe. Uncertainty, hatred and fear, destroyed their society. Something had been set in motion which could no longer be controlled.

During the final years of Emperor Nero's reign, the situation became unbearable.

The Roman consul of Syria tried several times to restore order and peace in Jerusalem and the surrounding regions, but without success. Suffering great losses in soldiers and equipment, he had to retreat. An all-out war seemed inevitable. Citizens who could foresee this escalation, started to leave Jerusalem. They were accompanied by the prophetic voice which year after year, could be heard in the streets: "Woe… Woe… A voice against Jerusalem and the temple…"

CHAPTER 3

A S ELIPHELET STARTED SPEAKING a profound silence fell on the meeting. All attention was directed at the honourable, grey headed man. The mere fact that he had not only known the apostles, but also the Lord Jesus Himself, gave him a certain authority. To be sure, at the time he had been only a half-hearted follower. But now, as an ear and eyewitness, old Eliphelet was able to relate many matters that had been told about Jesus of Nazareth. He was aware of the standing this gave him among his hearers. They noticed that he chose his words carefully, especially when describing the work which the Lord had done and the words which He had spoken.

Eliphelet didn't conceal the fact that after Jesus had risen from the dead, He needed to go to great lengths to overcome the unbelief of His disciples. And he himself was also one of those early Christians who had not stood out for their exemplary trust and faith – a fact that was reason for his present humbleness. But all this happened decades ago and the number of witnesses like himself, was dwindling. He understood that it was of utmost importance to accurately pass on to the next generation what he had heard with his own ears and what he had seen with his own eyes. He was thankful for the clarity of mind given to him and understood that this was special grace and not something simply for his own personal enjoyment. Rather, it was given to him so that he should serve the congregation, which put a great responsibility on him. The words which he had heard from the Saviour's mouth, were indelibly etched into his mind. It was clear to him that this could only be the work of the Holy Spirit. Guided by that same conviction, the Lord's apostles had endeavoured to put into writing what had been revealed in and about Christ. God kept watch over His Word. The gospel would continue its journey throughout the world.

Truly, it was a world that had been turned upside down.

Confusion ruled in Israel. In many places fighting had broken out. The country was in chaos and in Jerusalem there was growing resistance toward the Romans. Leading Jews, who had a better understanding of the situation and considered that a rebellion would not succeed, were being pushed aside or even murdered.

Eliphelet gave a brief outline of the current situation which reminded him and the other elders of what the Saviour had prophesied about Jerusalem. How at His triumphant entry into Jerusalem, He had mourned for her and prophesied that the days would come that her enemies would lay siegeworks against her. They would encircle Jerusalem, distress her from all sides, and raze her to the ground! Not one stone would be left upon another. The city and its inhabitants would be trampled underfoot because they failed to recognise the goodness God had shown them in the past.

"It's not that time yet," Eliphelet said, "but if it keeps going like this, it won't take long before the emperor will give the command to crush the rebellion by force. When we think about the fall of our city and the destruction of its people, our hearts bleed. The judgement is deserved, we confess it, because the sins of Jerusalem are great. But if the Lord mourned when He declared this judgement, then it's fitting for us to mourn as well when the judgement comes. We also remember the words of the Saviour, that when we see Jerusalem being surrounded by armies, her destruction is nigh. Those who are in the city should move away. Those in Judea should flee to the mountains. And those living outside of Jerusalem's walls, in the fields, should not come inside to look for protection. Considering then the signs and times, we see that haughtiness increases. It's as if our people have been struck with blindness and have lost all perspective. They set out to fight the Romans with primitive weapons and expect the Lord to help them, while ignoring His admonitions. They believe they can take the fight to the Romans like David did against Goliath, without the sincerity and humbleness of that servant of the

Lord. Our prayers are for Jerusalem and for our people over whom this judgement has been announced. It's not bad luck that strikes us but rather the fulfilment of the prophecy. The hand of the Lord is in this, according to the words of our Lord Jesus Christ, when He said: 'And they will fall by the edge of the sword and be led away captive into all the nations. And Jerusalem will be trampled underfoot by Gentiles, until the times of the Gentiles are fulfilled.'

We have prayerfully considered what we ought to do," Eliphelet continued. "Of course, we will not participate in the rebellion against our oppressors. And the exodus of leaders and commoners shows clearly that there are people who think like we do. The proclamation of the doomsday-preacher, who for many years has walked our streets, is a warning to us. No matter how much we love our people, we may not participate in their evil works. We therefore urge all Christians to leave the city before it is too late, that they may find a safe place to stay. By doing so we can be a witness against our rebellious neighbours. Let's pray that they will take it to heart. We are preparing ourselves to go to Pella on the other side of the Jordan, but you can make your own arrangements and put your personal affairs in order. While doing so, try to keep calm and trust in the Lord."

Although the people were daily confronted with the topics and events of which Eliphelet spoke, they were deeply moved by his warnings. Especially the prophecies about Jerusalem's future had an impact. People could hardly believe that these things were meant literally. Once you had seen and admired the enormous stones of the temple building, it was hard to imagine that not one of them would be left upon another. Great silence fell upon the meeting when Eliphelet finished speaking.

"And what do I do with my house?" Shobal asked, breaking the silence. "My father and my grandfather lived there and ran their business from it."

Eliphelet, with great empathy and sadness, looked him in the eye. "I think all of us have some difficult goodbyes to say, my dear brother. We aren't leaving for just a few weeks or even years. If we understand the words of the Lord properly, there will be no return here until several generations have passed."

Among the people, suppressed crying could be heard.

"Remember Lot's wife!" Eliphelet exhorted them. "Those who cannot let go of the world, will go down with her. Much of what we hold dear, we shall have to let go. But whatever we may leave behind, we have the Lord's promise that He will be with us all our days, even to the end of the world.

Take from your possessions what you can salvage but say farewell to your homes. We still have each other. Don't we together make up the body of Christ? It will be a hard lesson for all of us. But remember that here on earth we have no lasting home. Did the Lord not say that He was leaving in order to prepare a place for us in His Father's house? Let us find our comfort in those words. Our home is above in heaven, and we shall share in His glory if we persevere in faith.

A man like you, brother Shobal, will find work anywhere. Your pots and urns are famous. I have no doubt you will find clay, and you will most certainly find buyers."

At last people began talking again. Some of them started to make plans for working together. Of course, many questions still needed an answer. Eliphelet listened patiently and gave good counsel. Possessions which could not be taken along were best sold to others.

CHAPTER 4

A LTHOUGH RAPHA DID NOT have friends, had no social interaction, and lived like a scared rat in his house, not much escaped him of the goings-on in Jerusalem. He had therefore also heard of the intentions of the Christian congregation, to abandon their city. Even the fact, that they didn't expect to return to their homes had come to his attention. What had immediately sprung to his businessman's mind was that this might be a fine opportunity to do some good deals. It had excited him greatly. Under normal circumstances he wouldn't have been at all interested in buying houses. But this was an exception! Although houses were not really his interest, he could smell profits. A great deal of money!

He wanted to make sure that he was the first one in. These Christians were unlikely to announce their departure and that could be to his benefit. Of course, when they did offer their homes for sale, they wouldn't be able to ask the highest price, so interested buyers would have the advantage. Yet to risk waiting that long, did not seem wise. He would then be one among many bidders and the very thought that he would have to bid against them, made him feel sick.

Rapha decided to be ahead of everyone else and one evening he headed off to Gedor who lived nearby.

It was rather a shock to Gedor when, after hearing the knock, he unbolted the door and saw a shadowy figure in the flickering light of the oil lamp.

"Shalom," Rapha's scratchy voice greeted him. Coming from his mouth however it sounded more like a proclamation of doom.

"I would like to have a word with you in private, Gedor. I mean, just the two of us."

Gedor let him in and took him to a small room where they could speak freely.

"Is there something I can do for you?" he asked.

Rapha wrung his bony hands together and with a sly expression in his watery, blood-shot eyes, he said, "Is it true that you are going to leave the city?"

"What makes you think that Rapha? Who told you?"

"Nobody. I heard a rumour about it. Here and there people are whispering things and sometimes you can make out what they're saying."

Cunningly he bowed his head toward Gedor and whispered, "Those are not matters one shouts aloud on the streets."

"In a way you are right," Gedor admitted. Meanwhile, he was wondering what this sinister man's intentions were. "We don't shout it from the rooftops, but neither do we try to keep it a secret. You know just as well as I do, that war is imminent. As Christian congregation we are of the opinion that we are better off taking our chances in the countryside than to remain here in Jerusalem. And there are others as well, who think like we do. We believe that the sins of our people will be visited upon Jerusalem, Rapha. The destruction of our city has been foretold. If you want to listen to sound advice, you should also leave the city."

He noticed how those last words frightened the miserly man, who cringed and shook. Gedor assumed that the prophesied doom over Jerusalem made Rapha react as he did, but he was wrong. The greedy man was thinking about his possessions and trembled with fear at the thought of having to part with them. Leaving the city had never entered his mind.

"I will stay here," he croaked.

"So, you're also one of those who do not believe the message of the doomsday prophet?"

"Lies! Lies!" Rapha squealed, gesturing wildly as if he wanted to fend off the warning with his skinny hands.

Gedor shook his head. "I don't think so Rapha. What he announced we have certainly deserved. The unrighteousness of the city is great. It's wrong to ignore the warnings the Lord has spoken previously. It's simply grace that we've been given so much time. Isn't it four years already since the prophet started his doomsday calls in the streets?"

"Exactly because of that… um, um… exactly because it's been so long already!" Rapha said with a nervous chuckle, cracking his bony fingers. "Can't you see something is wrong? It's not true…um, else it would've already come true, wouldn't it? It's wrong, it's a lie!"

"Well, we have different opinions on that," Gedor said quietly. "But apart from that, tell me, what is the purpose of your coming here?"

"If you are all going to leave the city…," Rapha paused and observed Gedor with a sly look in his eyes, "and don't count on ever coming back here again… well, if you truly believe that… then you may as well sell your house straight away. It's no longer any good to you."

"Ah, so that's what you're after. You want to buy my house?"

"Well, yes, as long as you're not asking too much for it," Rapha replied. "You'll understand that under the given circumstances it's not worth anything."

"How come?" Gedor asked innocently.

"You believe there'll be war soon, don't you? Imagine that your house will be destroyed. Who would want to buy a pile of rubble?"

Gedor grinned and said, "Who? The only one I can think of is you."

"Me?" Rapha looked at Gedor in disbelief.

"Yes you… Oh Rapha, you are such a generous person. You're prepared to put your money into a house that will most likely soon be plundered or even destroyed by fire? No one believes that. All you can think of, is making a lot of profit by exploiting the situation. But still, you make a valid point: the house is not worth anything anymore."

Gedor stared at him intently. "If you read the signs of the times properly Rapha, you'll realise that, probably soon, the same goes for all the houses in Jerusalem. Yours as well! It's time to start thinking about other things than only making money. Your soul is at stake; think about that! Dedicate your whole life to the Lord and not to earthly possessions. He who trusts in his riches shall fall, as we read in Proverbs. True riches are only found in the Lord."

"Stories and more stories," Rapha squeaked, annoyed. Still, he was visibly disturbed by what Gedor had said. "But what are you doing with your house now? You'll have to leave it behind in any case. And what will become of it, if it's not sold? Who will take care of it?"

"I don't know how things will go with my house Rapha, but I cannot sell it. My brother would have to give permission for that as well."

"Pagiel?" Rapha lamented. "That hot-head?"

"Ah, so you know him?" Gedor smiled. "Like I said, my brother is co-owner of the house. You may go and try to come to some arrangement with him."

"You could have told me straight away!" Rapha replied sharply.

"Well, you should have told me what you came for when you got here. I don't hold a grudge Rapha, but you're busy with the wrong things. Don't try to make a profit from our adversity. Understand that what is to come, will also affect you. Shed tears for Jerusalem and over our people. Humble yourself before God and repent..."

"Repent? Me...? Of what? Why? Pagiel! No way!"

Rapha was seething.

He jumped up and left without another word.

Walking close to the houses, he found his way home through the dark street. It was hard for him to get over his disappointment. Anger raged in his head. Now and then he violently swung his arms in the air. This kept him so busy that he had a great fright when he bumped into someone. That person's ghastly screech made him freeze for a moment. Then he stormed off, hands over his ears, followed only by the sad cry of the prophet.

CHAPTER 5

"WE'LL HAVE TO MAKE a visit to your father," said Gedor. "Well at least I'm hoping that he'll be willing to receive us. He needs to know that we're leaving Jerusalem and that our house will be empty. I'll have to make some arrangements with him, whether he likes it or not and we shall have to say our goodbyes. I fear it won't be an easy conversation with him. And no doubt your brothers will regard what we're about to do, as treason."

Silla nodded. She realised that the visit was necessary, but also painful. While she longed to see her father again it was very likely that this farewell would be a permanent one.

"We'll go with the three of us," Tirza decided.

"I don't think that's a good idea," responded Gedor.

"I thought you would say that, but I'm coming in any case," replied Tirza smiling. "Your brother is a difficult person, but I've always managed to get on with him."

"Oh really? I can still hear him yelling at you."

"That may be so, but that's just how he is. He's angry with us, but we're not angry with him, are we?"

The servant who received them was visibly confused. Being well informed about the family's relationships he wondered how this unannounced visit would turn out. Requesting them to wait in the foyer, he went to ask his master for instructions. As expected, they had to be very patient. Pagiel's first reaction would probably be a refusal to see them. And although he might not act on those feelings, it would probably take him some time to get over them.

Eventually the servant came to announce that his master was ready to receive them.

Even though the reception was chilly it was an emotional moment for Silla. Pagiel was alone in the room, sitting on his chair like a king on his throne. He left it to his brother to start the conversation since it was below his dignity to show curiosity. Yet Gedor noticed how Pagiel showed emotion when he looked at his daughter Silla, who had become a beautiful young woman. Gedor also knew that his brother was broken-hearted by her separation from him and her four brothers.

"We're grateful to you for receiving us Pagiel. You'll understand that we've come on a very important matter."

Since Pagiel didn't respond, Gedor continued. "It's been a long time since we spoke with one another and I'm not sure how you see the situation, but to us it's clear that war will break out soon."

Pagiel couldn't resist blurting out, "Only a fool could have missed that." He was facing his daughter and she thought he looked old and tired.

"In our estimation such a war will be disastrous for Israel, and Jerusalem won't escape a siege," Gedor continued. "For that reason, we've decided to leave the city before it's too late… We'll have to leave the house empty and already someone has heard this and offered to buy it. But seeing I don't have the sole right to decide, I've referred him to you. Whatever you decide Pagiel, is fine by me. We'll have to leave it behind even though it hurts us very much. Our intent is to seek refuge in the Trans-Jordan area. But first we wanted to say goodbye to you, and we hope that before we leave, you'll also farewell Silla."

Pagiel turned to look at his brother. He tried to master his rising temper, but it was obvious that a storm was building up inside him, and suddenly he burst out, "So, you just run away? You disappear, whereas soon every man will be needed to resist the Romans? I know that a rumour is going around that the sect you belong to, is preparing to leave the city. But I hadn't imagined that my own brother would stoop to such a treacherous deed. Or perhaps I knew you would! Are your actions not typical for the doctrine you adhere to? War will certainly come! But then Jerusalem will be the safest place to be. Have you forgotten that the Almighty Himself has His dwelling place here? Or doesn't that mean anything to you anymore either?"

Gedor tried to make his voice sound as friendly as possible when he replied, "Pagiel, you know the Scriptures just as well as I do. We had the same upbringing. Indeed, Jerusalem is the city of God. But consider that when all of Israel forgot about the Lord, the Philistines managed to capture the ark of the covenant and take it away. Israel's sins were great in those days! The sons of Eli, Hophni and Phinehas, were disloyal priests. They caused the people to sin. You remember that don't you? Wasn't it inevitable that punishment would follow? And we know how the Babylonians destroyed Jerusalem and the temple of Solomon with fire. That also didn't happen just by chance, did it? There was good reason for it, wasn't there? And spiritually, is Israel in a better position today? Personally, I think it's worse now than in those days! The treasury of the temple is overloaded with valuables. But what about the state of the Holy of Holies?"

"What do you mean by that?" Pagiel fumed. "Watch that you don't speak blasphemy Gedor."

"May God graciously prevent me from doing so," replied Gedor, "but you'll have to agree with me that the sins of Israel are crying out to heaven. Have you forgotten that the curtain of separation in the temple, was torn in two? Do you still refuse to believe that it was a sign from heaven?"

Pagiel was furious. "Have you come to taunt me?"

"Is it taunting you if I remind you of an event which every Jew spoke about?"

"Do you have any idea how old that curtain was and how heavy? There was also an earthquake on that day so it's quite understandable that it finally tore!"

"It wasn't just any tear Pagiel, but it tore right through the middle. And from top to bottom! Neither was it just any earthquake. It happened on the day that Jesus was crucified... at the same moment when Jesus gave up His Spirit."

"You know very well that I don't want to hear that name in my house!" replied a fuming Pagiel. "You know that very well! So why do you mention it again? I should never have let you into my house! I could have known this would happen."

He rose from his chair but suddenly gasped for air and sank back again. His face was beaded with sweat.

Silla jumped up and took him by the hand.

"Father… don't be so angry," she begged of him.

The sound of her voice seemed to calm him a little.

Tirza came with a cup of water. She wanted to help him drink but that was again below his dignity. He grunted as he took the cup, drank a little and freshened up his face with a moist cloth.

"You'll get yourself into trouble like that," said Tirza.

"That's a bit rich coming from you!" Pagiel retorted.

"I'm sorry," she responded calmly.

"But I don't accept that apology! You come here, push me to the limit, and then think it strange that I could die of stress? Just leave! Go and get out of Jerusalem. Leave us to suffer alone."

"Don't be unreasonable," Tirza said with a smile. "You said a minute ago that the safest place to be is Jerusalem. Why then will you have to suffer?"

"Unreasonable? I'm being unreasonable?"

Pagiel wanted to get up again, but Tirza held him back. "Well, you just proved that you're not deaf brother-in-law." She smiled as she spoke. "What a blessing… But now let go of your anger and pay some attention to your daughter. Gedor and I would have loved to have her as our own child. You are unreasonably stubborn. Had you been a little wiser, we would have missed out on some very happy years with Silla. Therefore, despite everything, I'm still grateful to you Pagiel. At the same time, I feel sorry for you. Oh, I know you're too stiff-necked to admit it, but the reason you agreed to see us today, is that Silla is with us. You have inflicted much pain on her and on yourself with that terrible stubbornness."

For a moment Pagiel stared at her in disbelief. Then he angrily turned towards his brother. "It looks like you still haven't been able to change your wife's habits!" he snapped at Gedor.

"You're welcome to have a try," Gedor replied, "but I don't like your chances."

Pagiel growled back, "There was a time when women were stoned for talking like this!"

"Perhaps by men like you," was Tirza's quick response, "but fortunately there aren't many like you."

"That's an insult!"

"Well, it's certainly not a compliment," Tirza replied. She knew exactly how to handle her brother-in-law. "Come on Pagiel, we love you and you know it. Don't let this opportunity slip through your fingers to say a proper farewell to each other. Perhaps …" she hesitated for a moment but then added in a soft voice, "perhaps we'll never see each other again." It had not escaped her attention that the old man was still holding on to his daughter's hand.

With a deep sigh he said, "I see that you haven't turned back from your false beliefs."

He looked at Silla. His eyes seemed to be asking her that question.

"It's the only way that leads to life," Silla said. "I pray for you that one day you'll also see it."

He wanted to flare up again but held himself back.

Silla felt how he gripped her hands more tightly. "Father… I love you." With these simple words she knelt beside him. "I hate leaving you like this. Won't you give me your blessing?"

Suddenly tears welled up in his eyes!

Gedor and Tirza held their breath when they saw this wondrous happening.

Pagiel pulled his daughter toward himself, put his shaky hands on her head and cried out loud…

The words he spoke could only be heard by God Himself.

On leaving Pagiel's house, they met Nimsi in the entry. He had just come in, and taken by surprise, he stood glued to the spot.

"I never expected to see you here. What do you want?"

"We've said goodbye to your father," Gedor replied.

"Goodbye? Are you leaving the city? Ah, but of course. I've heard about that. Scared of the Romans, hey? And once we've cleansed the land of those vermin, you'll come back to enjoy the freedom we fought for. Isn't that right? But as far as I'm concerned you should never come back."

Gedor couldn't help but respond, saying, "That's very friendly of you! But are you sure there'll be a Jerusalem to come back to, Nimsi? Have you never considered the prophecy which has been proclaimed over the city and our people in recent years?"

"That fool you mean?" was Nimsi's sharp retort. "One of these days someone will bash him over the head with a rock! We won't be discouraged by such men."

"He's only confirming the prophecy of long ago, Nimsi! Not one stone will be left on top of another in this place. You simply don't stand a chance. You're inexperienced in warfare, have inadequate weapons and the enemy is mighty."

"God is with us!" Nimsi insisted. "You'll see!"

"The Lord is with the meek and humble of heart. I don't recognise that in you. I'm very worried for you Nimsi, for you and your brothers. The leaders you're following are false shepherds who lead the people astray."

Nimsi laughed in disdain. "Just you wait and see," he said, "you'll be surprised!"

He brushed past them and disappeared into the house without saying goodbye.

CHAPTER 6

"WAR...," RAPHA MUMBLED. PENSIVELY he stroked his middle finger along his nose. "Imagine war does break out. Everything will become scarce. Well, that's to say, that could happen... Especially if there's a siege... And if that siege lasts a long time, everything will run out... people will become hungry. Yes, they will. Then they'll pay whatever you ask, for a bit of food... if it lasts long enough..."

He tried to imagine that situation. The city besieged and all main roads in and out of the city blockaded. If it went on long enough, all food supplies would dwindle! And any food still available would naturally go to those doing the fighting. Ordinary citizens would be the first to suffer hunger. For a smart person it would be a marvellous opportunity to make a lot of money...

"You need to look ahead," Rapha laughed nervously. Tapping his forehead, he said, "Look ahead and use your brain. Take timely measures to be prepared."

Rapha's idea to buy houses had failed. He wouldn't even consider negotiating with Pagiel. That wasn't a man with whom he could do business. And when he made careful enquiries with several others, he hadn't been well received. No, they didn't like him. He couldn't really understand why.

But if they were to become hungry and he had something to offer them, things would be different. Then they would be only too pleased to receive his help. So, he ought to make plans to have something to offer them. Something to eat that would last and not go rotten. And then he wouldn't offer it for sale immediately when there was a need, but he would wait… Prices would creep up and he could ask whatever price he wanted!

He was already pleased with himself at the thought of it.

But of course, first there would have to be a war.

Fortunately, he was hearing more and more rumours about a pending war. Those Christians were probably right about that. Sure, the leaders of the city didn't feel like war, but the younger ones looked forward to it. There were more and more skirmishes. It would surely end up in an armed conflict.

Rapha began muttering to himself, "Barley, yes barley seems to be the best way to go. It's cheapest to buy and will provide the greatest profits. Once people get hungry, they'll gladly pay more for it than the best wheat, even if it's going mouldy! Oh yes, much more, if there's nothing else for sale."

No, he wouldn't be able to assist in fighting, but at least he could try and make sure there was something to eat. Well, that is to say, for those who could afford it. After all he was going to put all his hard-earned money into it. He was the one doing all the planning.

"That's being smart," he grinned.

The only problem was, he had to find someone who could help in executing his plan.

"A reliable person," Rapha whispered, "but not too smart."

It would have to be someone who could follow orders. But not someone who would ask him all sorts of awkward questions. Not someone who would want to know what he would do with all that barley. Nor someone who would want to be paid too much for buying in all that barley…

Where could he find such a person?

"Come in and tell me what the matter is," Gedor welcomed his nephew.

Pallu, the youngest son of Pagiel, looked rather worried.

"Father has taken a turn for the worse," he stammered.

"Did he send you to us?"

"No, he lost consciousness."

"Did you leave him on his own?" Gedor asked, all worried.

"The others are with him."

"Did they send you?"

"They don't know that I've gone to see you. They think Father didn't cope very well with your visit, and this will be his death. Nimsi says that he must have really got worked up from your visit. Did you have a fight?"

"No, but it was emotionally stressful for him. He wasn't looking all that well when we left. We'll come with you straight away."

He saw the hesitation in Pallu who said, "Actually, I came for Silla…"

Gedor put his hand on his nephew's shoulder and looked him straight in the eyes.

"Your father is my brother," he said gently.

"But the others…" Pallu hesitated.

"Nimsi didn't give your sister any attention when we met him at your father's house. So, I can't imagine that your sister will be warmly welcomed by her brothers. But do you think that in the given circumstances we should be bothered by that? It would be very harsh if they refused Silla and me from seeing him."

"They are not as reasonable as you may think," responded Pallu hesitantly.

"They have those traits from their father, but they are not inhuman, and neither is he."

Pallu sighed and shrugged his shoulders in resignation.

"I'm going to call both Silla and your aunt."

The women were rather shocked when they heard the news and without hesitation, they went along with Gedor and Pallu.

A servant immediately let them in and took them to Pagiel. Gedor had the impression that it was only because Pallu was with them, and he suspected that the servant had been told to expect them. Still, this should be a relief to Pallu.

There was no warm welcome from the three brothers. Silently they moved out of the way as the visitors approached the bed. Pagiel looked awful.

"Has a doctor been to see him?" Tirza asked, as Silla kneeled beside the bed, and with tears running down her cheeks took hold of her father's hand.

"Yes." Nadab answered sullenly.

"And? What did he say?" Gedor asked.

"Too much excitement, at least too much excitement for his heart."

"There was nothing else he could do for him," Hassub added. "I think he expects that Father will die without regaining consciousness."

"Let's call on the Lord," Gedor proposed.

"Which One?" Hassub blurted out. There was bitterness in his voice.

"The One and Only," Gedor responded gently. "The God of Abraham, Isaac and Jacob. There is no other God. There is no Redeemer apart from Him. As we read in Scripture, 'I, I am the Lord your God and there is no Saviour besides Me.'"

Hassub wanted to respond but changed his mind.

Everyone was silent.

Then Gedor raised his hands toward heaven and passionately prayed for the life of his brother. When he had finished his prayer, Pagiel slowly opened his tired eyes.

"Father," whispered Silla.

He looked at her for a while and then a glimmer of a smile appeared. After that his gaze went from one to another and a growing amazement showed on his face. It was as if he wondered what made him worthy of all that attention. As he tried to mumble something, he suddenly realised it was difficult for him to speak.

There was great sadness among all of them when they noticed that although Pagiel had come out of his coma, he was almost completely paralysed.

After a few days he regained most of his speaking ability. But his legs no longer responded and neither did his left arm. For the remainder of his life, he would be fully dependent on the help of others.

His name was Kish, but he was better known as Simpleton. On the face of it, he had some features that gave rise to this name. His appearance could give the impression that you were dealing with a somewhat clumsy, awkward person. Simpleton did not seem to be affected by that at all.

Now and then, some people were confronted with the real Kish. Usually they were so surprised, they attributed his responses to 'a bright moment' or pure coincidence.

Early on in life, Kish had cleverly learned to make use of what others may have experienced to be a handicap and something they would have struggled with throughout their life.

It wasn't as if he looked weird. When it came down to it, it wasn't even possible to clearly define what was different about him. His face was normal, he had auburn hair, beautiful brown eyes and a mouth that gave the impression of a somewhat sad smile. His arms and legs were of normal proportions. So essentially there was nothing wrong with him. And yet… Those who didn't look deeper, and had no real interest in people, would not hesitate to see him as Simpleton.

Kish had a presence that was uninspiring.

No wonder that Rapha conceived the brilliant idea to use this young man for his purpose. He was on the look-out for him, when luck was on his side. One evening Simpleton on his donkey, came riding past his house.

From his dark porch, Rapha tried to draw his attention.

"Hey you there… Hoi… psst!"

Simpleton halted his donkey and scanned the darkness for clues.

"Here… here in the porch," a soft voice called out.

Rapha stepped forward and waved his cloak around to show himself more clearly.

Simpleton clacked his tongue and steered his donkey toward the porch.

"What's up?" he asked.

"Shush!" Rapha quickly tried to silence him.

"What do you want from me?" Simpleton asked again.

"Do be quiet!" Rapha hissed nervously. "The whole city doesn't have to hear it!" He began to fear that there were some downsides to using such a simple person.

"Could you perhaps come down and join me here?"

"Why?" asked Simpleton.

"I want to talk to you for a minute. But not here in the street. I want to ask you something. Let's go inside for a minute."

Kish slid off the animal, tied him up and went inside with Rapha.

"Nobody needs to know what I want to discuss with you," Rapha grumbled. He carefully bolted the door and indicated a stool where his guest could sit down.

"You probably would like a drink?"

Simpleton nodded and Rapha fetched him a cup of water.

"Don't you have any wine?" Simpleton asked.

"Nothing is as healthy as water," Rapha replied indignantly. The request for wine was like a stab to his heart. Just imagine, wine for this oaf. He himself was satisfied with water so why could he not be?

"Wine tastes nicer."

"Nicer perhaps but not as refreshing! Water allows you to keep a clear head. That's much better if we want to talk business."

"I didn't come to do business," Simpleton assured him. "What do you really want from me?"

He had a loud voice and it made Rapha nervous.

"You should keep your voice down!" he reprimanded him.

"I always talk like that. But what did you want to ask me?"

"Well, how would you like to make a bit of money?"

"A bit?"

"Yes, a bit, if you can do a little job for me!"

"What little job would that be?"

"Run an errand. Really easy… just buy something for me."

"What do you want me to buy?"

"First tell me if you want to do it…"

"As long as it's easy I'll do it," Simpleton assured him.

"Oh yes, it's easy. Very easy. Listen, I will explain it to you."

They sat opposite each other in the bare room that was dimly lit by an oil lamp on the floor. The flickering light gave a sinister, ghostly look to their faces.

Simpleton slurped water from the cup and stared at Rapha across its brim. He in turn leaned over toward Simpleton as if plotting something illegal.

Rapha tried to act a bit fatherly when he said, "I've heard that you're an honest chap. I could have asked someone else, but I prefer to ask someone who is known to be reliable."

Simpleton nodded.

"I want to ask you to buy barley for me. Not too far away. Just outside the city are plenty of farmers who grow barley. I see that you own a donkey. Such an animal can carry heavy loads."

"Is that all I have to do?" Simpleton asked with relief in his voice.

"Rather simple, isn't it?" Rapha snickered. "Just collect some barley for me, nothing else. Easy enough to remember, isn't it? Buy barley from the farmers… that's all. Do you have money?"

"Yes, I have money," said Simpleton.

Rapha could have hugged him but restrained himself. He couldn't have wished for better proof that he had chosen the right helper. He was very pleased with himself. That Simpleton was simple. Anyone of sound mind wouldn't admit to a total stranger that he had money. It was another big relief for Rapha. He'd been racking his brain how to organise payment for the barley. The very thought that he would have to entrust his own money into the care of Simpleton had been the only draw-back of his plan, and a terrible one at that. He'd had nightmares about it.

"Wonderful, then you can pay with your own money. The advantage is that you don't run the risk you might get robbed of someone else's money. Or imagine you would lose it!"

"Then I would have to make up for it," Simpleton agreed.

"Exactly! You've said it. You do understand!" Rapha purred with enthusiasm. Maybe he even overdid it a bit, which caused him immediate regret. But then again, it would be good for Simpleton to keep seeing it as an honour that he was allowed to do this for him.

"So, you pay the farmer for the barley and then you'll get your money back when you come and drop it off."

"From the farmer?"

"Ha, ha. That's a good one. Would be nice, too!" Rapha laughed. "No, he won't be that generous. No, I'll pay you for the barley. At cost price of course."

"Because we are the generous ones hey," Simpleton laughed.

"What?" Rapha had a fright. He looked at him intently and asked, "What do you mean?"

"You're the generous one! The farmer may not return my money, but you will!"

"Um, yes that's right."

"And even a little extra on top."

"Yes, if you do your work properly."

"And what are you going to do with all that barley? Eat it all?"

Rapha was pleased that he had prepared himself for this question. Even a simple person would ask it, so he had prepared a nice answer.

"That's my little secret," he whispered and stealthily looked around like someone telling a secret. "There are widows and orphans in our city."

Simpleton nodded in agreement.

"And many sick and poor people too," Rapha continued.

Simpleton interrupted him and added, "And the Lord looks after them."

"You have guessed right," Rapha said.

"Not really, isn't that what the law teaches?" Simpleton corrected him.

Rapha was momentarily confused when he saw the joy on Simpleton's face. But then Simpleton picked up again, "And now … you … are going to buy barley … for them?"

"Yes, but nobody is allowed to know that."

"There's no need for it either because the Lord Who sees in secret, will repay you for it," Simpleton quoted.

Rapha didn't like that comment, but it suited his story nicely.

"And you're allowed to help me give those poor people food. The cheaper you manage to buy barley from the farmers, the more people I can help. But, as I said before, nobody is allowed to know. That's why you can't come and deliver the barley to me during the day, but only after dark."

"You're a good man," Simpleton said. "Sure, I will help you, no worries. I'm even happy to bring the barley directly to those people. I don't mind doing that at all. I don't even have to get paid for it. Shall we do that?"

Rapha felt his heart stop. For a moment he gasped for air. It took all his will power to control himself and not start screaming. He certainly hadn't counted on such a proposal!

"No!" he said with a shaky voice. "No, I want to hand it out myself. It's nice of you to offer, but I won't even let you know who these people are."

"That's a pity," replied Simpleton, "but I can understand it. Everything must happen under cover of darkness. That way, no one can say thank you…"

"I want to surprise them, you see?"

"Yes, I think I get it," Simpleton said, and washed his mouth with a gulp of water. Suddenly he stood up and held his hand to his ear. "Can you hear that?"

The doomsday call of the prophet resounded through the street.

"He's been doing that for years and I've stopped paying attention to it," Rapha replied. Yet he couldn't cover up the nervous twitch in his voice.

"Woe… woe," repeated Simpleton, "would that apply to us?"

"Don't be silly!" Rapha responded abruptly.

"Well, because it's so close by… It's as though he's right on your doorstep."

Rapha advised him not to listen to it, saying, "I don't do that either," but meanwhile his forehead beaded with sweat.

Simpleton sighed. "It's my bad conscience. You wouldn't know about that. You're someone who even wants to buy barley for other people and all that… But I have these frightening thoughts sometimes you know. I'm not such a nice person. And then, sometimes I think, when I die, where will I end up?"

Rapha nervously responded, "You shouldn't think like that!"

"That's easy for you to say. But it just happens. Of course, you've always kept the law, but I haven't. Moses already warned us, didn't he? He who breaks the law will be doomed… That makes me scared. In the village where I come from, our rabbi taught the same. He said that all of us will one day have to give account of our actions before God. I don't think I can ever do that."

Not only is he a simple man, Rapha thought, he's even mad! Stark raving mad! Rapha became increasingly uncomfortable with all Simpleton's talk.

He tried to lighten the mood with a joke, and said, "You're starting to sound like a rabbi yourself!"

But Simpleton didn't respond.

It seemed that the prophet had moved on to spread his message to other parts of the city.

Rapha didn't have to wait long for his deliveries. According to their agreement, Simpleton would arrive soon after dark with a heavily laden donkey. When it came to unloading, Rapha didn't lift a finger. But when everything was inside, he took over. Naturally he wouldn't allow Simpleton to help him store it away. Everything was going to plan, and the profiteer felt very pleased, except when the time came to pay the bill. That commitment pained him each time again.

CHAPTER 7

FROM BETWEEN THE FOLIAGE of the tree where he had hidden himself, Caleb spied to see if he could recognise any of the young men who were being led away by the Romans. He had come close to being caught as well and then he would have been among them.

He felt sick from exhaustion and when he thought about the future that awaited his friends, he didn't feel any better. The Romans had their own type of amusement. Perhaps the more fortunate prisoners were those who would be sold as slaves on the markets. However, most of them would probably die in the heathen games in the arenas.

Rome had taught rebellious Galilee a harsh lesson. When moderate tactics had proved ineffective, and the rebels only increased in boldness, more forceful measures had been taken. The renowned field marshal Vespasian and his son Titus had been instructed by emperor Nero to utterly quell the rebellion. He would have been hard pressed to find better qualified army officers.

Josephus, who would later become the Jewish historian, had been responsible for leading the revolt in Galilee. Eventually he had been forced to surrender and was led away as prisoner in the entourage of Vespasian and Titus.

Caleb had witnessed much of the misery which the rebels had brought upon themselves and the people of Galilee. Vespasian had made rapid progress and hadn't allowed any obstacles to block his path. One fortified city after another had been conquered. As usual, those citizens who refused to take part in the revolt, had suffered most. At any opportunity, they would defect because there was more chance of receiving mercy from the Romans than from their rebellious countrymen.

Although Caleb was now of fighting age, he had not joined the Zealots. His family had denounced him for it, but the more he saw of their style of warfare, the more he was convinced of his own point of view.

His father and brother had fallen in the struggle. Their fanatic hatred against the Romans, had often confused him. He couldn't go along with them but then he asked himself if that was treason. He'd often heard them say they were prepared to lay down their lives for the good cause. But what he had experienced of the raging of the Zealots only strengthened him in doubting the cause.

War was a terrible business; he had witnessed that. The Romans knew how to fight. Their organisational skills and iron discipline had always fascinated him. He had seen them in action and admired them, although he realised that if the Zealots heard him express these thoughts, it could cost him his life. That he had not partaken in the fighting was bad enough for them. Only out of respect for his late father, had they left him alone.

Caleb was a keen observer. Just as he had absorbed all the happenings in the Roman camp while caring for the sheep near the lake of Galilee, so he had experienced the fighting in Galilee. More as an observer.

Just today however he had narrowly escaped becoming an active participant.

The Romans had practically finished dealing with the organised rebellion and were pursuing the fleeing rebels to stop them re-joining other groups and mustering renewed resistance. Caleb had almost been arrested in one of their raids. As the column of soldiers disappeared from sight, he heaved a sigh of relief.

He slipped down from the tree and headed in the direction of Jerusalem. Close to the city, he filled his water skin on one of the farms.

"Galilee?" asked the farmer.

Caleb nodded.

"What's the situation there?"

"Pretty bad for us."

"Were you there with them?"

"Yes…The Romans have taken many prisoners. John and his Zealots have escaped… At least that's what I heard… I don't know where they've gone."

"There's a constant stream of people going to Jerusalem," the farmer said. "It would be dreadful if the fighting would shift to this area. Do you think it might happen?"

Caleb shrugged his shoulders. "Only the Almighty knows," he sighed.

"What do you think, Kish?" The farmer addressed Simpleton who was loading barley onto his donkey.

"I think he's right," was his reply.

"That the Almighty knows it? Sure, that's true of course," the farmer agreed. "After all, He knows everything. But do you think there'll be war?"

"War has already broken out, hasn't it?" Kish replied.

"Just go and have a look in Galilee," added Caleb.

"That's still a long way from here," the farmer said. "But would those in Jerusalem get involved in it?"

"Depends," was the sombre response from Caleb. "If the same madness comes over people here as it did over there," motioning into the direction from where he came, "then I'm afraid war will come here too."

"Is that why you lug all that barley to the city?" His question was again directed to Kish. "As far as I know there's enough food stowed away in your storehouses to last for years."

Simpleton laughed a bit but did not answer.

His donkey was loaded, and he departed.

He was city-bound and Caleb walked along with him. Thinking out loud, Caleb said, "These people live in fear. The farmers I mean. Actually, everyone who has his house or business here, so close to the city. They don't stand a chance if war comes here. I've seen it in Galilee. When the Romans besiege a city, they pull everything down. Homes and trees, the lot… They wreck everything. It's horrible to see it happen. And then they build ramparts for their own protection. It's terrible to witness but nevertheless it's impressive. Have you ever seen them in action?"

"Who?" Kish asked.

"The Romans of course, who else? That's what we're talking about, aren't we?" Caleb replied in amazement. He turned to have a better look at his companion and suppressed a smile. He hadn't noticed it before, but now he realised he was talking to a simple person.

"What I asked was, if you had ever seen the Romans march up in formation…"

Kish continued to play dumb.

"They form cohorts," Caleb explained. "Do you know what they are? They're groups of soldiers made up of about 600 men… in six divisions… called Centuriae. Those are ten rows of ten soldiers behind one another."

"Man, oh man," said Simpleton, feigning surprise.

This response encouraged Caleb to continue, "If they are pelted with rocks from above or shot at with arrows, they hold their shields above their heads, so it looks like one big roof… When you see how they do that… It's a bit scary to see it happen but at the same time you can't turn your eyes away."

"You sure know a lot," Simpleton said in admiration.

Caleb was modest in his reply. "Oh, well… It's always fascinated me. Do you think that's strange? The Romans have something we lack."

Casually observing his companion again, he asked, "What's your name anyway?"

"Kish… but most people call me something else… And you?"

"Caleb… A few days ago, I narrowly escaped from the Romans."

"That was fortunate… But why are you going to Jerusalem?"

"I have family there… A cousin of my father… I wouldn't know where else to go… Do you live in Jerusalem?"

Kish didn't reply but guided his heavily laden donkey into the city. They had arrived.

Although Caleb had been here before when they had celebrated national feast days, he was again greatly impressed. The massive walls, the strong gates and the enormous stones with which the large structures had been built, gave the impression of invincibility.

"What marvellous buildings," he sighed with admiration.

"Yes, for as long as they last," said Kish, to Caleb's consternation.

That sort of comment could easily be heard by the wrong person in this sea of people. And his fears proved right. It didn't take long for people to react. Someone turned around in anger and yelled at him, "You'd better watch what you're saying young man!"

"That's treason!" shouted another.

But then a third person laughingly said, "Just look at who's talking! It's only Simpleton... He must have heard something somewhere and is now prattling about it. We've gained yet another prophet!"

Fortunately, that realisation eased the tension. Some were still growling at Kish, but no one lifted a finger against him.

"Why did you say that?" Caleb asked when they'd moved away from the busy area. "They could have stoned you!"

"It's going to happen," Kish answered. "All these beautiful homes; nothing will be left of them... Not of the temple either... Not one stone will be left upon another."

He is mad, Caleb thought. His attention was drawn to a group of men making fun of a poorly dressed person. Despite his shabby appearance, he had a certain aura which commanded a level of respect.

Then suddenly he raised his hands toward heaven and with a loud voice he cried out the message of doom over his people, the city and the temple...

"Woe... Woe... Woe..."

"He's been doing that for years already," Kish commented.

"I had heard about him," Caleb said, "but it's scary to witness it from close by."

"They don't want to believe him… And now and then they throw stones at him or bash him up…"

"And what do you think of it? Do you believe him?" Caleb asked with some hesitation.

"Yes," said Kish, "just have a look at how they treat him."

Caleb shook his head. He was puzzled by the answer.

CHAPTER 8

For DAYS ALREADY, SILLA had suffered inner turmoil, but now she'd come to the point that she could talk about it.

"I've decided to stay in Jerusalem," she told her foster parents. "I've prayed a lot about it, to get clarity on what I'm supposed to do, but now I've found peace. It was a very difficult decision because the Lord has said that we ought to escape from Jerusalem when it's besieged, and I was afraid that I would be disobedient if I remained in the city. But I believe that I may not leave Father behind on his own. He is fully dependent on our care and his health is deteriorating. That's clear to all of us."

She remained silent for a moment, searching for the right words to continue. "I could never forgive myself if he were to come to his end in miserable circumstances, just because I had wanted to flee to safety. I can't bear that thought. My brothers look after him all right, but they can't really give proper care. Besides they're so busy with their great ideals. If it happens that the city is besieged, I'm afraid they won't be able to give him much attention. What do you think? The law tells us that we are to honour our parents, doesn't it?"

"Dear Silla," said Gedor, "your decision doesn't surprise us… True, isn't it Tirza?"

Tirza nodded.

"We too have brought these things in prayer before the Lord in the past few days," he continued. "Your decision obviously fills us with great concern, but truthfully, we hadn't expected anything else. On the one hand I'm happy that you stay to care for your father; on the other hand, it worries me greatly to think about what could happen if the city is indeed besieged. Have you given that enough thought? Not only that your life will be in danger, but you're a pretty girl Silla… In war many evil things happen, especially to women and children. They often suffer the most. Murder and rape…"

"I've brought it all before the Lord," was Silla's simple answer, "and I remembered the preaching of Eliphelet when he reminded us of the words of our Lord Jesus … I know that He will always be with us. We need not be afraid, Eliphelet said, no matter how great the danger… That's how I want to face it… No matter what happens…"

"We've seen it coming," said Tirza, "and your uncle and I have discussed the matter together. We agreed that if you decided to stay, we would postpone our departure as well. So that's what we'll do. If you don't come with us, we wouldn't have much peace in the trans-Jordan anyway. In our minds we'd be with you all the time, so it's better if we stay."

"It's been a strange turn of events," said Gedor. "No one could have seen this business with your father coming…"

"He can't do without you anymore," Tirza added. "The Lord seems to use you to soften his heart. Who knows how that will develop?"

"I'm very happy that you're willing to stay with me," said Silla, "but at the same time I feel very burdened by it. If later, you won't be able to leave the city, I will forever feel guilty about it."

"Silla, you're no longer a child. All three of us are adults and we've all made our own individual decisions in prayerful consideration," was Gedor's warm response. "Let's agree that in this matter no one can hold another guilty of anything. Your aunt and I have nothing to lose in this world other than the people whom we love, and you are number one for us. Whatever happens, you're not allowed to blame yourself where we are concerned."

"We're happy with your decision," said Tirza seriously. "We believe that it's according to the will of the Lord."

"Your aunt and I have had elaborate discussions on this," assured Gedor once again. "Securing our own safety is not the most important thing. Hasn't the Lord Himself taught us that?"

"I just hope that others in the congregation will understand what you are doing," was Silla's hesitant response. "Some have left already, and others are about to leave."

"Not all brothers and sisters will agree with us," Gedor acknowledged, "but you'll always get that. Circumstances differ. I think I would feel obliged to leave Jerusalem if our current situation didn't compel us to stay."

Tirza declared that most people would certainly agree with them. And others would, perhaps come to understand it later.

"And even if not, I think we're doing the responsible thing," Gedor decided. "For the moment at least, our house won't be for sale then. That will be sad for Rapha."

"Have you told your father that you've changed your plans and will stay here?"

"No," Silla answered, "I first wanted to share it with you. Perhaps also to hear your thoughts and to have confirmation on my decision."

Tirza said, "I'm keen to see how he will respond."

Rapha dragged the barley-filled sacks to his secret hiding place. "Just like an ant," he sniggered. It was the best comparison that came to mind. Not that he was at all interested in the animal world, but he knew just enough to recall that ants are diligent insects who are always busy gathering things and bringing them to their nest.

Had someone observed Rapha's activities, undoubtedly a different comparison would have come to mind. More along the lines of seeing a rat dragging its loot to safety.

If Rapha had been able to sing, he would certainly be singing now, but instead he mumbled a bit and occasionally produced a squeaky noise which supposedly indicated great satisfaction. It cost him a lot of effort to drag the sacks of barley from the entry hall all the way to the hidden rooms. But the very thought of the money he would make, gave him the power and energy to move heavy items which in most other cases would have been well beyond his strength. Especially descending the stairs demanded great effort.

Of course, Simpleton would have found it a lot easier to do. And had they been able to work together it would have cost very little effort. But such ideas were so offensive that it scared Rapha to even think about it.

"Do it all by myself, that's always the best," he whispered. "Then it's all for yourself."

Despite the hard work, he had no regrets whatsoever that he had started this enterprise. The only thing he had noticed was that his storerooms were so small. He knew he was unable to do anything about it, but sometimes it kept him awake. He wondered why the builders hadn't dug the rooms deeper and wider and although he tried to think of a solution, it was fruitless. It was impossible for him to dig out the hard rock. Stone masons with special tools would be required for that task. These thoughts troubled him and caused him to break out in a cold sweat. Seeking help meant that he would need to share his secret with others. And of course, that was out of the question!

So, even though he regretted it, he would have to be satisfied with the limited capacity the house offered. And being satisfied wasn't easy for him.

Wiping the sweat from his forehead he looked with great satisfaction at the goods he had already stored. "You've probably stored enough for a whole year," he recalled Simpleton saying, and he'd added, "By now you can just about feed all of Jerusalem."

"Ha ha... All of Jerusalem...! If only that were true!"

But certainly, he had quite a lot already. Although... not enough of course. To have enough would take a lot more than this! The concept of 'enough' was hard for Rapha to imagine. No, there was never enough...

Lovingly he stroked the bales of barley. You could be sure that many people would beg for a bite to eat when the time came. By now he was confident that an all-out war was certain. The rumours he overheard were not just stories. The rumblings were everywhere. If he understood correctly, the rebels had even captured the stronghold of Masada.

Suddenly Rapha froze!

Had something just run around him...?

He thought he had seen a shadow scooting around on the floor. He wasn't entirely sure because he hadn't seen it clearly. It was something he caught from the corner of his eye. Suddenly he recalled what Simpleton had said, that he should watch out for vermin getting into his barley, like mice or rats.

Again, he broke out in a sweat. Couldn't it simply have been the flickering oil lamp that played tricks on him and made him jumpy? After all, he had been deep in thought... He tried to calm himself down. Normally the entrance to the underground rooms was very well sealed so it would be impossible for such vermin to get in. Nor had he ever seen a mouse here!

No, he must have been mistaken... he thought... But then again, the storerooms had been open all the time while he'd been busy that evening, dragging the bales down the stairs. So, something could easily have gone down there without his noticing! He didn't want to think about it, but he couldn't stop himself...

Rapha searched across the floors, and moved everything as far as was possible; he searched up and down, and down and up again throughout his entire house but found nothing.

That however didn't give him peace of mind. Rats and mice were smart. Although he moved around quietly like a shadow from room to room, their hearing was very sharp. Totally exhausted, he had to end his search. But he couldn't sleep and spent a restless night.

The thought that some vermin was gobbling up his precious barley constantly plagued him. He gnashed his teeth in helpless rage.

Just as on other days, Simpleton appeared the following evening with his heavily laden donkey. In complete silence the goods were taken down and brought into the house. The men settled accounts in the entry hall.

"How much more do you still need?" asked Simpleton. He spoke very quietly without even realising. "Some farmers in the closer vicinity are moving away. Many villains are roaming around, and much is being plundered."

"By the Romans?"

"No, by our own people… Well, by thieves and murderers. So how much do you still want?"

"About three more loads," whispered Rapha, "or maybe four. Till I can't fit in anymore."

"Fit anymore in where?" Simpleton asked.

"In…" Rapha could have kicked himself. He'd nearly given himself away!

"I mean till it's no longer possible. When the farmers move out, they can no longer sell you anything."

"That's right," said Simpleton. "Then there's no more to get for the poor people. But at least you've done your best for them. Many will be very thankful to you, don't you think? Have you distributed much already?"

"Nearly all of it," Rapha lied.

"Marvellous! My father always said that 'he who gives what he has, is worthy to live'. Nice saying hey? And another thing he always said was, 'The rest of the righteous is sweet.' But I think he took that from the Scriptures."

Simpleton left quietly, but a few moments later he knocked on the door again…

"Hey… Rapha…"

Cautiously opening the door, Rapha wondered what the matter could be. He held up his oil lamp to see better. His eyes lit up with disgust when he saw the dead rat that Simpleton was holding up in front of him.

"I don't know if this one came from inside," Simpleton whispered, "but it was scurrying around near your door, so I immediately killed it… That's what I was talking about you see. You need to watch out for those vermin. Before you know it, they'll eat all the food of the poor people. It would be a shame of all the money you spent on it too. Do you want to keep it, or shall I toss it out?"

"Please throw it away!" Rapha hissed and slammed the door shut.

Shaken to the core he searched his house again for rats and mice. He found none. But he wasn't convinced there weren't any.

"Silla…"

She went to his bed.

"When are you and the others leaving?"

"I'm not going anymore."

Pagiel looked at her intently.

She added, "I was just about to tell you."

"But you were all going to leave the city?"

"I'm staying with you."

He pondered this for a moment, visibly shaken.

"Out of pity for me?" he asked.

She shook her head.

"Why then?"

"Because you are my father… and because I love you…"

After a few moments he asked, "And what do they say about it?"

"They totally agree with me."

"So, they're leaving without you? Leaving you to fend for yourself?"

"No Father, they're also staying in Jerusalem."

"Ah, so they have changed their minds, have they? They're no longer convinced that things here will become dangerous …"

"No that's not it, Father. They love you and they love me. They don't want to go away without me and neither do they want me to leave you by yourself under these circumstances."

"So, they pity me after all," grumbled Pagiel and for a moment his old temper flared again.

"No, not just out of pity Father. But even if that were true, is it such a bad thing to feel sorry for someone?"

He stared at her for a while. Then his face relaxed and with a smile on his face he said, "No my child, compassion is not a bad thing at all. But it's a bit harder to accept when it concerns yourself. At least for someone like me…"

"We love you," Silla repeated.

"After all that's happened?" Pagiel sighed.

"Perhaps because of all that's happened," said Silla.

There was confusion on her father's face.

"I've been doing so much thinking the last few days Silla, and I've started to wonder if I've done the right thing. I mean by behaving like I did. First towards Gedor and Tirza… And then even more so toward you. They took you from me. That's how I experienced it…"

"They didn't do that Father," Silla protested.

"Oh, but they did," Pagiel said. He surprised Silla by the calm way he said it. "I'm convinced you've all gone in a wrong direction… Don't get angry my dear child," and he reached out to her with his healthy hand. "That's how I see the situation. It tears me apart that such a spiritual rift has come between us…"

He saw that she wanted to object, but motioned that she should keep quiet, and continued, "But I'm ashamed of the way I've responded to the situation. Instead of showing from the Scriptures where you went wrong, I allowed myself to get angry and eventually told you to leave."

"That was ages ago Father," Silla said, in an attempt to soften the hurt.

She saw the tears in his eyes.

"Yes, but the past can't be erased," Pagiel said. He searched for her hand.

"Forgive me Silla," he whispered.

Filled with emotion, Silla replied, "Father, I already forgave you a long time ago. It was dreadful that we were no longer welcome in this house, that's true. But uncle Gedor, aunt Tirza and I, have always kept loving you and the boys…"

"Gedor and Tirza?"

"We love you Father, please just accept that now… Every day we pray for you and the boys… We were taught that we should even love our enemies… and pray for those who persecute us. Would we then forget our own family, when we know they love us?"

"But we're family who sent you away… I've been the cause of much misery Silla. The sad thing is that I've only just realised it. Or rather, only just admitted it to myself… now that I'm bedridden and largely paralysed and helpless…"

"I've missed you very much," said Silla, "but I was never unhappy. Uncle Gedor and aunt Tirza have taken such good care of me."

"I'm grateful to them for that. And I've never doubted that either. But it only increases my guilt toward you… As boys, Gedor and I spent a lot of time together. He had a more placid nature, but you knew that already. I've always been quick to fly off the handle… Despite our different characters, we always got along. I suspect that was mostly thanks to him. Together we also studied the Scriptures. We kept that up until… well, you know what happened. Let's not keep talking about it. All these years you've kept praying for me. And I've pleaded with the Almighty that He would return you to the right ways."

For a moment he was quiet and then smiled at her.

"You've become a very beautiful girl Silla… Yes, I can say that as your father… And frankly I'm surprised that no one else has said this to you yet."

"Uncle Gedor did!" Silla said and blushed.

"Uncle Gedor…? Another old fellow like me! But you know what I mean. Many girls of your age are already married. Has no one come with a marriage proposal? Or are you so unapproachable that you scare off all the young men?"

"I don't know," was Silla's answer.

"But you must have thought about these things?"

"It's not the right time for that now."

"Because you're taking care of your old father…"

"No, it's not that. Besides I do that with love… But there's a war looming… You would also have heard that prophet crying out?"

"You call that a prophet?" scoffed Pagiel. "Nowadays anyone can claim to be a prophet. A foolish chap! Yes of course, I've heard him many times. He roams around the whole city. Is that what scares you? The prophesying of that man…? If war breaks out, you don't have to be scared, my dear. Not as long as Jerusalem exists. There's not a Roman that will enter; the Almighty Himself will see to that. The time of those Romans has come to an end…"

He fell silent. She saw that speaking cost him a lot of effort. She re-arranged the pillows and kissed him. He nodded to her to show his thankfulness and closed his eyes, saying, "Silla… I'm so happy that you're staying… and that you're here with me. My days are numbered but days like this are still good days."

Outside the cry of the prophet was heard. Most people paid no attention to him, but some became increasingly afraid.

"A voice against Jerusalem and the temple. A voice against the newly wedded men and women… A voice against this entire nation…"

"Don't let him frighten you, my child," Pagiel mumbled, half asleep.

CHAPTER 9

WHAT COULD HE DO to prevent the rats eating his precious barley? In all his searches through the house, he hadn't caught a single one, although on several occasions he thought he saw one scurrying by. He had lashed out with his club but never hit anything except the floor, or the wall where the shadows caused confusion. Were his nerves getting the better of him? Or was it his poor eyesight and the fickle light of the oil lamp? The only rat he had seen with his own eyes, was the one Simpleton had shown him. Beaten to death in front of his door… outside, on the street…

But of course, they could easily slip inside even if the door was ajar. And even more so when it was dark…Then such vermin became active!

Unfortunately, it was important for Rapha to have his goods delivered under cover of darkness. At least during the day, you could see vermin.

He was worrying about it so much, he hardly slept anymore. But then he hit on a good solution. He could bring his bed downstairs and sleep right between the barley in the storeroom. The slightest noise would wake him, and the rat who dared touch his precious possessions, would meet a speedy death. Rapha was particularly pleased with this brilliant idea and wasted no time implementing it. He gathered everything he needed, which was really very little, dragged it downstairs and made the bed. When he realised that his money would be right beside him while sleeping, he began to whistle from sheer joy. From that point on, he slept in his treasury, with a club near at hand.

"What's bothering you son," asked Shobal.

Thomas looked up, surprised.

"I see that you're worrying about something. Is it something I can help you with?"

"Silla is staying in Jerusalem with her family," Thomas answered hesitantly.

"Yes, that's what I heard too," said Shobal. "She's made a courageous decision. I heard she's taking care of her father. She doesn't want to leave him behind while he's helplessly lying in his bed, paralysed... Gedor told me. He and his wife are also staying here. And I can understand that. She's like their own daughter to them ever since her hot-tempered father refused to keep her in the house. The decision to stay was not made lightly. It was a matter of much prayer for them."

Shobal inspected the urn which he had just taken from the kiln.

"Speak up son," he encouraged him, while appearing to give his full attention to his work.

"I've thought about staying here as well," Thomas said, keenly watching to see how his father would react.

"You've decided to stay here you mean," Shobal corrected him. He put down the urn and approached Thomas. Putting his hand on his shoulder he looked at him seriously.

"To tell you the truth, I expected something like this to happen... Most of our people have left already. Others are leaving soon. We'll go too... but I've struggled to arrive at a decision. You'll understand that better when you have your own family, the Lord willing... I suspected it... and then I weighed up if we should take a gamble and stay here with you... I didn't want to burden your mother yet, so I quietly prayed about it. But I've decided that for the sakes of Miriam and Joseph, we can't take such a risk. I see it as my responsibility toward my family to flee the city, Thomas. The words of our Lord were very clear. The prophet has been warning us for many years, and I see that too as a sign that doom is near. The news that comes to us gets worse and worse. The rebels are becoming more daring. The Zealots who stir up the people increase in fanaticism. They've lost all perspective on reality. They are blinded. And the Romans are getting fed up with it. Before long they will take drastic action."

He smiled sadly.

"You care about Silla, right? No, don't be shy about it. I've observed you lately son, and I noticed that you can't take your eyes off her when we have our meetings. She's very beautiful Thomas. But the flower fades and the grass withers… It's more important that she's caring and faithful, and that's obvious in how she's willing to stay and care for her father despite the risks! You'll need to face them too, my son."

"Do you mind if I stay here?" Thomas asked.

"Son, you're a grown man now. What gives me the right to forbid you? You love her."

"But perhaps she won't love me… I've never spoken to her about it. It's just that the very thought of what could happen to her, once Jerusalem is besieged, makes me feel sick."

"When I fell in love with your mother Thomas, I would have taken on the whole world to protect her… What I want to say is, I understand your feelings. But then, I didn't have to take on the whole world. But you do. War is coming. If her father doesn't pass away before it starts, so you can still leave the city, everything you can possibly think of will be stacked against your survival. That hurts me son. And perhaps even more so because of the sorrow you may experience because of her."

"The Lord is with us, Father."

"That's His promise."

"You approve of me staying then?"

"You have my blessing, son. Watch over her. Perhaps you won't be able to accomplish much, but do your best… I'll let your mother know, and we'll pray for you day and night."

CHAPTER 10

CALEB ROAMED AROUND AIMLESSLY in the vicinity of Jerusalem. The search for his family had been unsuccessful. And the house in which they had lived was now occupied by other people who were unable to give him any forwarding information. They only knew that the previous owners had left the city. Eventually he found a sheltered place on the mount of Olives and made it his temporary home. Meanwhile he explored the surrounding area.

At a small farmhouse he asked for some water. Caleb had the impression that the owners were preparing to abandon their small farm. Initially the farmer wasn't very helpful but when he discovered that Caleb was alone, he became friendlier. In response to his questions, Caleb explained that he was a refugee from Galilee. He told about the battles for the fortified cities and how much the people had suffered from the war, including the misery which he had experienced first-hand. While expressing sorrow about the loss of his own family and the defeats his people had suffered, he couldn't hide his admiration for the achievements of the Romans.

"As a young lad I already admired them," he admitted. "If you see how they tackle problems, you stand amazed. Cities which seem impregnable, they take anyway. Nothing seems to hold them back, nothing at all. I've even seen them fill massive ravines, and then build a causeway across, to get to the city wall. Once they've reached the wall, they're unstoppable. They have battering rams which are fully covered with cowhide. Their soldiers are well hidden underneath and totally protected unless you manage to set one on fire. Then they become rather uncomfortable."

"You know a lot about it," the farmer said admiringly.

Caleb answered, "I don't know why but they really impress me. Perhaps I just have an inquisitive nature, but I've always been like this."

"But you're not a soldier?" asked the farmer.

"No, I'm not."

"What about when you were in Galilee? Did you fight there?"

"It depends on what you call fighting. A few times when I was too late to escape, I was stuck in a besieged city and then it was hard for me to avoid fighting. But I'm not really a fighter. I would help to provide materials needed for combat when the battle drew near."

"I've heard," the farmer said, "that ordinary citizens were forced to fight as well. Is that true?"

"I'm sure that happened," Caleb answered. "They also resented my not fighting with them. But it didn't bother me much. As I said, I didn't entirely withdraw… I helped with provisions. You see, I always have the urge to see what's happening… it's odd really. On the one hand I abhor war, but on the other I like to experience it all."

"Yes, that's certainly strange," the farmer remarked. "As far as I'm concerned, the war can stay far away. That's why I won't stay here any longer. The fighting will come here too, mark my words! No, I'm not at all keen to see all their fighting equipment. Anyway, you describe it so well, it's like you've built it yourself!"

"You need professionals for that," Caleb laughed. "You should see how cleverly it's all been designed. The battering rams I observed, had some sort of turret built at the top. Inside were archers. They shot at anyone on the wall who tried to interfere with the ramming. Also, in that tower, they had buckets of water to douse potential fires started by our people. It's a scary thing to behold such a battering ram. It's unstoppable."

"When I listen to you, I get the impression that you could replicate one of them," the farmer said, "although it wouldn't be of much help to us because we're always on the other side of the wall… But I agree, whether you live in Galilee or here in Jerusalem, you're not safe anywhere. There are also many villains roaming around so that we're even robbed and plundered by our own people. I'm not going to wait for something to happen. I'm leaving with my family today. If I were you, I wouldn't hang around here either."

"I'll take care," Caleb promised.

As he went on his way again, he saw more deserted farmhouses. There was something ominous about deserted houses. It gave the surroundings a gloomy atmosphere.

Caleb came to a wooded area and decided to have a rest. He looked for a secluded spot among the bushes where he wouldn't be easily seen. While making himself comfortable, he thought he heard noises. Mindful of the farmer's warning, he decided not to take any risks and carefully crawled in the direction of the sounds. Coming to an open space he noticed a person busy with some activity. Staying close to the ground, he slid forward with utmost care… so as not to give away his presence…

The clearing in the bush was about ten paces in diameter. Right opposite him, a long, straight branch was stuck in the ground like a spear. Closer by a man was standing with his back to him, but so close that he could probably have touched him.

While Caleb was wondering what was going on, the man, with a swift action, threw something that hit the top of the branch with a thud. Then he walked over to retrieve the thrown item and returned to his previous position. Immediately Caleb recognised the man as Kish, and feeling relieved he started to get up, but suddenly he changed his mind. Since arriving in Jerusalem, he hadn't seen Kish, and he was curious to find out what the man was up to. Was he playing a game? Again, Kish flung out his arm with lightning speed, and a second later the object hit the target dead centre. It appeared to be a long, sharp knife with a small blade. At first Caleb thought it was a lucky strike, but when the knife hit the target again and again, he had to reconsider. He understood this stunt could only have been achieved with a great deal of practice and few would be able to imitate it. He was about to come out of hiding but again held back when he heard voices. Five armed ruffians approached, making no effort to go unnoticed. They seemed to trust their own brutality and strength and besides, here they were well off the beaten track. Although their arrival took Kish by surprise, he had removed the branch and pocketed his knife before they entered the clearing. For a moment the men seemed startled, but on seeing that Kish was by himself, they relaxed. Besides, Kish again radiated the simpleness of mind that had earned him his nickname.

"Look at that," said the biggest of the five men who seemed to be their leader. "We didn't expect to see anyone here! Let's see what you've got on you."

He headed for Simpleton and was about to search him for any valuables that may have been tucked in his belt or hidden on his person. But he stopped when Kish waved him away with one arm and putting a finger to his lips, let out a warning "ssssh!" His whole being expressed fear, but obviously not because of the five men, for when their leader laughed at him and roughly knocked his arm out of the way, Simpleton again responded angrily with "ssssh".

The men looked at one another in amazement and even their leader hesitated. Angrily he asked, "What do you mean ssssh? What's your problem?"

Involuntarily his voice had dropped to a whisper.

"He seems to be scared of something," said one of the others.

"Of us, I reckon!" their leader suggested.

"Of course not! Can't you see that?"

"And still I say, he's scared of us!" their leader insisted.

"Okay then, let's say he is scared of us... But he's even more scared of something else! Just look at him; he's shaking all over."

"Because of us!" the leader repeated. It seemed he only had command of a small vocabulary and proved to be a stubborn fellow.

And yet the whole conversation was held in whispers.

"No! I'm not afraid of you lot!" Simpleton whispered with a teary voice. "I hoped you were coming to help me!"

"Help? What do you mean help? What do you need help with?... Against what?"

"Against soldiers!"

"What soldiers? What on earth are you talking about?"

"The soldiers that are following me! They're searching for me."

"Why do you think that?" the leader asked.

"Because I ran away."

"Why did you run away?"

"Man, stop that nonsense!" one of the other men interrupted angrily. "That man is a nervous wreck. Just ask him how many soldiers there are and where they're located!"

"Don't you interfere!" barked the leader, insulted.

"If I don't interfere, we won't be alive much longer!"

"They're very close!" Simpleton whimpered. He wrung his hands and desperation showed on his face.

"How many soldiers are there? Three…? Four…? How many?"

Simpleton raised both his hands and fumbled around with his fingers.

"Very many," he whispered. "Many more than you lot."

"I reckon he can't even count," growled their leader.

"Maybe, but I'm sure he can tell if there's more or less than us," another challenged him, and continued, "I'm getting out of here!"

"Which direction are they coming from?" the leader quickly asked.

Simpleton made a gesture with his arms in all directions.

"I've heard enough!" moaned one of the men nervously. "Soon we'll walk straight into them! We've wasted enough time here!"

"Be quiet!" snapped the leader, suddenly worried.

While they held their breath, they heard rustling in the bushes and to their strained nerves this could mean nothing else but soldiers approaching. As fast as they could, they stormed off in the opposite direction, into the dense shrubbery, searching for safety.

Once they had disappeared, Caleb came out from the bushes. In his hand he held the stick with which he'd made the rustling noises to frighten the bandits.

"Shalom," he greeted Kish with a smile.

"Shalom," Kish answered, "and thanks for the help. Your timing was perfect. But now, let's get out of here."

"Scared of the soldiers?" Caleb teased.

"Not so much of soldiers, but of bandits like those fellows. They're more dangerous at present. I'd rather not meet them again."

"But you fooled them really well."

"That could be, but I'd rather not play games like that."

"You were perfect in that role."

"I think you've amused yourself more than I have my friend. It was deadly serious for me. My life was at stake. These guys would slit your throat for a shekel."

"I don't think that will happen to you in a hurry."

"No? Why not? I wouldn't stand a chance against five of those fellows. Who do you think I am?"

"You know how to handle yourself… I had already watched you for a while, before those fellows arrived."

"Oh…" Kish replied.

"I saw enough to stand amazed at you," Caleb said. "I saw how you hit that branch every time again."

"Luck was on my side…"

"Nine out of ten times you hit the target! Lucky? No, you don't fool me Kish. Sure, I believe in a bit of luck, but this wasn't it… I just hope you never aim for me."

Kish walked on, deep in thought. He set a firm pace and didn't respond to Caleb's comments.

"You don't have to answer me," Caleb continued, "but perhaps I can wonder aloud what kind of person you really are? They call you Simpleton. And I hope you don't mind me saying so, but sometimes you give a very good rendition of that. As you did just now with the bandits… Do you do that on purpose? That sort of thing really fascinates me… I realise that I'm also a bit of an odd fellow in other people's minds. However, what I've seen of you is rather special. You don't mind me saying this, do you? Because I mean it in admiration really. No one else could have pulled off, what you did back there."

"Caleb, I'm not going to give you the whole story," Kish said eventually. "I don't think I'll ever tell anyone, as matter of fact. I have my secrets, as have most people. But I'll share a few things with you. When I was young, I suffered from being called by that name. Especially as a child. Later on, I learned to use it to my advantage. The things you see me do, and the way I act, are quite natural. I don't put it on… Although I can do that as well, when I want to… If and when it suits me, I will pretend. Sometimes that line is blurred so that I'm not even sure what's real or put on," he laughed. "And just forget about the rest…"

"And what about that knife throwing then?" Caleb asked.

"That's just for fun," Kish answered light-heartedly. "And you never know when it may come in handy," he laughed.

Suddenly he turned serious, "As far as I'm aware, you're the only person who knows these things, Caleb. Please keep it that way, will you? Let me be Simpleton. You seem a fine sort of fellow and if you remain here, we'll probably see more of each other. But for now, just let me potter around by myself."

"As you wish," Caleb said. "You must have your reasons for it… I'm not sure what I'm going to do yet, whether I'll stay here or move somewhere more peaceful. I wasn't able to find any trace of my family back in Jerusalem. They've left without any further notice. I'll see what I'll do. The way things are going, life will soon get tougher."

"We can count on that," Kish agreed.

"Vespasian is slowly but surely cutting off all access roads to Jerusalem," Caleb said. "Just wait and see what happens next. He's not in a hurry, that cunning fox. He knows exactly what he's doing."

"Yes, I think so too, better than the leaders in Jerusalem at least," Kish agreed. "They allow everyone to enter the city and already the place teems with criminals and adventurers."

"If that wasn't bad enough, they've even taken in John of Gischala and his Zealots!" said Caleb. "What a pleasant lot! They pretend they achieved much, but were actually defeated by the Romans and driven out of Galilee… I saw them there … they wanted nothing to do with Josephus. They suspected him of being a Roman sympathiser… You should have heard them! Or rather seen what crimes they committed! No, it wasn't smart to allow them into the city. They were welcomed with open arms but by now everyone would rather see them disappear."

"That's not going to happen," remarked Kish.

"No, we'll never get rid of them now," Caleb sighed. "Where could they be safer, than in Jerusalem? But it gives the Romans even more reason to besiege the city."

"And that will most certainly happen, mark my words."

"When it does happen, will you also leave?" Caleb asked.

"No, I'll stay," Kish answered.

"Well, I've already told you that I'm not sure what I'll do," Caleb said, "I've seen enough warfare for now… But just in case I stay… We may be needing one another again soon…"

"That's very well possible," Kish agreed.

"But then we should know where to find each other!"

"We'll make sure of that, shall we?" said Kish.

CHAPTER 11

JERUSALEM'S CITIZENS HAD REBELLED against the Zealots' reign of terror, including all those who, rightly or wrongly, identified with them. Crimes which had been committed by the ruffians defied description. Respectable people, such as priests and members of the royal house, were falsely accused and imprisoned, tortured and murdered. Anyone who from a position of some authority disagreed with the rebels, was in danger of being killed. By their actions the rebels gained some support, particularly from reckless youths, but the majority of the population wanted nothing to do with them. For a long time, the common people had lacked the courage to openly speak up against the bandits. But now that they themselves were severely threatened, the time had come for indignation to triumph over fear. High-priests and others in authority, called upon the people to rid themselves of the lawless rebels. Heavy fighting broke out during which many were wounded and killed on both sides. Although the citizens were poorly armed and less battle-hardened, they outnumbered their opponents by far. And no matter how tough a resistance the Zealots offered, eventually they were forced to retreat.

Once cornered, they sought refuge in the temple. Their indifference, or perhaps their fear was so great, that they were not ashamed of defiling the sacred place with their blood.

Taking advantage of the circumstances, John of Gischala, who had fled from Galilee, played a treacherous game. While he pretended to be on the side of the common people, he schemed to attain a position of power. Using a wicked lie, he called in the assistance of the Idumeans, saying that the citizens of Jerusalem were about to surrender to the Romans. On hearing this, the Idumeans, angry and keen to fight, gathered twenty thousand men and attacked the city. However, the city gates were kept shut and the citizens refused to let them in.

During the night a fearful thunderstorm developed, which forced the Idumeans to abandon their camp and huddle for shelter near the city wall. With their shields they protected themselves as best they could against the heavy downpour.

Meanwhile some of the Zealots, under cover of the thunderstorm, opened the gates. Embittered by the resistance they had encountered, and humiliated both by the leaders and the wild weather, the Idumeans vented their rage on the citizens of the city. Together with the rebels they attacked them like wild beasts. The chief priests were hunted down and killed. No one crossing their path was shown any mercy. After killing the leaders, the common people were targeted, and thousands were murdered.

At first Thomas was unable to identify the noises he heard. It was still night-time, and the thunderstorm was still raging, although it had eased since he had gone to bed. From afar came an ominous rumble of what sounded like an approaching tidal wave. This had awakened him from his sleep.

Because of the situation in the city, he had prepared for all eventualities. He no longer slept in his ground-level room behind the workshop but had moved his bed to the attic which could only be reached by a ladder. He put on his overcoat and opened the door giving access to the roof. The rain impaired his visibility, yet in the distance, in the direction of the temple, he detected a faint glow. As his eyes grew accustomed to the darkness, he thought he could see dancing flames, or perhaps they were torches. The noises that had sounded to him like the surf of the ocean, must have been voices. It was the sound of raging and cursing, mixed with screams of anguish and despair.

Were the Zealots perhaps making an attempt to escape their imprisonment? Had they perhaps been successful?

The sounds came closer. What could they mean? He thought he could hear shouts and screams of women and children. Perhaps the Zealots had managed to break out and were now avenging themselves on the citizens! But how was that possible when the people of Jerusalem had posted six thousand guards at the temple gates…?

Now the sounds were coming in his direction!

From his vantage point on the roof, he could see a wide surging stream of people, branching out into smaller streams, filling the streets. The speed with which it happened made him realise that this wasn't a struggle between two equally matched parties. It reminded him strongly of a wild chase. Or of an angry mob, successfully destroying and mercilessly slaying anyone in its path, because no resistance was offered. Thomas wondered if this was an attack on the unsuspecting, sleeping citizens.

A wave of desperate, panic-stricken people swept past his house. One of them spotted him on the roof and paused for a second to yell at him in desperation, "Idumeans! Get out of here! They're killing everyone!" The man then continued his flight.

Thomas hesitated. Should he leave the house and try avoiding the marauding bands? In silence he prayed for wisdom. But he had no chance to choose because he had already run out of time.

Another group of people stormed through the street, chased by armed hooligans who smashed down doors, entered houses and trashed whatever stood in their path. Thomas rushed back into his attic room and picked up the iron bar which he had laid next to his bed for self-defence. He heard how the door downstairs was bashed in … The sounds of earthenware being smashed revealed they were vandalising his workshop. Hurriedly they searched the house. He prayed that the empty rooms downstairs would make them conclude that all the inhabitants had fled. He heard the assailants leave the house in a tirade of yelling and screaming and waited a little before he dared to cast an eye on the street from his rooftop.

Suddenly a loud scream was heard. A few houses away two men appeared, dragging a woman by her hair.

Thomas felt his heart miss a beat and could barely suppress a cry of horror. For a moment he felt stunned and stared at the events below that would forever be burned into his memory. Somehow, he associated that desperate woman with Silla. It was the sort of thing he didn't want to think about. This was the reason he'd stayed in Jerusalem. Only now did he realise how utterly foolish he'd been in thinking that he could protect Silla from the very worst he could imagine: that she would fall prey to people like that. He heard the laughter of the ruffians even while the woman was begging for mercy.

Suddenly, a raging anger flared up in him, suppressing any thought of self-preservation. He opened the attic trapdoor, lowered the ladder, and rushed down, iron bar in hand as if wielding a sword. Uttering a shrill cry, unfamiliar even to himself, he flew at the men.

They were totally taken by surprise and before they could recover, he had floored one and knocked the sword out of the other man's hand. He pulled the woman to her feet. "Get yourself to safety!" he ordered her and then proceeded to fall upon the second man who had managed to retrieve his sword and intended to attack. Although Thomas had no experience whatsoever in sword fighting, he laid into his attacker with such great power, that the other's every attempt to fend off the blows was to no avail. It wasn't till his opponent hit the ground and remained motionless that Thomas started to calm down…

He looked around him.

The street was empty.

The woman had disappeared.

The sound of shouting and crying people had faded into the distance.

In dismay he looked down on the men whom he had struck down. Never before in his life had he fought like this. Never before had he realised that such a raging, destructive force was hidden inside him. The powerful monster that had emerged in those terrible moments, filled him with shame and fear.

In great turmoil he entered his house again and dropped to the floor between the shards of broken pots and jars. He felt sick and miserable. What had he just done? Was this a sample of things to come? Could war with the Romans be any worse? He found it hard to imagine. The desperate cry of the woman he had managed to save, still rang in his ears. There would have been many like her who would have cried out in vain.

He thought about Silla and got up. Hiding the iron bar under his cloak, he went outside…

"I couldn't sleep because of the storm," Gedor said, "but when I realised that something far worse was about to happen, I woke up Tirza and Silla… They're safe for now. Well, as far as anyone can be safe in these circumstances… We had already taken some precautions and prepared a hiding place… That's where they are now… it was more with the Romans in mind and a siege of the city… I'm not sure what's worse. No, the rebels haven't been around here fortunately… But another time it could be different."

In response to Thomas' insistent knocking, Gedor had opened up and let him in, but only after making very sure that it was a friend and not a foe at the door.

"I don't know how they managed to get into the city, but it must have been by treachery," Thomas said. "On my way here, I talked to some other people who managed to evade the Idumeans in the nick of time. They told me that among these brutal men, there were many Zealots who had been locked up in the temple… No one had any idea how they managed to get out."

"With the aid of the Idumeans no doubt," Gedor suggested, "that seems to me the most obvious answer."

"And what about those six thousand men who kept guard?" Thomas asked. "We must assume the worst… We'll find out soon enough… But it doesn't look good…"

"I saw them coming…" Thomas began his story with some hesitation. Now that he knew nothing bad had happened to Silla and that for the moment she was safe, the tension left him. But he felt tired and depressed. Gedor had looked surprised when he produced the iron bar from under his cloak and stood it against the wall.

"They came from the direction of the temple… Like a tsunami they flooded the streets. I was on the roof of my house… Fleeing people ran past, followed by their pursuers. When most of them had passed, I saw a couple of men dragging a woman out of a house… And then…"

He nervously pulled with the corner of his mouth and found it hard to find the right words… "She cried and shouted for help… She begged for mercy… I don't know exactly what came over me, but I ran downstairs…"

Helplessly he looked at Gedor. "I think I beat both of them to death," he whispered, and his eyes revealed his deep pain.

It was quiet for a moment.

"What do you think would have happened if you hadn't done that?" Gedor asked.

Thomas left the question unanswered.

"I don't know what came over me," he said. "I scared myself… I became so enraged with those two men… Is that hatred? I thought they were so disgusting, so utterly brutish. But I'm scared of what I discovered within myself. I wanted to destroy them! Completely annihilate them… And I think that's what I did. When I stormed at them and yelled at them, it was as if someone else was doing it."

"What lives in you, lives in us all," Gedor said calmly. "I'm an old man. I'm no longer young enough to play the brave protector… But if someone would try to do something against my wife or Silla, I can't vouch for my behaviour. If I even imagine what could happen to them, I catch myself busy killing such evildoers… That's the sad reality of life, Thomas. Our inclinations don't make it easy. On top of that we live in a world where we need to protect everything that is dear and precious, against the evil around us…"

"I feel like I'm a murderer…," Thomas said with a sad face, "and we're not allowed to kill."

"Was there another way of dealing with it?" asked Gedor. "They could have killed you as well… They were already in the process of taking a life, my boy! You endangered your own life in order to save a defenceless woman… Isn't that vastly different? What do you think you'll do if you end up in the same situation again? Just imagine they want to molest Tirza or Silla…! I would protect them with my own life, I can assure you. It's just that I won't really be able to do much anymore… What can I expect from you Thomas? Should the weak be left undefended?"

He bent over to Thomas and looked him straight in the eyes. "Why did we stay in Jerusalem? Wasn't it to protect Silla…? But she isn't the only one in danger. We made the choice to stay here and that includes dealing with situations like you found yourself in, my lad. We're often forced to make a choice Thomas, just like this evening. You didn't hesitate for a moment as I understand it."

"It was terrible!"

"But it was also the right choice…"

"I'm not even sure it was a choice I made… I became enraged… It came over me… It just happened…"

"In any case you couldn't suffer the injustice. You prevented a crime from happening. Thomas, you saved her!"

"I want to follow the Lord Jesus," Thomas said, "and that makes it so difficult… How can I reconcile killing people, with that?"

"I understand…," Gedor sighed, "but how do you think you can protect Silla if you would shrink from the ultimate consequences? No don't worry. No one has talked about you. But we know why you stayed behind in Jerusalem, Thomas. As yet there's nothing wrong with my eyesight. You love Silla… She doesn't know, but my wife and I have noticed your attitude towards her. We won't tell her though. That's something you'll have to do yourself when the moment is right."

"This isn't the time to talk to a girl about that," Thomas said dejectedly.

Outside they heard the sad call of the prophet, "A voice against the newly wedded men and women… A voice against this entire people…"

The Idumeans had ignored him or else he would have succumbed to their rage.

"Yes, it's wiser to await better days if you're planning a wedding feast," Gedor agreed. "But if you declare your love for a girl in difficult times it can be a great support for her."

"So, you think, you suggest that…," Thomas sounded surprised.

"It's you who has to think," Gedor answered with a smile.

"Maybe she has no feelings for me!"

"Then you can still leave Jerusalem," said Gedor.

"No way!" Thomas declared.

"So, I'm wrong?"

"I love her," said Thomas.

"I think we noticed that already," smiled Gedor and he patted Thomas on the shoulder in a fatherly way. "Love is stronger than death, says Solomon in the Song of Songs. I fear we'll have much to do with death Thomas. The only thing that overcomes death is love."

"The love of God," Thomas responded.

"Yes, amen… which was poured out in our hearts through Christ's merit."

When the raging madness of the Idumeans came to an end, they discovered that the inhabitants of Jerusalem had never intended to hand the city over to the Romans. Perhaps it was embarrassment because of their gruesome misdeeds but more likely because they were appalled at the fanaticism of the Zealots who even exceeded them in wickedness, that they rather suddenly left the city. For both the citizens and the Zealots this came as a surprise. The Zealots didn't appear to miss them but continued with their attacks and murderous frenzies. Only the poorest citizens escaped their predatory raids.

Although it appeared as if the Romans weren't interested, these events didn't escape their attention. The officers urged Vespasian to make use of this turmoil and internal fighting and attack Jerusalem, however the experienced commander was of the opinion that by going against them now, the Jews would consolidate as one. Why not simply wait till they had wasted as much energy as possible on each other? All the effort the Jews put in to destroy each other in a civil war would only make things easier for the Romans, but not less glorious. It was his opinion, that it was easier to win the war with patience and self-control than with the sword. As long as the Jews were fighting among themselves, they wouldn't have time to prepare to fight the Romans. It also prevented them from sharpening their weapons, fortifying the city and building a well-prepared army.

Vespasian was proven right.

Jerusalem was busy destroying itself.

CHAPTER 12

"I NEED YOUR HELP," SAID Kish.

"Tell me what I need to do," Caleb replied.

"This evening I need to go to Jerusalem to make a delivery to someone who never allows me to enter his home beyond the entry hall. It's important that I learn some more about him but that's only possible if I can be inside his house without his knowledge."

"Sounds a bit suspicious," Caleb commented.

"Yes, you're right about that," Kish admitted. "However, I assure you that I don't have bad intentions."

"As long as you're not out to steal something."

"Do I look like a thief?"

"Honestly? No, not really. Tell me what you want me to do."

"Just come along with me at dusk and while I'm busy with the man, make sure he doesn't see you. Once I go inside with the last load of goods, you quickly run and stand next to the donkey and wave your hand to say goodbye. But make sure you don't say a word. After that, take the donkey to a place which I'll point out to you, and wait for me."

"Meanwhile you'll be inside? How long will that take?"

"No idea, but I don't think it will take longer than half an hour."

"A strange arrangement. But sure, you can count on me."

Rapha was very angry with himself.

He'd been out to do some debt collecting, making sure to charge the right amount of interest. One person he had to visit was a shop keeper, only a few streets away from where he lived. But it turned out that the shop had been looted, and the shopkeeper was killed!

From listening in on conversations, he understood that the shop had been raided, like so many other places in this chaotic city. While on the street, he'd controlled himself and resorted to some angry hissing and gnashing of teeth. Back home however, he let himself go. He pulled at his hair and ranted and raved about the misfortune that he'd suffered. He blamed himself that he hadn't gone to collect the debt a day earlier. But he was even more angry with the shopkeeper who had managed to get himself killed without paying off his debt.

Rapha's day had been ruined! Instead of being able to add a nice sum to his possessions, he now had to write off the debt. Loss was a terrible word for him. Especially where it concerned money. Besides, he already felt things weren't going his way. Of late, Simpleton hadn't been regular with his deliveries. The first time he missed a day, Rapha had given him a firm telling off. After all, he was the boss and Simpleton was receiving his pay. But the ignorant chap had told him that many farmers had moved away and now he had to go further afield to buy the barley.

Well, that may be so, but really it wasn't Rapha's problem. He just wanted more barley. He wanted to see his storehouse filled up. It was getting there but he could still fit in some more.

Fortunately, he hadn't suffered any loss by the rats.

Oh sure, he still thought he saw them scamper off when he went on his daily inspections through the rooms, but they hadn't touched the barley. It had been a rather smart idea of his to go and sleep downstairs.

Close to his money and his barley; things couldn't be better. Besides, he was hidden from the ruffians who wanted to rob other people's possessions. That shopkeeper should have been just as cunning. Then at least he could have paid his debt.

Rapha was really in a foul mood when Simpleton arrived again after dusk. But when he saw the heavily laden donkey, his bad mood subsided somewhat.

"Well, well. Good to see you again… Managed to find another farmer hey? That's a nice load!"

"It's all he had left for sale," Simpleton replied. "I got there just in time. He said he was also leaving…So just a few more and then I'll stop doing this. It takes me too long to find the farmers. Everyone is leaving. And by now, you should have your house full of barley anyway. Enough to feed a lot of poor people in this city for a few years."

"Mind your own business," Rapha growled. "I'll tell you when it's enough."

"But what if I can't find any more farmers?"

Rapha wasn't sure how to reply to that.

"Just have a good look," he said. "Don't forget you're also making some money." He felt that was his strongest argument.

"Just a little," Simpleton said contentedly.

"Right, and if you're frugal it will continue to grow. As long as you save it up. And now you'd better bring that barley inside."

Simpleton dragged the bags into the entry hall and received his pay.

"Oh, wait a minute!" he said suddenly. "I think there was one more bale."

He brought it inside and while Rapha turned to put the bale with the others, he carefully gave the front door a push so that it closed.

"Fool!" Rapha scolded, assuming Simpleton had gone straight outside again. But he sniggered scornfully. He hadn't paid Simpleton for that last bale and the extra profit gave him a happy feeling. It made up a little for his bad day!

He smirked when he held the door ajar and raised his hand. The dark shadow on the donkey waved back. After bolting the door, Rapha rubbed his hands together, lit a lamp and started his tough job to get the barley downstairs.

CHAPTER 13

"OVER EIGHT AND A half thousand people dead," Pagiel repeated softly to himself. "They've humiliated and butchered respectable people…! Homes have been plundered; women raped! Who are the animals responsible? What did you do to prevent it?" He looked sternly at his sons, one by one. "Well? How did you try to stop it?"

Hassub shook his head… "There was nothing we could do. Try to imagine! An army of tens of thousands of crazed men, out for blood! And you expect the four of us to stop it? Do you think we would even be sitting here if we had tried?"

"You have no idea what's going on in the city Father," Pallu said. "Your life is in danger if you dare to disagree with them."

"And that's Jews among themselves! Jews who sought the help of scum in order to butcher other Jews," Pagiel said with disgust. "I even heard that blood was pouring over the temple walls! … The blood of Jews…! O Creator of all life, how is this possible!" he said as he raised his healthy hand to the heavens. "How is it possible? What has come over us that such things are happening in the city where Your Name is proclaimed? Is this Your judgement over our sins?"

He turned to Hassub, "Is there no one left who raises his voice against them? No righteous person who would rather die than keep silent amid so many atrocities?"

"There were some," answered Hassub, "but they're the ones who indeed have been butchered."

"For example, the high priest Annas," Nadab said in support of his brother. "He spoke up. You know how he was opposed to the rebellion and warned the people... And there have been more like him. And no doubt there are others who would want to protest but they don't because they know what will happen."

"And what about you?" Pagiel asked. "What are you going to do now? In these circumstances there can surely be no justification for a righteous battle against the Romans. Because even we ourselves are trampling the law under foot!"

"Right now, no one has the courage to say that to our leaders," said Nadab. "But perhaps they will come to their senses. The rebellion against the Romans is going ahead in any case."

"But surely without us! You will withdraw!"

"Father," said Hassub, "you really don't have a grasp on what's happening out there... To withdraw is seen as treason and immediately punished with death."

"They seem like they're possessed," said Nimsi, taking part in the conversation. "It's really much worse than you can imagine Father. All common sense has gone out of the window. You can't trust anyone. Hassub is right... I fully support the revolt against the Romans, but what's happening now has nothing to do with it. I reckon that at the moment the wrong people are in power. I think I'll stay out of it for the time being."

"How do you want to do that?" Hassub asked with concern in his voice.

"How does he think to do that?" Pagiel flared up. "You should all simply follow his example! The very thought that my sons could be involved with this marauding mob..."

"But not long ago you had a very different opinion," Hassub said indignantly.

"Well, then you've misunderstood me!" Pagiel barked angrily. "Not in my wildest dreams did I ever want you to grow up as criminals. Our motivation in chasing away the Romans, has always been zeal for the service of the Lord and His temple."

"Yes, that's indeed our motivation and as far as I'm concerned that doesn't change," Hassub responded angrily. "But what Nimsi now wants to do is lunacy! It will cost us our lives. They'll search us out, I can assure you! I agree with him that the leadership of this movement has fallen into wrong hands. But that can be changed. I reckon we should simply bide our time. If we desert the cause now, we'll need to flee Jerusalem or go into hiding. We'll also miss out on any news to which we as insiders are now privy."

"Insiders…? Information…? Were you aware that they had called in the assistance of the Idumeans?" Pagiel asked.

"No," Hassub had to admit. "but…"

"No ifs and buts! You simply didn't know! And how they entered the city… Do you know that?"

"No, we don't know that either… But that's not to say…"

"It's a great relief to me that you know nothing about it," Pagiel said mockingly. "But it does prove that you as ordinary boys, are no closer to the source. By joining in with the leadership, you run the risk of being involved in similar atrocities."

"If we desert now, it doesn't only put us at risk, but you also," said Hassub. "I promise Father, that we won't participate in any criminal activities. If the leadership doesn't take control of the situation, the time will come that we withdraw from the rebellion."

"Despite the consequences," Nadab said in support.

"Perhaps it's better if we wait and see how things develop," Pallu chipped in. "As long as we participate in the revolt, you and the family are less likely to be at risk…"

"Don't fool yourselves!" said Pagiel. "After all the things I've heard in the past few days, I'm starting to think the prophet may be right after all."

"Silla my child, I'm so grateful to you," said Pagiel.

"You don't have to say that all the time Father," she smiled.

"But I need to say it. I want you to know. I have some catching up to do…"

He looked at her with sorrowful eyes.

"Silla…"

"Yes Father?"

"The events of recent days have caused me great concern. It's never occurred to me that we as Jews would one day wreak havoc amongst ourselves. Perhaps I was naïve, but there it is… Of course, bickering between us is not a new thing, but a civil war… And when I hear the latest news, that's what it's starting to look like …

I'm aware that you are trying to spare me; I've noticed that. But when I talk with Gedor or your brothers… I remember I said with conviction, there was no safer place than Jerusalem… That was when you came to tell me you were leaving the city. I could only think of war against the Romans. I would never have believed that the danger was already within our city walls… That's what I was thinking about while I saw you busy just now. Suddenly it got to me…

No, don't worry, I'm not bringing up the past again… I've already told you how sorry I am about all the things I inflicted upon you… Right now, I'm terribly concerned about everything that's happening around us… All of a sudden, I realise how dangerous it really is for you in Jerusalem… I can't stand the thought that something might happen to you… Silla, it's better that you leave the city… Actually, I'm starting to believe the mad prophet is not so mad after all. His message is starting to weigh heavily on me. I'll only be at peace if I know that you are somewhere safe… Go! Leave together with your uncle and aunt… Silla…"

She knelt down beside his bed and took his hand.

"Father," she said, unable to hide the emotion in her voice. "We've known from the outset the dangers we are facing. Naturally we're shocked by the events, but we're not exactly surprised by them. I understand that Jerusalem is no longer safe for me. But then, it's not safe for anyone really. A curse lies over the city. Sometimes I think the prophet is bringing a final warning from the Lord. He's a strange man, but he's definitely not crazy. For about six years he's been prophesying the same message. And that in spite of so many people trying to silence him. Isn't that remarkable? They've abused him and beaten him; he's even been tortured, but he continues nevertheless."

"I'm afraid you're right," said Pagiel earnestly. "That's exactly the reason why I want you to leave while it's still possible."

"Who would take care of you if aunt Tirza and I would be gone?" Silla asked. "No Father, I can't leave you behind in your helpless state. And for you, fleeing would be impossible. I'm staying with you."

"And if I order you to leave?" Pagiel asked.

"That would be terrible because I would have to be disobedient."

"Silla!"

"Don't send me away Father," she begged. "I'm convinced that my place is here right beside you, and that the Lord wants me to stay with you."

"He wants you to honour your parents, so you should listen to your Father and do as he says." Pagiel tried to be stern with her, but his voice was hesitant.

"I can't believe that the Lord would want me to abandon you."

"My dear child, you wouldn't be doing that. I'm asking you to leave. I would dearly like to be assured of your safety. It will make it so much easier for me when the time comes for me to die."

"The Lord told us not to be afraid and not worry about anything… Where would we really be safe anyway, Father? All of Israel is in turmoil. The Romans are cracking down on us. Dangers lurk everywhere… The only One we can rely on is the Lord and that's what I want to do."

"That gladdens my heart but still doesn't give me peace," Pagiel said. "Perhaps that doesn't sound very pious. I know I can only blame myself, nevertheless I'm very concerned. For the boys, but more so for you… If only I wasn't so incapacitated, maybe I would feel a bit different. But now… Anyone coming here with evil intentions can easily dispose of me and I wouldn't be able to protect you… I'll have a talk with Gedor."

"He agrees with me," Silla assured him. "We believe this is the only way for us. We're staying with you."

"Sadly, it seems you've inherited your father's stubbornness," Pagiel sighed.

"I don't want to be stubborn, but believing," Silla said.

"That's what I want too, my girl. But alas we differ in what we believe. I think it's better for you to go."

For a moment he was quiet and looked at her intently.

"You know," he began, searching for words. "I actually know so little about what really motivates you… I'm talking about that faith of yours… We've never really spoken about it… And I know that was my fault and not yours. The thought that you had fallen away from serving the one and only true God, made that impossible for me… I know I've lashed out terribly too. First against my brother and his wife and later, also against you… But really, I was in deep despair and didn't know how to deal with the situation… And I still don't know… If we're not one in the faith our forefathers delivered to us, then in reality there is a deep abyss between us. Then we speak as it were, two different languages and don't actually have proper contact with one another…

But when you're here, I don't experience it like that. On the contrary, I feel that we understand each other very well. Like we are of one mind… Or am I mistaken? Do I only experience it like that because I want it to be like that…?

That troubles me you see…

What do you think Silla? Am I wrong?"

"No Father, I experience it exactly like you… And that's not so strange really, is it? When uncle Gedor prayed for you, he even reiterated it with Hassub. We believe that the Lord is the Only God, the God of Abraham, Isaac and Jacob."

Pagiel shook his head in confusion.

"But don't you see then that you'll have to renounce that Man from Nazareth…?"

He couldn't even make himself say the name Jesus.

"What do you know about Him, Father?" Silla quietly asked him.

"I don't want to make you angry," he sighed and squeezed her hand a little tighter, as if he was afraid she might leave him.

"I would really love you to come to know the truth about Him," said Silla.

"I know that child, because I know the Scriptures."

"Uncle Gedor thought so too."

"Sadly, he let himself be…" he stopped.

"What did he let himself, Father?"

"Ah, we'd better stop now."

"I would so much like to talk to you about Him."

"I'm scared you'll get angry Silla… And I don't want to upset you! It's tearing me apart and I'm not sure if it's causing me to sin. Actually, I do know that we're not to love anything or anyone more than God… But I don't want to lose you again…"

"I won't get angry," assured Silla.

"Or sad…?"

"I would still really like to talk about it."

"Okay then… What I wanted to say was that Gedor has allowed himself to be misled by that Galilean. Sure, I can believe he was a very friendly man. I was still young, and I never met him, but I've heard much about him… Silla, over the years there've been so many who pretended to be the Messiah. He wasn't the first to do so. But I reckon … he was the worst…"

"Why the worst?"

"Because he made himself equal with the Most High God, praise His holy Name! That's why, Silla…! How can you not understand that? I find that inexplicable… And you were just a young girl. Still so immature… But Gedor was a Scribe. He should have known better… They've pulled you along in their thinking."

"But it was *I* who asked *them* about it," said Silla. "I saw something in their lives that attracted me. I wanted to be like that too. There was something about them that I missed in so many others."

Pagiel looked at her sadly.

"When I heard you and the boys talk about the Messiah, it was always about someone who would come to set us free from the oppression of the Romans. Uncle Gedor and aunt Tirza however, told me that the Messiah had already come. That He had healed the sick and raised the dead to life again, and proclaimed peace to those tired and humble of heart. That He had come to redeem us from our sins. That He did so by taking upon Himself the punishment for sin and bearing it in our place. That He did so on the cross."

"Silla," said Pagiel, and his voice was full of compassion, "they told you a beautiful story. But I know what really brought him to the cross. It was his own sins! The high priest and the whole Sanhedrin heard from his own mouth that he considered himself equal to the Almighty! That's blasphemy my dear child. Think about it. A mortal man who elevated himself to be God! According to the law there's only one punishment for that."

Silla nodded silently.

Pagiel thought he had hurt her deeply.

"Forgive me if I cause you grief," he begged her, "but I can't see it any differently. I'll give anything to make you see the truth. That's my only motivation. Please believe me."

"I don't doubt that at all, Father. I know your intentions are well meant… But you are truly mistaken if you think we followed a human being who made himself God. That's just impossible! That idea is just as objectionable to us as it is to you… We don't believe in a man who wanted to be God, but in God Who wanted to become man in order to save us."

For a moment Pagiel was speechless.

He looked so bewildered that it scared her for a second.

"What's the matter?" she asked him and lovingly stroked his hand. But he shook his head and put her at ease.

"No, it's okay," he said. Then he quietly repeated to himself, "God who became man!"

CHAPTER 14

T HE CHAOS ONLY GREW worse.

The stronghold of Masada had become a robber's den from which the surrounding towns and cities were raided. And there were more places used for this purpose. The people endured intolerable suffering. The various rebel leaders tried to outdo one another in brutality and cruelty. It seemed that the Romans didn't take much notice and only intervened when it became necessary for political or strategic reasons. It suited Vespasian that the Jews were fighting each other and weakening themselves. He continued with his plan to close off all Jerusalem's access roads and to prepare a siege against it.

However, in Rome things weren't peaceful either. The contest for power was ignited when the notorious reign of emperor Nero ended abruptly in suicide. For thirteen years this cruel man had ruled the Roman Empire. Especially the Christians had suffered much because of him. When Nero had wanted to clear space in Rome for his building plans, he first caused a great fire to burn through the city, and then blamed it on the Jews and Christians. Whereas the Jews were afforded some protection, the Christians had become victims of the uncontrolled hatred of both the government and the populace. Many died as martyrs. Nero had even used some of them as living torches for his garden parties.

As soon as Vespasian heard about the death of the emperor, he delayed his siege of Jerusalem. He wanted to wait till the situation in Rome had stabilised and the government was once again in firm hands. Those hands would become his hands because law and order were not restored in Rome till the legions proclaimed the experienced Vespasian to be the next emperor!

His son Titus received orders to continue the war and to lead the siege against Jerusalem.

For the Jewish people, things continued to go from bad to worse. More and more citizens became convinced that they had less to fear from the occupying forces than from their own people and therefore sought protection with the Romans.

Moreover, another scourge plagued Jerusalem. A certain Simon, a strong and bold bandit, had managed to gather a large following. After he had terrorised the land, he succeeded in establishing himself among the other gangs in Jerusalem. There, together with his son Eleazar, he ruled with frightening terror, increasing the desperate plight of the citizens. Unfortunately, those same citizens had first invited him in.

John, who wouldn't tolerate another tyrant beside himself, fought against Simon and Eleazar in a battle of life and death. The battle ebbed and flowed with disastrous consequences. Whenever they had opportunity, they set fire to each other's provisions. Food which could have fed the inhabitants of the city for many years, went up in flames. Both parties fought with bitter hatred. The immediate surroundings of the temple where the fighting took place, were transformed into a desolate, burnt-out waste land.

The prophet continued to deliver his warnings, "A voice from the East... A voice from the West... Woe Jerusalem... Woe the temple... Woe this people..."

"Silla tells me that you want to talk with me."

"Yes, that's what I asked. It was good of you to come Gedor."

"You like to discuss what we believe... Did I understand that correctly?"

"Yes Gedor, that's right."

"Pagiel, to be frank, I'm hesitant to do so. I think of all those times we've tried, both Tirza and I. For years you banned us from coming here… And when I recall your tirades, I shudder. Not so much for my sake but for yours."

"Because of my hot-tempered nature."

"Yes, correct, your hot-tempered nature… I'm not scared for myself but… We really don't want to lose you…"

"You mean that I might cause myself harm."

"Yes… The excitement might prove too much for you."

"You've always managed to deal with it Gedor… I've had a lot of time to think… I've thought back of the days when we were children. Two such very different characters and yet we could always get along, couldn't we…? You were always very patient with the weak… I still remember that you came home with a lamb which you'd found in the fields. It had been abandoned because it was too weak… A weak animal. You pampered it and cared for it till it could stand on its own legs and return to the fold again. However, it wouldn't be separated from you anymore."

"You enjoyed it just as much as I did Pagiel."

"But that patience, Gedor, that patience… only you had it. With me the lamb would have died. Like so many other things have nearly died around me…

You're wondering if I've been talking to Silla?

Yes, I have. And something has happened Gedor… She said something that struck me like lightning. Something I could have thought of myself, but its significance never dawned on me… That's what I wanted to talk about."

"Why talk to me, if she said it to you Pagiel?"

"I don't think she even realises what caused this confusion in me Gedor… I could have asked her to talk some more. But I'm afraid that I may not have dared to say everything I wanted to. With you I can shout, with you I can quarrel and get angry… You can take it… I can't do that to Silla. I don't want to lose her again Gedor… I know I've already been much too hard on her."

"She won't leave you Pagiel."

"It's not that Gedor. But I don't want all her thoughts of me to be associated with fear and sorrow. Not again! I'm so happy to have her close to me, however I want to ask you to take her to safety somewhere outside of Jerusalem…But let's talk about that later. First, I want to talk with you about those things that have so unsettled me."

"Go ahead then."

"I tried to make her see the fallacy of what you believe. Did she tell you?"

"No, she didn't."

"Okay then… I won't go through all the details, but it came down to this: I wanted her to see that the Galilean only had himself to blame for his death because he had declared before the high priest, to be equal to the Almighty… I tried very carefully to tell her that according to the law, only one punishment is possible for blasphemy, and so he was justly crucified… I'm not sure if it's because of my illness Gedor, but I've changed. I felt miserable when I said those things and feared that I had caused her much grief. But to my great surprise she acknowledged what I said…

At first that confused me because I hadn't at all anticipated such a reaction. But what she said next, left me totally bewildered… Perhaps I would have heard you say the same words if I'd taken the time and effort to listen to you previously and had discussed it with you. You probably think it's dumb, but it was all new to me… She said: we don't believe in a man who became God, but in God Who became man in order to save us… And while she spoke, it dawned on me that the first part I could rightfully dismiss as blasphemous, but not the latter! I can't deny that He could do it if He wanted to… The whole idea has become something of an obsession to me because, if it's *possible*, it could also *happen*."

He hesitated for a moment.

"Or could even really have happened?"

Pagiel looked at his brother helplessly.

"Help me please… Let's talk about it together. And put up with me if I fall back into my old habits. I have questions and perhaps you have the answers… We both know the Scriptures… But what do you know more than I, Gedor?"

Deeply touched, Gedor had listened to his brother. He understood that the Lord had brought Pagiel to this point. Quietly he prayed for wisdom, for the guidance of the Holy Spirit so that he could be a blessing to his brother.

"I don't think I know more than you," he answered. "But it's the Lord who has to shed His light on the letter of the text, so it comes alive for us. The righteous will see the light, as the psalmist says. Why would it not be possible for the Almighty to come to earth as a man? Why would He not be able to make Himself the same as us?"

"Why would He do that?" asked Pagiel.

"Yes, that's the next question," Gedor answered. "But let's first establish that it's possible for Him to reveal Himself as a human being."

"If that's what He wanted to do, yes He could."

"Isn't it even most likely, that if He reveals Himself to mankind, He does so in human form…? Hasn't He created us in His image? Something of the eternal invisible God, must be visible in us. There must be some resemblance. He made us in His own likeness.

When He appeared to Abraham, didn't He also appear in human form? He wasn't ashamed to lower Himself to do that. He spoke to Abraham as a man with his friend…

The wife of Manoah was also addressed by a Man, who announced the birth of Samson, while she was out in the fields. Scripture tells us it was the Angel of the Lord who appeared to her. Read it again, Pagiel. When the Man performed a miracle, ascending in the flame of offering, they realised it was God Himself who had been and spoken to them. And they feared greatly. Manoah even thought he would die because 'they had seen God'. But his wife understood more clearly: the Lord does not appear to people to kill them, but that they may live…

And what about Job when he complained that the Lord is not a man like himself, with whom he could reason if He would take him, Job, to court? Doesn't he show a strong desire for a Mediator who can lay a hand on them both? And in my opinion, he prophesied of this, when he says that he knows his Redeemer lives and will appear in the flesh."

Pagiel listened intently to his brother.

"All these things you know already," Gedor smiled. "I'm really giving a lesson on things you've learned long ago…"

"Please continue, I'm listening," said Pagiel.

"Very well then," said Gedor, "when we consider the appearance of God revealed in human form, the vision at the time of the prophet Ezekiel's calling stands out. I'm sure you'll recall it… He describes something that looks like a throne… and on that throne something that looks like… a man! If you like, I'll get the scroll of the book for you and show it to you Pagiel. The prophet says that the person's appearance was like that of the glory of the Lord!"

"But He was not a man."

"No, God is not a man. But when He wants, He can appear like a man."

"So here we arrive at the question, why He would do that," said Pagiel.

"To make an end of sin. To save us from death. Isaiah speaks of this already, Pagiel when he says, 'But He was wounded for our transgressions, He was bruised for our iniquities; The chastisement for our peace was upon Him and by His stripes we are healed.' That's why He had to become like one of us. He suffered in our place and believed in our place…!"

"Believed?"

"Yes, He has done for us what we could not do: Believe! Through His death and resurrection, He demonstrated that we can fully trust in God's mercy."

"Please explain that…"

"On the cross, Jesus was deserted by God. That's what He cried out in His agony. Yet He continued to trust in God and addressed Him as His Father… You and I wouldn't be able to do that Pagiel. No one could! Not a single person. Only He, Who by His resurrection from the dead, proved to be the Son of God."

"Are you implying that the Lord Himself is the Messiah?" asked Pagiel with bated breath.

"Can the Messiah be anything else but equal to God?" Gedor replied. "Doesn't God say that besides Him there is no Saviour…? And concerning the fact that He came into the world as a man, doesn't Isaiah prophesy: 'For unto us a Child is born, unto us a Son is given; and the government will be upon His shoulder. And His name will be called Wonderful, Counsellor, Mighty God, Everlasting Father, Prince of Peace'? How is it possible for the Messiah to be just a man, if such things are prophesied about Him? Isn't that totally impossible? Who can be Child and everlasting Father at the same time? This can only be said of the eternal Creator!"

"A Child… a Son…," whispered Pagiel. There was excitement in his face.

"I'm wearing you out!" said Gedor, suddenly concerned.

"A Child… A Son…?" Pagiel repeated. "Almighty God… Father and Son…? No, you're not wearing me out Gedor… I never wanted to listen and even now I feel strong resistance. But at the moment I can't think of counter arguments… Perhaps I was afraid years ago… Afraid that you could be right…"

His eyes drifted though the room.

"Where's Silla?"

"Would you rather talk with her now?"

"No, it's not that, but I suddenly wondered where she is. Didn't she come with you?"

"Yes, she did, but she thought you wanted to talk with me. Shall I call her?"

"There's no need. She probably has something to attend to. She won't be bored."

"We brought along a young man from our congregation who has also remained in Jerusalem. His name is Thomas, son of Shobal the potter; and that's also his trade. I think you know his father. I'll introduce him to you when we leave."

"Why hasn't he left Jerusalem with the others? Is he looking after the business?"

"Something like that… But he's already experienced some terrible things with all those riots. During the raid of the Idumeans he had to fight for a woman's life and his home was totally smashed

up. Things are going from bad to worse in Jerusalem, Pagiel…
There's a threat of disaster hanging over the city."

"God can still turn the tide," Pagiel said.

"That will take a great miracle."

"That's what I'm hoping for."

"As is your son, Hassub. But I don't believe we're allowed to count on that. Among the leaders in Jerusalem there's no hint of regret or remorse, let alone humbleness. No, it doesn't look good at all… Only 'he who dwells in the secret place of the Most High shall abide under the shadow of the Almighty…'"

And Pagiel added, "'I will say of the Lord, He is my refuge and my fortress; My God, in Him I will trust.'"

"Amen." Gedor acknowledged.

"Gedor!"

"Yes, what is it Pagiel. What can I do for you?… I see that you're tired."

"Please come back soon, will you? Then we can talk some more… I'd like to know more."

———

"I heard you had a visitor, that young man and son of Shobal… Gedor introduced him to me before they left. He looks to be a nice person Silla, and handsome too. Have you known him long?"

"He was a member in our congregation."

"So you already had contact with each other?"

"Father… He doesn't even know I exist."

"Well, he would have to be blind as a bat if that were true!" Pagiel blurted out. "I don't want to make you vain, but he'll have to search a long time to find a woman more beautiful than you."

"Father…," she begged him.

"Sorry, that was silly of me. You're even blushing. I apologise. Don't mind me… But he seemed such a bright young man…"

He was observing her closely when a sudden thought occurred to him. "Silla," he said quietly, "would you want him to notice you?"

From afar the call of the prophet penetrated their home…

"Now is not the time for such things," she replied.

"Love is as strong as death itself," Pagiel said. "And neither take any notice of circumstances."

CHAPTER 15

"HAVE YOU HEARD THAT John wants to take the wood dedicated for the temple, and use it for the war effort?" Pallu asked Nimsi.

"I've even seen it with my own eyes," replied Nimsi, "they've already started. Beautiful timber from the Lebanon, massive trees with perfectly straight trunks. It would have cost a lot of money… Not to mention the effort to get it here…"

"But it was destined for the temple! That's shameful! How dare they lay their hands on it! It's a wicked thing to do! I heard they want to make war machines. John has ordered the lumber to be cut into planks and beams, to make towers for fighting here in Jerusalem. As if the mayhem isn't bad enough already. I don't even dare to tell Father about it… People trip over the corpses. And let no one try to bury even one of them because there'll always be some people around the corner who'll kill you for it… Where will this end? This was never our intention, was it Nimsi? Not mine in any case. I thought we'd fight the Romans together but until now, I've seen nothing but the blood of our own people flowing in the streets. How can we justify this before God?"

"I don't think we can," Nimsi answered. "As far as that goes you're right… It's also becoming increasingly risky, to not participate in things. They're starting to notice. They appointed me to help with cutting up the dedicated timber, but I ran away. I don't think I'll be showing myself there again… Father was right. We need to end this, Pallu."

"We should have done that a long time ago!"

"I agree but that's speaking with the benefit of hindsight. We'll need to find a good hiding place somewhere."

"The best thing to do is to leave the city altogether."

"And how do you propose to do that? They're keeping a close eye on the gates. If they suspect that we're defecting to the Romans, we're done for!"

"And what about Hassub and Nadab?"

"Nadab has already expressed similar thoughts but I'm not so sure about Hassub. He still wants to see how things develop. But what else is there to wait for? The streets can hardly be navigated anymore because of the rubbish and the dead bodies. The temple surrounds are destroyed. The city stinks like one big rubbish heap."

"It's all going wrong. And let's be honest, we've seen it coming for some time already. We let ourselves be fooled by our hatred of the Romans. We can't claim that we've only just realised it. We didn't *want* to see it. We allowed all kinds of strange elements to enter Jerusalem. We thought to gain fellow freedom-fighters. And what are they doing? They're butchering one another. And the common people are being plundered... I'm worried about Father and Silla... I'm not sure what you want to do but I'm pulling out. Come what may."

"I'll talk to the others again, if I can find them. But in any case, I'm with you. We have to pull out of this mess. But it won't be easy."

"One thing still bothers me... Can we just leave Father behind?"

"Of course, I've thought about that too. But what can we do for him if we stay here? And it's impossible to take him along. At least here he's well taken care of... Besides, he's told us himself that we should quit."

"Perhaps he won't be able to stay in his house though. Won't they be looking for us there if we disappear?"

"We'll warn Gedor and ask him for advice."

"Aren't we simply taking the easy way out?"

"Maybe so, but what else can we do? Our lives are at stake, don't forget that!"

Nadab was nowhere to be found and, as usual, Hassub wanted to delay making a decision. Pallu and Nimsi confided in Gedor and went into hiding, while waiting for an opportune moment to flee the city. Attempts to flee were quite common when disenchanted rebels became fed up with the shedding of blood among brothers. They risked being caught and tried because no mercy could be expected from their former brothers-in-arms.

CHAPTER 16

KISH REINED IN HIS donkey and dismounted. Although few people frequented the area, he proceeded with caution. He had heard a soft rustling in the bushes and when his donkey also pricked up its ears, he was on high alert. It could simply be an animal trying to run off. However, on closer inspection he discovered a broad trail that led toward the undergrowth. That made him suspicious. They weren't animal tracks. Would it be a trap? The area was isolated, and it wasn't likely that he would meet other people. And yet... he'd made a habit of being prepared for anything.

He inched carefully toward the bushes from where he thought the sound had come. As he cautiously pushed aside the foliage, he saw a man sitting on the ground a little further on. He was a Roman. He had removed his helmet and placed it on the ground beside him, but held his sword in his fist, ready to defend himself.

It was immediately clear to Kish that he didn't need to fear this Roman. The very fact that the soldier didn't jump to his feet and approach him with his sword, showed Kish enough. The man was wounded and couldn't walk. They appraised one another for a few seconds.

"Don't think I won't put up a fight," the Roman growled and defensively held up his sword.

"Is your leg broken?" Kish asked.

The soldier looked at him suspiciously.

"I'm on my own," said Kish, anticipating the man's thoughts.

He saw that the soldier didn't believe him.

"On your own… in these times… in this area?" He kept his sword at the ready.

Kish believed that the Roman wouldn't throw his sword at him. After all, if he missed, he would be helpless and at his mercy. A true warrior would see the sense of that.

"You have nothing to fear from me," Kish said. "Don't be scared that I'll attack a wounded man."

"Scared?" the soldier mocked.

Kish tried to calm him down, "No I didn't mean it like that. I would consider myself a coward for attacking a wounded person. Put that sword away and let me have a look at you."

"Stay away from me Jew!"

Kish shrugged his shoulders and sighed. "I'm sure you're a brave man," he said, "but not a very sensible one, it seems. I understand that you don't immediately trust me, but really, what do you have to lose? Your lips are cracked due to thirst. That means you've been here for a long time without a drink. You're not counting on your mates to come and rescue you, else they would have found you by now… There's no water around here and… just hold on," he interrupted himself. He went back to his donkey to get a water skin.

"Here you go," he said when he returned, and threw the sack to the surprised man. It was clear he hadn't seen that coming.

"Once you've had a drink you might think clearly again… Come on, drink up or do you think I'm trying to poison you?"

The Roman observed him with a peculiar look in his eyes.

Then he put the sword down, eagerly grabbed the water skin and gulped down the water.

"Here are some dried figs for you as well," said Kish and threw the food to him. "If you don't want my help, there's nothing else I can do for you. But realise what you're doing! If you want me to leave you here like this, you'll die of hunger and thirst. Or, if bandits find you, they'll kill you. The chance of being found by your fellow Romans seems very slim. I've offered my help but now it's your choice.

Of course, you're not really such good friends with us Jews … I wish you well… You can keep the rest of the water…"

Kish turned around and started to walk off. However, before he had reached his donkey the soldier called him back.

"So, you're really on your own?"

"Yes," said Kish. "I told you that didn't I? Shall I have a look at your leg now?"

"What do you know about broken bones?" the soldier asked grumpily.

"One can at least look," Kish answered without giving anything away.

"Just having a look won't do any good. I've done that myself already. My right leg is broken, and my left foot appears to be sprained. There's no way I can walk."

"How did you end up in these bushes?" Kish asked while examining the broken leg.

"I rolled my way here."

"I'll try to apply a splint… May I borrow your hatchet?"

The soldier hesitated for a moment.

"I need it to chop up some bits of wood," Kish explained. "How else am I to make a splint? You may do it yourself if you think that's safer."

The hatchet was handed to him, and he found some branches suitable for splints. He cut some strips of cloth from his own clothes and after setting the leg as well as possible he bound it up.

"Just grit your teeth for a moment," he told the soldier. But the latter scorned his advice.

When the sprained ankle had also been bandaged, the Roman attempted to stand up.

However, although he bore the pain unflinchingly, he was unsuccessful.

"It's hard to see you march even half a mile in this condition," said Kish, "and that's nothing to be ashamed of." Kish saw the soldier had broken out in a sweat at his attempt. "Where can I take you?"

Despite his hopeless situation and the pain which he no doubt suffered, he managed to look at Kish with a grin on his face. And he noticed something that must have escaped him earlier. The Jew had something so innocent about him, that all distrust toward him instantly vanished.

"If you can just drop me off at the tenth legion, I'll be most grateful," he said sarcastically. "But I suspect you won't feel like doing that."

"Are you stationed with them?" Kish asked.

"More or less… But in any case, I know the tenth legion is coming to Jerusalem from Jericho."

"So, you need to go there too? To Jerusalem, I mean?"

"It's no secret so you may as well know. Yes, to Jerusalem. If I can offer you some advice, stay far away from it."

"I live there."

"Well, this will be a good opportunity to relocate."

"But where to?"

"Good question. Wherever you go, make sure it's not where we are going to be."

Kish picked up the sword and gave it to the Roman. Then he reached under his arms and pulled him up.

"Just lean on me and I'll support you as best I can," he said.

They left the bushes and walked over to the donkey. There Kish helped the surprised man into the saddle and took the reins.

For a while they travelled without talking. The Roman was first to break the silence.

"So, what are you planning to do next?" he asked. "Don't tell me you want to bring me to Jericho?"

"Well in any case, some way in that direction," Kish admitted. "Perhaps we'll find a solution on the way… But if not, I'll deliver you to an outpost in the vicinity of Jericho."

"You must be mad!" the Roman replied. "I meant what I said before! If you have any sense at all, stay away from us!"

"Do you want to go on by yourself or something? That means you'll have to walk because I'm not giving you my donkey."

"You don't seem to understand that you're in danger! There's a war on, man! Surely, it's no news that Galilee is destroyed. And because you people don't know how to quit, we'll take Jerusalem as

well. And whatever resists us on the way, we'll trample underfoot…
I'm not exactly tender-hearted, but in light of what you've just done
for me I don't wish that on you… And I must admit that I still
don't understand… If the roles had been reversed, you would still be
sitting there. You're a strange one… By the way, what's your name?"

"Kish," he said. "My name is Kish, but most people know me by
a different name."

"My name is Gaius," the Roman said, "but if you were to yell
out that name by night in the middle of our camp, half the legion
will jump to attention. Everyone knows me as the Ram… What do
they call you?"

"Simpleton…"

"Sim…" Gaius swallowed his words and grinned to himself. So
there… he wasn't mistaken. "You're a good fellow Kish."

"I've heard that before," Kish replied innocently. "But tell me,
how did you end up in those bushes back there, wounded and all on
your own?"

"That's a bit of an odd story. Those scoundrels will laugh for
years to come I reckon. It happened like this. We were on our
way with a column of heavy equipment when suddenly I needed
to go urgently. I was sitting on the last wagon. As I jumped off, I
already sprained my ankle. Then while looking for a sheltered spot,
I stepped into a hole in the ground made by some animal… Well,
the rest you know. I could shout all I wanted but they couldn't hear
me because they'd moved too far away already, and no one missed
me. In hindsight I should have reported what I was doing. But who
would expect something like this? I had no provisions with me
either… And I couldn't walk anywhere. I couldn't even stand up. I
implored all the gods I could think of."

"Except the only true One," said Kish.

"What do you mean?"

"There's only One God," Kish responded, "the God of Abraham,
Isaac and Jacob."

"You mean to say that our gods are no good?" Gaius grinned. "If
I could walk, I would knock your block off Kish."

"If you could walk, I wouldn't let you ride on my donkey."

"If I had been able to stand on my own two legs, I would have simply commandeered your donkey. There's a war on Kish and things get a bit rough. But you are partially right, of course. Not one of the gods came to the rescue when the Ram needed them most."

"And then the Eternal God sent this simple Jew to you," said Kish.

For a moment Gaius was stunned but then he burst out into loud laughter.

"That's a good one!" he shouted.

"I meant to say the Only true God," Kish corrected himself.

Gaius wiped the tears from his eyes and the sweat from his forehead.

"Do you know," he started, "that one time, I spent a whole night talking to a rabbi? It was very interesting. He knew a whole lot about the faith of your people. I really liked it but found it difficult to combine it with the life of a legionary soldier. I would happily have spent more time talking with him, but the next day he was executed. I'm not sure why but there must have been a reason for it. I was sorry because he had a lot of knowledge…

You are a strange people Kish. We Romans take life a bit easier…

And then there are those Christians as well. I never understood whether they belong to you or not, because they're not all Jews, are they? They believe in Jesus who was also a Jew. But they claim that He is God and He's been put to death… That would be true because Pilate had Him crucified, and when we do something like that, we do it properly… Yet they claim that He's alive again… It's quite something to believe all that, I tell you.

Hey Kish, surely that's not the same God as yours…? Or is it?"

"The Lord our God is One," answered Kish.

"You don't mind if I say that I don't understand at all?" Gaius asked with a smile. "I've seen a lot of crooks die on the cross but a god… no I don't think I've been privileged to see that… I don't think too much about those things Kish. I don't expect the gods to descend to earth any time soon. They don't even pay attention when you lie there with a broken leg! Who knows what would have happened if you hadn't found me by chance…"

"I don't believe in chance; I believe in God," replied Kish. "How's your pain, by the way? Are you all right?"

"You're reminding me of it now, but I'm doing alright… Indeed, you're a good fellow Kish…What you're trying to tell me is that my gods abandoned me, but your God sent you to come and help me. Am I right? I don't want to disillusion you, but who's to say that those gods of mine didn't have a late change of heart and sent you to me?"

"Well, I can clarify that! Those gods of yours can't change their mind because they can't think. Our God is gracious and merciful; that's why you're still alive. Otherwise, I would have killed you when you lay there so helplessly in the bushes."

"Wow. Do you know there's a death penalty for saying such things? Watch what you're saying once we're among the people again, because they won't stand for it… I think we would get on well with each other Kish. Pity you're in the other camp. Pity…

By the way, if I haven't yet made it clear, I'll spell it out for you: I'm very well aware that I owe you my life. If you hadn't found me and helped me, I would have been rotting away in a few days' time…I realise that very well, Kish… They say I'm hard as nails, but I'll never forget this, although I can't understand your motivation. You ascribe it to your God, and I'm inclined to believe that because I can't think of another reason. This country is consumed by hatred but then I meet a Jew like you… If we survive this war and I can help you out with something…"

"Who knows, perhaps one day I'll call upon you for a favour," said Kish.

"I hope you'll take my advice and stay away from Jerusalem."

"I can't do that," said Kish. "All my friends live there."

"Then they should also make themselves scarce."

"Many of them believe that Jerusalem will never succumb."

"And what about you?" Gaius asked.

Kish didn't respond but had again taken on that look of a simpleton, causing the Roman to wonder.

"I'm not a leader in the army Kish. But I can tell you for a certainty that Rome has determined to quell the rebellion once and for all. And everyone understands that to do so, Jerusalem must be taken. Truly, you should not be there. Leave, before it's too late."

"I won't abandon my friends."

"That I can understand," sighed Gaius while thinking: you don't even abandon your enemies.

"In case I need to call upon you one day, where do I find you?" asked Kish.

"What, after the war?" Gaius asked.

"No, during the siege of Jerusalem."

"Have you totally lost your senses, Kish? Do you really not understand what the situation will be like? On the walls and in their close vicinity, it will be a matter of life and death. And anyone who tries to get out of the city runs the risk of being killed on the spot."

Such a simple soul, Gaius thought.

"Only in extreme necessity of course," said Kish. "You never know what may happen. It won't be easy, but is there a way I can find you?"

"Listen Kish. I've already told you, we're on the way to Jerusalem with heavy equipment. I'm not part of the infantry or cavalry. I'm in the 10th legion and I specialise in taking responsibility for the heavy war machines. Those heavy implements have always been the love of my life. Catapults and battering rams are my pride and joy and I'm always thinking of ways to improve them. Hence also my nickname: the Ram. So, if I can be found anywhere, it will be near those things. But it's insanity to try and find someone in the heat of a battle."

"I'm not saying *that* I'll do it but just *if* … Please keep in mind that it's *possible*. And then don't forget who I am."

"I won't forget you," Gaius assured him, "but I sincerely hope you forget all about those stupid ideas. My rank is that of centurion… I'm only called out when there's trouble, you see. That heavy machinery requires a lot of manpower, so there will be many soldiers around and you'd be dead before you could ask about me. In time of war hatred boils over, and if confronted with an enemy you would first chop off their head and then ask questions."

Kish nodded. "That's clear enough," he said.

"That's what I thought," Gaius grinned. He pointed into the distance. "If I'm not mistaken, we're getting visitors."

"A patrol," said Kish. "I'll hand you over to them."

CHAPTER 17

"**W**E'LL WAIT TILL NIGHTFALL. If we're given the opportunity to escape the city, they won't be able to catch us in the dark," said Nimsi.

"Yes, that's assuming we can get out. But that's the hard part, getting through the gate. Did you still manage to see Nadab?"

"Unfortunately not. I haven't seen him for days and I don't dare mention it to Father. Who knows, he may have perished in one of the street fights. It's such a chaos out there. Father has no idea how bad things are. I must confess, I'm finding it difficult to leave him behind like this. We won't see him again, Pallu."

"I ask myself how we could have been so blind as to believe in this whole business, Nimsi. We're now obliged to flee the city to save our skins and we must leave our loved ones behind. I feel so guilty."

"I did tell uncle Gedor. He'll make arrangements for Father if it becomes apparent that he's no longer safe in his own home."

"We don't have a choice."

"No, we don't."

"I just hope they won't take it out on Nadab and Hassub once they notice that we've left."

"It's no use thinking about it. After all, we asked them to come with us. It's their choice to stay."

As they waited in the ruins of a plundered and burnt-out house for darkness to fall, the hours ticked by and the tension grew. The hideout was one that held no interest for bandits who might be out for spoil. The ruins showed evidence that others had been there already. Only refugees might consider using this place as a shelter.

When at last the streets were cloaked in darkness, they left their hideout and made their way toward the gate they had chosen for their escape attempt. At a safe distance they staked out the area.

In the torchlight, they could make out groups of armed men. It seemed impossible to get past them.

"We're asking to be killed if we try," Nimsi whispered. "We'll have to wait for a better opportunity or dream up a clever strategy."

"I can't think of anything," Pallu whispered. "I've already racked my brain over it."

"In that case, we may as well go back because this is not exactly a safe place."

But at the very moment of their intended retreat, some men carrying a bier, arrived at the gate and sought permission to pass. The conversation that ensued appeared to stir the emotions as their voices sounded more and more agitated. Pallu and Nimsi saw the guards recoil and make threatening gestures.

"Probably someone who died of pestilence, whom they seek to bury outside the city," Nimsi suggested.

"I don't think they will let them."

"But it's also not permitted to bury them within the city walls. And the corpses are piling up."

"Perhaps it's an important person... I'm curious to see if they succeed. They don't seem to take no for an answer."

"They're taking a big risk if you ask me. Just listen how excited they're getting."

"But the guards don't dare to get close to the bier."

Suddenly Pallu grabbed Nimsi by the arm.

"Look there!" he whispered excitedly. "Look who's standing there in the shadows. I'm sure it's Nadab!"

"I think you're right!" Nimsi answered softly. "Would he have been assigned to guard duties?"

"It sure looks like it."

"He won't get a better chance to escape."

The commotion at the gate continued to grow as the dispute raged. More and more guardsmen involved themselves in the altercation. At the same time people came in through the gate who apparently had permission to enter.

"Perhaps this is an opportunity given to us by the Lord!" whispered Nimsi. "Let's make use of it. We won't get a second chance! Come on!"

They started off towards the gate. As inconspicuously as possible they walked past the groups of loudly disputing men …

Making their way against the stream of people coming in, they reached the gate, taking great care to avoid the torchlight. Nimsi hoped to meet Nadab, but he was nowhere to be seen…

The short escape through the gate seemed an hour-long torture. Their nerves were stretched to breaking point. In their hearts they prayed…

At last they reached the exit but there they encountered the greatest danger! Four armed rebels who were checking those who wanted to enter the city, were just processing the last group of people!

In a few moments the gates would be shut, and the heavy bars secured in place.

The brothers realised they had no time to waste. Caution was no longer an option. They needed to act and would most certainly draw attention to themselves…

Only a few people stood between them and their freedom.

Quick as lightening they sprang into action, knocking down the men who stood in their way! For a moment there was confusion but then two of the guards rushed out with drawn swords, trying to stop them. As the brothers knew that any delay would mean a certain death, they didn't hesitate for a moment. With all their strength they rushed at the guards, striking them with their swords so that they fell. Then they stormed away and fled into the darkness.

It all went so quickly that the onlookers hardly realised what was happening. The other two guards who hadn't been wounded, made an attempt to follow, but soon abandoned the chase. Outside the walls there was total darkness and they realised that pursuit was futile.

Nimsi and Pallu however didn't take any chances but ran as fast as they could to get away from the city. The terrain outside the gates was difficult to navigate in the dark, because of the many vegetable gardens, interspersed with drainage channels and ditches. The parcels of land were often separated by fences or stone walls, presenting the fleeing brothers with almost insurmountable obstacles.

Panting, stumbling, falling and standing up again, over obstacles and through ditches, they didn't allow themselves a break until it was impossible for them to continue, and they were close to exhaustion. Their hearts pounded to bursting point and their breath wheezed through their lips.

They stood with their arms around each other's shoulders, breathing heavily when suddenly they froze in fear. The sound of running feet came from behind them and before they knew what was happening, they were forcibly knocked to the ground. In the dark of night, it was hard to distinguish friend from foe and thinking they were being arrested, they fought back furiously.

At last Nimsi panted, "I've got him Pallu!"

"Pallu?" stammered the man, whom he had subdued in a headlock.

"Nadab!" Recognising his brother's voice Nimsi immediately released him.

The three men cried with joy. Even though they realised their difficulties were far from over, the tension of the last few hours fell away.

"I had determined that tonight I was going to make a run for it," Nadab explained when he had rested a while. "I managed to be assigned to guard duties at the city gates."

"We saw you, but then lost sight of you again," said Nimsi.

"When some refugees requested entrance, I waited for an opportune moment. First the guards' attention was drawn away by those citizens who wanted to bury someone and then the refugees added to the confusion. Meanwhile, you two showed up. It couldn't have worked out better for me. Of course, I only realised that in hindsight because at the time, I didn't know it was you. I only saw mayhem developing, and a couple of men rushing out through the gates. So I immediately ran after them. Without hesitating I chased after the sound of their footsteps till I bumped into you in the dark… Praise the Lord!"

"May He be merciful to Father and the others… May He also forgive us our wrongdoings," Nimsi sighed. To which Pallu added, "May He protect Jerusalem and His holy Temple."

The temple! With shameful hearts the three of them reflected on their last sight of the place where God Himself proclaimed His name. Contaminated! Lustreless and defiled! Not by the hand of the enemy, but by that of His own people.

It was as if the words which the prophet had in vain proclaimed for many years, still echoed from the darkness of the city. "Woe… woe… woe… Woe to Jerusalem and to the temple… Woe to the people…"

"Come on," said Nimsi, "let's move on. We have to leave the city as far behind as possible before daybreak… And try not to get caught by the Romans."

CHAPTER 18

H UNGER!

Rapha had pricked up his ears when he first heard the word mentioned. It had taken him completely by surprise. He had expected that there would only be talk of hunger in Jerusalem after the Romans had besieged it for many years. While only the supply of fresh food to the city was prevented by the enemy, the city itself had not been enclosed, so there shouldn't have been reason to experience hunger.

And even then, what was hunger? Food was scarce. That was the fault of those foolish rebels and their foolhardy activities. For a cunning businessman it was even an opportunity to make a profit. The thought made Rapha laugh to himself. Making a profit out of scarcity! One had to be smart to do that.

Hunger and scarcity were big words. After all, a person can get by with very little. He himself was the perfect example. Frugality gets you a long way.

No, Jerusalem didn't know yet what real hunger was. The abundance was gone! That was evident. He had heard that the gangs in the city seemed to be taking turns in burning each other's food stocks.

Whatever the case, real hunger or not, the prices were rising and for him as a businessman that was a good thing. He had already been sorely tempted to make use of the situation, but he had managed to restrain himself. In the current circumstances shortages would only increase. He had to wait for the right moment.

Just imagine that he would now sell barley for a tenfold profit. At first glance that would make him a tidy sum. But he dreaded the thought that later on, when there really was nothing left to eat, he would miss out on making a hundred or even thousandfold profit. The very thought excited him. No, he was going to wait. But he had to make sure that no vermin could touch his barley and that no one would discover he had a stash of food in his house.

It hadn't escaped his attention that some awful things were happening in the city. When according to habit, he went on his evening walk along the houses, his path had been hindered numerous times by dead bodies left lying in the streets as prey for the dogs and birds. Rapha wasn't interested in politics as long as it didn't interfere with his business. But the inconvenience caused by the terrible fighting in the city made him realise that there was something badly wrong. Still, he was far too busy to get involved in it. He had enough worries of his own.

Then, one morning, he was harshly confronted with reality when some men held him up in the street.

He'd been on his way to collect interest on a loan when he heard his name being mentioned.

"That's Rapha, the man I told you about."

Rapha immediately cringed and made himself look as small as possible. By quickly crossing the street he attempted to evade the men. But he was unsuccessful, and it soon became clear they intended to do him harm. They were faster than he and blocked his path.

"On the way to the bank are we, Rapha?"

He trembled and shook his head fervently.

"Now, now, you don't leave your house for nothing!"

His eyes were bulging, and he broke out in a sweat.

"We'd better have a look then," said one of the men, grabbing Rapha firmly by the neck with one hand, while searching his clothes with the other.

"Nothing!" he growled. "He has nothing on him. The stingy skunk!"

"But of course, he keeps all his money in a chest under his bed," another supposed. "Let's go with him to have a look."

Rapha started to resist and squealed in fear. The men however slapped him firmly and dragged him along to his house. They took his key and opened the door.

"Home sweet home," they taunted him and sat him on a stool.

"Now tell us where you keep your money, Rapha. We've never taken out a loan with you but now seems to be a good time. Come on! Where's your money?"

Rapha almost died and moaned quietly to himself but didn't answer the men.

"A bit deaf, are we?" the fellow concluded, and smacked Rapha so hard in the face that he tumbled off his stool. When the little profiteer tried to scramble to his feet, he received another blow which knocked him hard against the wall. There he lay dazed for a few moments.

"Don't kill him straight away," he heard them say. "He has to talk to us first."

"We should be able to find it without his help anyway."

"You never know. He's a crafty little ferret. I'm sure he has hidden it very well."

"Let's have a look. Who knows, maybe it's really hidden under his bed."

They searched the house from top to bottom but returned without success to the entry hall, where the slightly recovered Rapha sat bewildered on his stool, guarded by one of the crooks.

"Didn't find anything?"

"Nothing at all."

"I thought so."

"He'll have to help us then, won't he?" their leader said. "Come on Rapha, be brave now. How do we get to your money? Where have you hidden it?"

"I don't have anything in the house," hissed Rapha.

"Then where is it?"

"Not here!"

"Where then?"

"Outside of the city!"

"He's lying. Just give him to me for a minute."

"Let him tell his story first," the leader fended him off.

"Come on then Rapha, where outside the city? Then we'll go and get it. Give us your money and we won't harm you; then we'll let you live."

"In Emmaus, that's where I've brought it for safekeeping. But it's not much. Not worth your while really. I'm just a poor soul."

"He's lying through his teeth! That sly fox knows we wouldn't dream of going to Emmaus. The Romans are stationed there! Shall I make him squeal?"

"I think you're right. You may as well," the leader admitted. "Brace yourself Rapha, you're in for it now!"

They laid into him and broke nearly all of his bones. They invented the most painful torments, but Rapha maintained that he owned nothing. The closer to death they drove him, the more convincing his denials sounded. Eventually they had to believe him and disappointedly they left the house, leaving him for dead. And truly, he wasn't far from it.

Kish felt uneasy. There was no response to his repeated knocking on the door. That had never happened before. Rapha shunned the light, and he had poor eyesight, but his hearing was excellent.

Kish had a horrible feeling that something was wrong. He tried knocking once more but when again there was no answer, he decided to take action.

Opening the door wasn't difficult for him. Anyone observing his actions would have sworn he was a hardened burglar. He slipped inside and carefully closed the door again. He remembered where the oil lamp was kept and carefully felt around to locate it. Having found it, he lit it. The first thing he saw was the pathetic little human bundle in the middle of the floor. Initially he thought that Rapha was dead, but when he kneeled down and examined him, it turned out there was some life left in the little man. He looked terrible however and Kish guessed that he must have been lying there for several days. His lips were parched, and he didn't make a sound. Kish rummaged for a bowl and brought some water. He was hardly surprised to see that the house had been ransacked and turned upside down - as far as that was possible in the scantily furnished house.

Back with Rapha, he moistened his lips and carefully let some water run into his mouth. He washed his face and hands and tried to restore him to consciousness. But it didn't work. Although there were some signs of life, he was too far gone to respond properly. Kish realised that if he wanted to keep the miser alive, he had no time to lose, and Rapha would need better help than he was able to give him. He didn't hesitate long. He went to bring his donkey inside and unloaded the dried figs which he had been able to buy for Rapha. Then he locked the house and hurried through the streets to the house of Gedor, who was rather surprised to see him. He let Kish in, who then explained the situation to Gedor and Tirza.

"In a city where innocent people die every day, my request may seem somewhat strange. The person for whom I'm asking help, is not a likeable chap. That's why I wouldn't know where else to turn. I found Rapha in a terrible state. He was close to death. I think they tried to steal from him. And it's obvious that they tortured him.

I can't do any more for him but thought that maybe you could. I want to ask if I can bring him here and if you'll tend to him until he can take care of himself again. That's if he even makes it. He's a miserable chap. A merciless chap too. But I can't just let him die there."

"We know him a little," said Gedor. "Had he been conscious, he would never have given you permission to bring him here. We are Christians."

"I'm aware of that," said Kish. "That's why I turn to you first."

"You can bring him," said Tirza. "Perhaps we can keep him alive and care for him till he is well again. We don't expect to have a thankful patient, but we'll receive him in the love of Christ."

"Very well, then I'll go and bring him here."

"I'll give you a hand," said Gedor.

They collected Rapha, and Gedor wondered at the decisiveness with which Kish acted, the speed of his actions and his silent tread as he carried Rapha in his arms through the dark streets. A peacefulness emanated from Simpleton.

Tirza had already prepared a bed for Rapha.

"Why do you concern yourself with him?" she asked Kish, not mincing words.

"Because the Lord has pity on us," he answered to her surprise.

"I thought he may have been a distant relative or so."

"We're all relatives in a way... He's a human being... Once created in the image of God... But now there's not much evidence left."

Tirza was surprised to hear him talk like that. Like most people in the city, she knew Kish. But only from a distance. As Simpleton. She had never really met him.

"In a city where you are confronted by so much hatred nowadays, what you are doing is rather special," said Gedor. "That you have pity on this man... Precisely this man... He came to our door when he wanted to buy our house. He had heard that we would be leaving and thought to buy it for next to nothing. He lives for money. I wonder how he'll react when he gains consciousness."

"Not very well, I'm afraid," said Kish. "Probably in a manner that would make most people get rid of him quickly. I know he's an impossible man."

"Most people...? And what makes you think we won't? Honestly, I'm surprised you sought us out."

"In a city full of hatred that's not too hard to understand," said Kish. "All the Christians have left and rightfully so. Jerusalem is going to be levelled. And the temple as well. The prophet speaks the truth. You know that... And yet you stayed. For the sake of your brother... And he's not the easiest person either."

Gedor was stunned!

"What makes you say that?" Tirza asked. "How do you know?"

Kish shrugged his shoulders and laughed a bit. All of a sudden, he was Simpleton again.

"I heard about it," he said. "That's why I came to you."

From the room where Rapha was lying, a soft groan was heard. He had regained consciousness but when they went to see him, he didn't respond to their presence.

"He's exhausted," said Tirza.

"Mark my words, he will recover," Kish assured Tirza. "As long as he can think about money he'll be up and about in no time. He's a pitiful human being. I've tried to appeal to his conscience, but he closes himself off. Perhaps you can achieve something with him. He doesn't realise he's a lost soul… He's obsessed with money, and his soul doesn't seem to matter."

"What does it profit a man if he gains the whole world and loses his own soul?" sighed Tirza.

Through the good care of Tirza and Gedor, Rapha was soon well enough to start worrying about his possessions again. It went as they had expected; he showed little in the way of thankfulness. He regarded his benefactors with suspicion for the simple reason that he couldn't imagine that any person would help another except for a substantial reward. He considered that the cost of care received would only increase if he expressed his thankfulness. They wanted to feed him as well as possible, but he refused to eat more than the bare essentials. He had despaired when at first he couldn't even sit up, and had fretted in silence... The idea that he was dependent on people, whom he had only ever considered as money making objects, was intolerable. He was consumed by his desire to get out of bed and return to his own home.

Sometimes they heard him mumble in his sleep, but even when he was awake, he would repeat to himself, "I didn't tell them anything. They found nothing."

But the agonising uncertainty would return, that in his semi-consciousness he may have let something slip, which he would later come to regret. It was impossible for him to wait patiently for his recovery. He intended to leave as soon as he could walk again. Tirza and Gedor had spoken to him about the Gospel on several occasions. Silla also tried to draw his interest, while Tirza relieved her from caring for her father. But all of them had the feeling that they were sowing the seed on stony places.

Rapha realised full well that if he answered the call of the Lord Jesus Christ, the most precious thing in the world would be taken from him.

Nice stories! Don't gather your treasures here on earth. Yes, that's what they were telling him. And they threatened with moth and rust etc... As well as with thieves who could come and steal your treasures. Of course, they said these things just to make him scared!

He was intensely suspicious. They only said these things, so that he would crumble and give them something for the care they provided.

Fortunately, they didn't have many expenses on his behalf. Water was free and that little bit of food...

He had shown them that he could manage on very little. And he couldn't stand to hear them pray because they also prayed for *him*. It made him feel as if one day he would have to pay for it. Nothing for nothing, that's true, isn't it? Everything has its price.

He hardly said a word, and then mainly 'yes' and 'no'. Only if it was absolutely necessary. But most of the time he responded with an unintelligible growl.

Even when Simpleton dropped by now and then to inquire about his health, he never let it develop into a conversation.

All he longed for was his house and his money...

One morning, when he felt that his legs could support him again, he had simply left without saying goodbye. "Poor wretch," said Tirza when she found his bed empty.

Rapha dragged himself along, finding support against the houses, tripping over anything that lay in his path.

He was able to take care of himself again. He no longer needed anyone else!

He moved slowly and although it was agonising, he managed to get there. With his heart pounding in his chest, he came to his house and entered, trembling and afraid of what he might find.

After he had closed the door and lit the lamp, he was seized with trembling at the sight of the stool and the blood stains around it where he had lain on the floor. The stack of bags with dried figs, puzzled him for a moment but he soon managed to connect them to Simpleton, who had found him there.

When he opened the door to the cellars, he shivered with excitement. It took all his energy to keep his balance as he descended the steep staircase. Now and then he had to take a break to rest and catch his breath. In his weak state the emotions were almost too much for him. Having reached the bottom, he supported himself on the wall.

When he saw the great stockpile of food still safely piled up, the oil lamp almost slipped from his grasp. The tension of the last days suddenly erupted, as he broke down and cried hysterically.

Totally distraught, he dragged the chests of gold and silver towards himself, placed them next to each other and opened the lids. He continued to sob for a long time, while he allowed his eyes to feast on all his treasures... Then he fell to his knees, submerged both his hands in the money and let it run through his fingers. He caressed it, kissed it and eventually burst out in raucous laughter.

It was the laughter of a madman. Uncontrolled and frightening.

It sounded hollow and cold as metal.

Rapha was happy again.

CHAPTER 19

"**H**AVE YOU HEARD ANYTHING from the boys recently?" Pagiel asked his brother.

"It seems that they've managed to escape," Gedor replied.

"So, you've had word about them?"

"Yes, I did."

"From whom?"

Gedor smiled.

"Why are you smiling?" asked Pagiel.

"Because the man who told me, is probably not someone you esteem very highly. It was Kish, the Simpleton, who told me that one evening something happened at one of the gates. During an altercation some men took the opportunity to flee the city. And he's certain that they haven't been caught."

"That Simpleton…" said Pagiel.

"I've already told you that I've learned to see a different side of him. He's recently been at our house a number of times. I can assure you Pagiel, that if everyone in Jerusalem was as simple as he, things would look a whole lot rosier for us."

"Well, I hope the boys made it. Getting out of the city is one thing, but what's next?"

"You're right, they're not out of the woods yet… But nowadays it's better to fall into the hands of the Romans than of the rebels. If you could come for a walk through the city, you wouldn't believe your eyes."

"I've been told that many times already."

"That's because each time again we are shocked by what we see, Pagiel. Words can't describe it. I know it sounds repetitive. And it's almost too gruesome to talk about. We're not yet under siege but already food is becoming scarce. A lot of people are suffering hunger. Food stocks have been destroyed because Jews are fighting Jews. It's unbelievable what's happening, Pagiel. I can see it as nothing else than the judgement of God. It seems as if people are possessed. The daily offerings are still faithfully made but the temple service has become a disgrace. Everything is unclean. Death reigns on the streets. The ideals you and your sons dreamed about have been drowned in blood. The ordinary, good-hearted citizens suffer the most. It's even gone so far that many people are now praying for the Romans to come. That's ludicrous, isn't it? They would just about be welcomed as liberators."

Pagiel sadly shook his head. "Is it that bad?"

"Worse," Gedor assured him. "The leaders of the rebellion are at each other's throats, while they deceive the people with pious talk about the imminent arrival of the Messiah. As if the Most Holy One would give His blessings on the shameful injustices they are committing. They act shamelessly, cruelly and deceitfully."

"Have we then truly been so wrong?" Pagiel asked himself aloud. "How could this have happened?"

"If you would see it for yourself, you would think that God had left the city to its own devices."

"You really think so, Gedor?"

"I think it's a judgement being executed Pagiel. At the same time things are happening which prove that the Lord is not abandoning His own. Amidst all that misery there are signs of love and mercy. Kish who was merciful to Rapha… And Silla who takes care of you. And fortunately, there are more examples."

"But Jerusalem is the city of God, Gedor. Would He give her over into the hands of heathens?"

"Why not Pagiel? Hasn't that happened before? Wasn't Nebuchadnezzar a heathen? And why were our forefathers led into captivity? Wasn't it because of their disobedience to the Lord? Besides…"

"Besides… what?"

"The destruction of the city and the temple has been foretold."

"Ah, you mean that prophet…"

"No, I mean by the Lord Himself! Jerusalem won't survive this Pagiel. If only you could have a peek at the temple, it would be easier for you to believe me. If the Jews continue in this way, we won't even need the Romans anymore. By the time they get here everything will have been destroyed."

"Would it come to that?" Pagiel asked.

"I'm afraid it will," said Gedor. "I think about the words of Isaiah, 'Who gave Jacob for plunder, and Israel to the robbers? Was it not the Lord, He against whom we have sinned? For they would not walk in His ways, nor were they obedient to His law. Therefore, He has poured on him the fury of His anger and the strength of battle; It has set him on fire all around, yet he did not know; and it burned him, yet he did not take it to heart…'

The Lord cried over Jerusalem, shortly before he was given over to the heathens to be crucified."

"We intended to talk some more about that," said Pagiel. "I've given a lot of thought to the question if it was possible that the Most High could have come to us in the form of a man and why He would do that… That He *can* do it is beyond doubt. But that He would do it in the way you believe it has happened, is still a frightening thought for me, Gedor."

"Initially I also felt that way. But it shows us the terrible depravity of sin Pagiel. He had to humiliate Himself to that extent, so He could reconcile us to Himself. He died on the cross, to save us from eternal death."

"He, Who is life itself, would die on the cross? That's difficult for me, Gedor! That's not possible! He is the eternal and immortal God!"

"That's why He became man, Pagiel. Then it was possible! I read in Isaiah, 'Your dead shall live; together with my dead body they shall arise'… I've always wondered whom Isaiah was prophesying about, himself or the Messiah. We've been looking for the coming of a triumphant Messiah and indeed, we read of that in the Scriptures.

But we forgot to consider the prophecy of His suffering. Wait a minute, I'll get the book of Isaiah."

Gedor went to get the scroll from the ark in which his brother kept the Holy Scripture. Then he read:

"'For He was cut off from the land of the living; For the transgressions of My people He was stricken. And they made His grave with the wicked but with the rich at His death, because He had done no violence, nor was any deceit in His mouth. Yet it pleased the Lord to bruise Him; He has put Him to grief. When You make His soul an offering for sin, He shall see His seed, He shall prolong His days, and the pleasure of the Lord shall prosper in His hand.' Here Pagiel, I'll hold it in front of you so you can read it for yourself. It's all been foretold but we haven't understood it. When He came, we rejected Him… After His resurrection He even pointed out that everything was foretold by Moses and the prophets. And the Psalms are full of it, that the Christ had to suffer in order to enter into His glory… God Himself provided the perfect Lamb of which Abraham had prophesied!"

Pagiel listened and asked helplessly, "Who can believe such a thing?"

"Isaiah already queried that," replied Gedor. "He wrote, 'Who has believed our report? And to whom has the arm of the Lord been revealed?' And he explains why it will be almost impossible to believe, 'For He shall grow up before Him as a tender plant, and as a root out of dry ground. He has no form or comeliness; and when we see Him, there is no beauty that we should desire Him.'

Do you see how Isaiah foresaw that you and I would have great difficulty with it? The Lord knew that what He did for us would be unfathomable, Pagiel! We can't understand it, but we can believe it… Because God says it…! The righteous shall live by faith…

Let's read on a bit: 'He was despised and rejected by men, a Man of sorrows and acquainted with grief. And we hid, as it were, our faces from Him; He was despised, and we did not esteem Him.'

Israel didn't recognise Him, Pagiel. We even ridiculed Him and mocked Him and gave Him over to be crucified. But it all happened because He willed it so! It wasn't a tragic accident! He took it all onto Himself willingly! Just keep reading. I know it's familiar to you; you would have read it a hundred times already. But suddenly it can become new to you, like it happened to me some time back. It's when the Lord opens our hearts to the truth. From then on you read with a new understanding… Then you realise that He did it for Israel; that he did it for me…!

'Surely He has borne our griefs and carried our sorrows; Yet we esteemed Him stricken, smitten by God, and afflicted. But He was wounded for our transgressions, He was bruised for our iniquities; The chastisement for our peace was upon Him, and by His stripes we are healed. All we like sheep have gone astray; we have turned, every one, to his own way; And the Lord has laid on Him the iniquity of us all.'"

Pagiel was visibly impressed. "Gedor," he said, "have I been so blind? You are my witness that from childhood I've been instructed in the Scriptures. And that I've been immersed in these things my whole life. Now I'm asking myself how I could have read those verses so often without finding the explanation you provide. Did I perhaps push it away because it caused me anxiety? I don't know. And even now I'm afraid that I sin by following this line of reasoning. Am I afraid of the truth…? God only knows… In all honesty I have to say that I'm afraid to go astray."

"Just like us? Tirza and I… and your daughter… and so many more upright Jews?"

"Don't get angry now Gedor, that's not what I meant to say. I just don't know what to think anymore."

"I'm not angry with you at all. I just want to say that there are upright people, like your daughter Silla, who are also afraid of going astray but still they've come to see these prophecies in a different light. Light has been sown for the righteous, as you know. In His light we see light."

Deeply touched, Pagiel prayed, "Oh, send out Your light and Your truth! Let them lead me; let them bring me to Your holy hill and to Your tabernacle."

CHAPTER 20

THOMAS WONDERED WHAT WAS happening. Suddenly he found himself among a mass of people who didn't seem to know where they were going. He was pushed from before and behind. A commotion had developed because someone had shouted out that the Romans were coming. The reactions to this varied in the extreme. There were those who expected the Romans to appear on the walls any minute and fearfully sought a safe place to hide. There were others who, driven by curiosity, wanted to go and have a look on the walls or near the gates in order not to miss out on the spectacle. The confusion only increased when groups of armed warriors on horseback stormed by, chasing up the crowds to try and clear a path for themselves.

Thomas felt uneasy in the crowd. It cost him great effort to weave his way out and he was glad to reach the fringes of the masses.

Someone spoke to him, "Panic is life-threatening. I've experienced that a few times in Galilee. Once the crowd stampedes, woe to you if you find yourself in the middle of it. But sometimes it comes on so unexpectedly that you don't have a chance to get away. If you fall, you'll be trampled underfoot."

"What do you think is happening?" Thomas asked.

"I'm not sure yet. Someone yelled that the Romans were coming. But I'd better have a look on the wall. Not here, because they'll soon be pushing and shoving each other, and accidents are likely to happen. It's better to go a bit further along because there we'll see it just as well and have no one to bother us. Are you coming? I know a good spot."

Thomas followed the man to a quieter place where they could get on the wall without all the jostling. Here they had an ideal vantage point.

"There come the Romans!" Thomas' companion pointed out. "Before I forget, my name is Caleb."

"And I'm Thomas," said Thomas. "You seem rather pleased to see them."

"Not really, but I'm always impressed by their tactics."

"They're such gentle people, aren't they!" Thomas mocked.

"I mean their organisation… Today they haven't come to make war, that much is clear… How many would there be? Five hundred men perhaps? All mounted soldiers… They're following the main road directly toward the wall. If you ask me, they're on reconnaissance. But that does mean that soon we can expect them to besiege us."

"That's not cheering me up," Thomas remarked.

"I beg your pardon," Caleb apologised. "As a Jew, I also dislike seeing them here!"

"So, what do you like about them? Because you still admire them, don't you?"

"Yes, to be honest, I do admire them. If you see them march in their legions for example… So disciplined. Frightening and impressive at the same time. If we want to save Jerusalem from destruction, it would be best to open the gates for them right away."

"Don't let the authorities hear you!"

"What authorities? Those rebel leaders who currently order people around? How long have they been fighting each other already? Do you really think they stand a chance of stopping the Romans? Do you realise there's very little food left in the city? And do you know whom we have to thank for that? The same strategists who want to take up the fight against Rome!"

"I don't know if you always speak your mind like this to a stranger. If you do, it surprises me that you're still alive."

Caleb looked at him and smiled. "I know you're a Christian," he said. "You won't report me."

Thomas was taken by surprise. "Are you also…?" he began.

"No, not really but I've heard about it. And I like observing. I've seen and heard quite a bit in the city. I know where you live and also that they smashed up your pottery workshop. That happened when the Idumeans were invited into town."

Thomas looked at him in amazement. It made him feel very uncomfortable that someone knew so much about him.

"My father and brother were involved in the uprising in Galilee. I've experienced several sieges. I don't hold any illusions that we can achieve anything against Rome. We can only make things worse. You would have heard that prophet who walks the streets day and night? I believe he's right. Jerusalem and we all, are headed for destruction…"

Thomas didn't respond.

"That's the smart thing to do," said Caleb. "Say nothing. I talk a bit too much, I admit that. But don't think that I talk to just anyone. I've been searching for some of my family, who lived near you and that's why I know more about you than you expected. My search was futile because they've already left. Look!" he interrupted himself, "they're turning into a side road, do you see that?"

"What about it?" Thomas asked.

"In itself it's not important but it shows that they are scouting out the lay of the land. If they would now be attacked from the city, it could be rather dangerous for them. They're not wearing their armour and there are too few of them to engage in a fight."

"You sound like a field marshal or something," Thomas mocked. "Just as well they don't have to face you as their enemy in battle."

"I observe things, it's a sort of compulsion I have," laughed Caleb in return. "But I never really take part in fighting. I'm not suited to being a soldier."

"You might make a good historian! I notice that you're gathering a lot of information."

"It takes a bit more than that," Caleb answered. "I'm only a Jew from the countryside. Historians move in higher circles."

Suddenly they heard loud shouting and a large group of armed warriors on horseback streamed out through the gate. They fell upon the horsemen, concentrating their attack on those who were still near the main road. A victory cry arose from the walls as if Rome had already been defeated through this attack. Obviously, that was not the case, but the Romans certainly found themselves in a precarious position. Through the unexpected attack they had been separated in two sections and a rumour that the field marshal Titus himself was among the soldiers, rapidly spread to the onlookers on the wall.

Caleb quickly recognised him.

"There!" he pointed out to Thomas. "See how fiercely he is defending himself? He's courageous all right. No helmet, no shield… As I told you, they weren't looking for a fight… But he knows how to handle a sword, doesn't he? They're all going for him. If you ask me, he's trying to fight his way back. He has nowhere else to go. On terrain like this, close to the wall, they can't deploy their usual defence tactics. There are all sorts of obstacles down there such as fences, retaining walls and ditches."

"I think he's succeeding," said Thomas and he couldn't avoid the admiration in his voice. "See how he uses his horse to make room? He's going to get out! Look at that!"

"See also how the others protect him by surrounding him closely? All because of their great discipline, tactics, and a great deal of practice. Plain brute force is no match for that."

And indeed, the Romans managed to join up and escape their attackers. Although many of them were wounded, only two of them had been killed. Titus returned to his army unharmed.

"The beginning of the end," Caleb predicted. "This attack will only cause them to be more determined to teach us a lesson which we'll remember for a long time. Soon they'll be back but not just with a few hundred scouts. I expect the legions will be here very soon, Thomas. Just to be on the safe side, I won't go back to my own home."

"So where do you live?" Thomas wanted to know.

"I found a nice spot on the Mount of Olives and that's where I've been spending the nights. But now I'll stay within the walls, I think. I expect they'll overtake my camp within a few days, seeing it's not very fortified there. Would you know a place for me to sleep?

During the day I'll keep myself busy and rustle up a bit of food. But when I need to close my eyes, I prefer to do it in a safe place."

"Nice of you to ask me," laughed Thomas. "I'm guessing you already know what my answer will be. Tell me, what does the law say I should do?"

"You shall love your neighbour as yourself, so…"

"You're welcome… Come along with me and we'll organise a bed for you."

Caleb appeared to have evaluated the situation correctly. Already the next day, Titus marched with the two legions at his disposal, to Mount Scopus, from where he had an excellent view and could oversee the enormous terrain of the Temple grounds. On the way, the fifth legion, which had travelled via Emmaus, also joined them. Approximately a kilometre northeast of Jerusalem, he instructed the legions to set up two camps. They had just started when the tenth legion arrived from Jericho. The tenth was ordered to occupy the Mount of Olives which is to the east of the city and separated from it by a deep ravine called Kidron.

From within the city, Caleb observed the preparations for the siege with a fearful heart for what was about to happen but at the same time full of admiration for the craftsmanship with which the enemy worked.

Incidentally, he was not the only one who was impressed by the approaching Romans. It seemed at last to penetrate the rebels that the time had come to end their battles against each other and to unite in preparing for the siege and the defence of the city. John and Eleazar ceased their infighting and focussed their attention on the Romans.

But for them, as for the notorious Simon and his rebels who controlled the upper city, this realisation came much too late, as they would soon experience to their own detriment.

CHAPTER 21

"IT SEEMS THAT I'LL be a cripple for the rest of my life," Gaius grumbled as he tapped against his splinted leg. He was sitting beside the driver on the front of the cart.

"You have to give it a chance to heal. A broken bone needs time to grow together again. It doesn't happen overnight."

"Give it a chance to heal!" Gaius mocked. "What would you know about it? Suppose you tell me how I'm supposed to do that."

"By resting."

"Come to your senses!" barked Gaius, tapping the side of his helmet with a pointed finger. "How is a man like me supposed to rest? Tell me how I should do that! Have a look what's on the back of the cart, as well as all the gear that's following behind. Soon that all needs to be assembled again. Or do you think it will happen by itself!"

"Surely that's our task?"

"Who do you mean by 'our'?"

"Me and the lads. The whole team."

"Goes to show how little you know!" Gaius sighed. "Who needs to tell you each time again how to do it? If I didn't constantly keep an eye on you, nothing would be done right… Rest… Ha! How can you even suggest it!"

The cart driver grinned and didn't seem too impressed by the ear bashing of his superior.

"Rest," repeated Gaius, "that's what they said in Jericho too. That was the only thing they could suggest. When I asked them if there was anything else that could be done, they said, 'cut if off...' The audacity of it! And I even think they were serious about it."

"Scum," the carter grinned. "There's no respect for officers nowadays."

"If you're not careful, I'll knock you off the wagon," Gaius threatened.

"If that means you'll send me on paid leave, bring it on."

Gaius laughed out loud. "You would be missing out on all the excitement, my boy! No, I wouldn't be so cruel as to keep that from you. We're going to have a battle."

"Ramming!"

"Exactly. We'll teach these Jews a lesson that will stay with them for a long time. We shall see how strong their buildings are... Strange, isn't it, that one can get so much enjoyment from it? To smash to pieces things that others have so carefully and painstakingly put together... Have you ever been to Jerusalem?"

"No, never."

"Neither have I. I've been told it's a beautiful city with a grandiose temple. It's supposedly still packed with gold... The temple I mean. We'll see. It appears they used enormous stone blocks for the building. An officer told me that. He had been there several times. He said to me, 'I'm not convinced that you can tackle it with your ordinary ram.' So I replied: 'there hasn't yet been a stone that didn't move aside for me.'"

"A bit of a challenge for you," said the carter.

"You can put it that way, yes," Gaius admitted.

"And does it give you satisfaction?"

"Yes and no..."

"That's a clear answer!"

"Well, that's because... Well, it gives mixed feelings. When I'm busy with a wall or a tower, I can work myself up as if I'm fighting a man. Do you understand?"

"Yes, I think I get it."

"If it doesn't give way, I can get enraged and hate it as if it were a living being. Then I even talk to it."

"Really?"

"I swear it. Even in my sleep I'm busy with it and sometimes make long speeches."

"To one of those stone objects?"

"Yes. Do you find that strange?"

"You have to admit it's not quite normal."

"Because you don't feel what I feel… You see, at a certain stage those stones are no longer stones to me but real adversaries with a will of their own. Then I just keep going till they have to give up. That's the challenge… I'm not sure how else I can explain it…"

"It's clear enough to me now," the carter grinned.

"Up to now I've always been successful," Gaius continued, "so I've yet to come across a stone that gets the upper hand… But here's the strange thing… If a tower or whatever eventually gives up, I kind of see a giant collapsing in front of me… Why do you laugh at me like that? Just because you can't imagine it… But as crazy as it may sound to you, for me it feels as if a good acquaintance is dying…

Just as I thought, you're shaking your silly head again! Because you can't feel such things… Whatever! But that's why you're still a driver and not a commander of heavy equipment like I am."

"I never knew it works like that," the carter grinned again. "But look over there," he pointed with his whip, "that's a lot to take in."

From the slopes of the Mount of Olives they looked down on the city. And indeed, for a while, both were lost for words.

"Magnificent," the carter exclaimed. "And by the looks of it, that officer may even have been right. It looks terribly strong. I'm curious to see if we can knock that over."

"Just watch me," Gaius promised. "As long as they give me the opportunity and don't start moaning about my leg again. Nor should they leave us here on the mountain. As far as I'm concerned, we need to get to that fortress. Do you see what I mean? That fortress adjacent to the enormous temple square. I would love to have a closer look at it."

"I figure that we'll first start shooting at them from this hillside," the carter said. "Who knows, they may quickly surrender so that we don't need to ram the fortress. I would even prefer that option because of the beautiful buildings."

"Those Jews won't surrender so easily," Gaius assured him. "From what I've heard they are terribly fanatical. They are a kind of possessed people who will fight to the last drop of blood. They'll cause us a lot of work."

"That would be good for your leg. It will have plenty of time to heal. We'll keep shooting those Jews off the wall and you can just sit and watch." He grinned and added, "and tell us how to do it of course, otherwise we won't hit anything."

"I regret I ever promoted you to decurion," grumbled Gaius, feigning insult. "I'll never cite you for a medal again! Not even if you were to take the city all by yourself! All that nagging about my leg and resting. I've had enough of it… One of these days I'll rip these splints off and take you for a run! Then we'll see if you still have the courage to patronise your superior."

"It's all because we're concerned about you, commander."

"I don't doubt it for a moment, Marius!"

And he was right about that. Having both grown up in the slums of Rome, they had been friends from an early age. In adulthood they had lost track of each other but then, far away from home, they had met again as legionnaires.

After Titus had settled in on Mount Scopus and the army camps were set up, he began levelling off the whole area between his headquarters and the city walls. He had every tree chopped down; every fence removed. Farmhouses and cabins were demolished; everything that blocked his views. It all became one flat area. Ditches and holes were filled in. The whole area was being prepared for a battle according to the Roman custom. Not just for meeting the enemy in a man-to-man battle, but also to allow movement of the rolling equipment toward the walls. Besides, this way it was a lot easier to oversee everything and keep track of the enemy's movements if they ventured outside the walls.

When the Romans had completed this enormous task, they set up two other camps, this time much closer to the city, but just outside the range of the catapults, approximately four hundred metres away from the wall. One camp on the north-west corner of the city and the other one opposite the Antonia fortress, the citadel that stood adjacent to the temple square.

Titus then started his attack on the north side of the citadel, by ordering three legions to build up an embankment that would enable the battering rams to reach the fortress. Meanwhile the soldiers of the tenth legion kept the rebellious Zealots busy by continuously bombarding the temple from the hillside of the Mount of Olives. With their enormous catapults they shot heavy stones weighing about fifty kilos into the besieged city. The large chunks of stone hit the pavement of the temple square with deadly force and crushed anything in their path. Many people were killed and others severely maimed.

Despite the bombardment, Caleb couldn't refrain from choosing a spot from which to observe the activities of the enemy. Being a keen observer, he noticed that if you paid attention, one could spot the oncoming projectiles. The stones were of a light colour and contrasted clearly with the dark background of the Mount of Olives. When he made others aware of this, observers were placed in strategic locations who warned when they saw a projectile coming. They would also point to the place where the stone would most likely land. As a result, everyone tried to avoid its path and flattened themselves to the ground.

Gaius however soon picked up on it.

"We're doing something wrong," he growled. "The first shots were effective but now they manage to avoid being hit. They must be able to see the stones coming. In this way we're wasting our efforts."

His eyes fell on the nearest stash of projectiles lying near the catapult, when it suddenly dawned on him.

"Just look how well these shiny things contrast with their background," he yelled at the gunners. "We'll soon put a stop to that! Colour them dark, make them black or whatever."

He sent a soldier to the catapults to pass on the order and the results had an immediate effect. The projectiles no longer reflected the sunlight and again wreaked havoc and death in the temple square.

"He picked that up very well," said Marius to his mates with whom he operated one of the heavy catapults.

They worked up a sweat.

It was hard work to first load and fire the catapult followed by re-tensioning the spring. The latter action required a lot of muscle and had to be done with several men working together. Once they released the trigger which unloaded the spring, the slide would shoot forward in the guide with enormous power and the rock would fly over a distance of several hundred metres.

The people had no defence against the projectiles once they were darkened by the Romans. Caleb too was unable to determine where the danger came from and kept himself at a safe distance, out of the firing line.

Gaius purred with satisfaction. He made himself comfortable and surveyed the battle scene. Every time again his eyes rested on the mighty Antonia fortress, slightly to the right in front of him where the legions were busy building an embankment in preparation for storming the city. Once that was finished his real work could start.

For now, he felt as if he was being kept occupied supervising the men on top of that platform. Once his leg was fully healed, he would be able to move around a bit faster. He had especially felt handicapped when the 10th legion was still busy taking its position and building a defensive wall and he and his men were putting together the war machines. At that moment the Jews had chosen to make a raid on them. It was done so unexpectedly and with such brute force that the surprised Romans had to retreat, and almost succumbed. By the level-headed conduct of Titus who had come to their aid, they had eventually been able to push back the enemy from the hillside.

Particularly with that Jewish assault, Gaius had experienced how much his movements were impeded. To his great annoyance, he could do nothing but try and stay out of the hands of his attackers and even that had cost him much effort...

But now he was organised again and prepared for anything. He could be satisfied.

Soldiers came and went. They carried instructions from the high command and Gaius in turn reported back to them. Everything ran like a well-oiled machine.

"How is the splint going, centurion?" Marius inquired.

"A few more days," answered Gaius, "and it comes off! You just take care of your job!"

CHAPTER 22

"I'M GLAD YOU'VE MADE contact again, Hassub. Your father kept asking about you but I had no news for him. I had hoped you would come and visit him. It's been a long time since we heard from you. We were afraid you may have perished in the fights between Jewish factions."

"I don't really dare to face Father, but please pass on my regards, uncle Gedor, and tell him all is well with me. I won't ask you anything about the others, but I think my three brothers have managed to get away. They had asked me to come with them, but I couldn't bring myself to do it. I still believe our cause is a just one."

"Do you also believe things will end well?" Gedor asked.

"If the Messiah comes…" Hassub responded hesitantly.

"He won't come."

"No! According to your beliefs He has already come," Hassub mocked. "I forgot about that! But I look forward to the Messiah of the Scriptures, our King. With one sweep He will cleanse our land of the Romans! That's what I believe. And that's what kept me here."

"Would you otherwise have gone with your brothers?"

"Yes…" Hassub replied doubtfully.

"May I tell you why, Hassub? Because deep down you're an honest man. An upright Jew, just like your father. You're shaken up because of all the things you've experienced recently at the hand of those so-called freedom fighters. Murder and killing, hatred and disdain. Injustice which is crying out to the highest heavens! Have you seen how much the ordinary citizens are suffering? And I'm not talking about the other factions that fought against you but the ordinary people who would simply love to live in peace and serve the Lord. Haven't you seen the bodies of women and children on the streets? Don't you see that your commanders and fellow fighters have much more reason to *fear* the coming of the Messiah than to long for it? He, Who is the King of justice, do you think He would choose to side with *you*? Are you so ignorant, my boy? Don't you realise that thousands in the city would gladly surrender themselves to the Romans if you didn't stand in their way? And despite that, many still seek to flee from the city.

Have you let that sink in and considered what that means, Hassub?

It means that for us ordinary citizens of Jerusalem it's now better to fall into the hands of the heathens than into the hands of you rebels!"

Hassub's temper flared briefly, but then he dropped his head.

Gedor put his hand on his nephew's arm. "I think that you despise this whole business," he said.

"I've kept myself far away from anything that's against the law," Hassub assured him. "But I don't dare to visit Father because I'm scared he'll ask me all sorts of questions for which I have no answer."

"You mean questions you don't want to answer!"

"Father believed in this uprising just as much as my brothers and I did. I can't tell him the truth and I won't lie to him. I know what he's like. It could be his death."

"How do you envisage the future for your father and sister in this city, Hassub?"

"No Roman will ever set foot into our streets!"

"I can imagine that's what you hope for, but I'm convinced of the contrary. But if you're right, would there be less danger for us? The Romans don't spare women, children or the elderly when they besiege and capture a city, but what can we expect from the rebels? From our own people? It seems to me that question has already been answered! It could hardly get worse, Hassub.

Now already children are dying of hunger. You know who is to blame don't you? It's not the fault of the Romans! They've only just set up camp outside the walls.

Israel is fighting a lost battle, my boy…

The temple is desecrated, the city polluted… The blood of thousands of innocents cries out to heaven."

"Only recently I heard a rabbi read a passage from the prophecies of Zechariah. God Himself shall save the city! He will destroy our enemies. The Romans will rot away where they are standing!" Hassub responded fanatically.

"I know that prophecy, but I can assure you that it's not referring to this siege Hassub! The passage the rabbi was reading, speaks of a distant future. The Lord tells us that in those days, He 'will pour on the house of David and on the inhabitants of Jerusalem the Spirit of grace and supplication'. And then He adds, 'and they will look on Me whom they pierced.'

That refers to the second coming of the Messiah… 'The Spirit of grace and supplication', Hassub. We need them to come from heaven! But right now it's the prince of darkness who is filling the hearts of people and leading the uprising… What we are currently experiencing will lead to the destruction of Jerusalem, just as the Messiah foretold some forty years ago!"

"I love Jerusalem and the Temple is holy to me!" Hassub flared up in anger.

"And so they are to me," Gedor assured his nephew. "It cuts me to my heart and soul, yet no stone will be left upon another."

"Because of the prophecy of the Galilean?"

"Yes, He is the Christ and He knows what He is saying!"

"He is a liar!" shouted Hassub. But Gedor saw his desperation.

"He is Truth Himself!"

"Only the Eternal One is Truth!" Hassub yelled.

"Exactly!" said Gedor.

"That's blasphemy!"

"No, rather what you are doing is blasphemy, Hassub! Desecrating Jerusalem and the temple with the blood of the innocents. Robbing and stealing and raping! And then to think that the Messiah will come and help you! That is blasphemous! Just listen to the prophet who has wandered these streets for many years! Woe to Jerusalem and the temple. Woe to all the inhabitants…

Why don't you believe him? Why did you seek to kill him all these years, and who has protected him from you? Hassub my boy, dare to be honest with yourself! Look around and see how the city is headed for destruction. Understand what's been happening. God doesn't give blessings on godlessness…!

Hassub… It must be tearing you apart… I think your heart bleeds, my boy. Stop closing your eyes to all that injustice and don't foster a false hope."

"If you're so sure about all that, if you believe it's a lost cause, why have you stayed in the city?" Hassub hissed.

"In the first place because of your father. We would rather die here with him than abandon him. We love you, Hassub, all of you. I hope you believe these are not empty words. And that's why I tell you these things, even risking that you'll be enraged with me. It pleases God to preserve and not to destroy."

Staring ahead, Hassub sat thinking for a while. Eventually he looked Gedor straight in the eyes.

"I don't want the Romans to have Jerusalem, uncle. I do know about all those terrible things, and it makes me sick thinking about the state of the city. That's why I don't go to my father, for fear he'll ask me all sorts of questions. What's happening in the city? And what's happening with the temple? I don't dare to tell him the truth… And still, I feel obliged to continue fighting and do what I can to defeat the Romans. Perhaps a miracle will happen."

CHAPTER 23

THOMAS KNELT DOWN BESIDE the prophet. Some miscreant must have come upon the man and knocked him out because he was lying half dazed in front of a house. Blood ran down his face. When Thomas inspected the head-wound, the man opened his eyes. "This will need to be treated," said Thomas, pointing to the wound. "It's more than just a scratch. Have they only hurt your head or are there more injuries? Can you still walk?"

The prophet did not answer but straightened himself up and staggered to his feet.

"Just lean on me," said Thomas. "I'll bring you to someone who can help you. It's near by."

He had never looked at the man closely but now he noticed a remarkable glow burning in his dark eyes. The expression on his face revealed great sadness but also willpower. Thomas felt increasingly impressed by the man's personality.

Even if Silla was surprised to see Thomas and the odd companion he brought along, she certainly didn't show it. She immediately gave all her attention to tending the wound, cleaning and bandaging it.

During the treatment the prophet remained silent, simply looking from Silla to Thomas, in turn. Silla gave him something to eat and drink. There was no word of thanks. He accepted the aid and food as something he was entitled to and didn't respond to Silla's offer that he stay and rest a while. Promptly after receiving their care, he left again.

Coming outside he immediately sounded forth his words of warning, which had already for so long resounded through Jerusalem, "Woe to Jerusalem… Woe… a voice against the temple… a voice against the newly wedded men and women…"

"A strange man," Thomas pondered. "But I do believe he has been sent by the Lord. He too is suffering a fate foretold by the Lord. Jerusalem does not listen to the prophets sent to her. The man would not have lived this long if it wasn't for the Lord's care over him. But the people have ignored his warnings. Oh, the patience the Lord has with us… But now the destruction of the city has come very near, Silla… I was on the city wall and saw the Romans arrive. They go about their work with great deliberation. You can see they have much experience in warfare. I do not understand that the rebels don't realise this. They keep on believing that they can outsmart the Romans. They must have been struck with blindness."

While he spoke to her, Silla appeared engrossed in her work. Thomas tried to focus his eyes away from her but failed miserably. She was so attractive to him, that he couldn't resist looking at her constantly.

Everything about her fascinated him.

Her busy hands, the playful curls which popped out from beneath her head-cloth, the display of her beautiful, long eyelashes when she looked down on the work in her hands, the smooth movements of her slender body…

Thomas felt shy and embarrassed, as if he was doing something wrong by looking and admiring her beauty. There was no real excuse for him to be in Pagiel's house any longer, but he tried to stretch the time. He couldn't get enough of it. Her nearness gave him an overwhelming sense of happiness.

At the same time he felt sad.

First of all because of the circumstances in which they found themselves, but also because he felt so helpless, not knowing how to approach her. She seemed so out of reach. Thomas tried his utmost not to let her notice that he was watching her. He tried so hard that Silla couldn't help but notice it.

It made her heart beat faster.

For several years already her heart had gone out to Thomas, choosing him from among the young men in the congregation. As a young girl she had often lain awake, dreaming about him. But it had seemed as if Thomas never regarded her as special, but simply saw her as one of the young people he grew up with.

But today she was aware of the way he looked at her, though she did her best not to show it. In this she was a lot more successful than Thomas.

She would have preferred to run straight into his arms.

However, she was not only sensible but also playful and a bit of a tease, just enough to play this game and let herself be won by him.

Thomas prepared to leave.

"I had better be going again," he said. "Thanks very much for your help, Silla."

"Will you be careful Thomas?"

He looked up in surprise, but Silla appeared to focus her attention on her work.

"Why?" he asked.

"Well, I assume you remained in Jerusalem for a good reason?" she answered. "Everyone is in danger here. Almost all Christians have left the city. Why did you stay and not go away with the others…? It would be terrible if something happened to you."

He felt cornered and stammered shyly. Especially the fact that she seemed to care for his safety, confused him greatly.

"Well, you stayed here too, didn't you?" he said.

"But I had a good reason to stay."

"I did too," said Thomas, a bit shocked by his own words.

Silla tilted her head and looked him in the eyes.

Something in the way she looked at him set him alight. Suddenly he got the courage to tell her how he felt about her. In his thoughts he had often rehearsed a lengthy speech to prepare himself for this moment. But now that the moment had arrived, he simply said, "Silla, I love you!"

The next moment he embraced her in his arms.

Pagiel had been calling and was not a little surprised when Silla and Thomas appeared at his bedside, hand in hand. However, that amazement gave way to emotion when Thomas asked if he could have his beloved daughter as wife.

"Unfortunately, this is not the time for a wedding," said Thomas. "We'll have to see if we survive this war. But if you give us permission and grant us your blessing, we will already be very happy."

"If Silla is happy, then I am too," said Pagiel.

They knelt beside the bed, and he brought them before the Lord in prayer. Together they could experience unforgettable moments.

CHAPTER 24

IN SPITE OF THE Roman siege of Jerusalem, skirmishes broke out again between the rebel gangs. While on the walls they had to fight the enemy from without, on the streets they were fighting each other in a civil war.

It had become virtually impossible to lead a normal life within the city. The fighters demanded food for themselves and when this had become increasingly scarce, they went on raids and took everything from the people that was edible. Most people hardly dared to cook or roast their food for fear that the smell would betray them and others would come and steal it.

Tables were no longer prepared.

Food was eaten in secret and as quickly as possible.

John, who with his troops occupied the temple and controlled the area around it, stole from the temple treasures and took possession of the holy oil and wine which he then distributed among his men. To the dismay of many who heard about it or became helpless spectators, drinking parties were organised which usually ended up in violence. And each time again, the ordinary citizens who didn't participate in the uprising, had to pay the price.

Titus gratefully made use of this division and chaos among the Jews, and his legions worked hard to completely close off the city from the rest of the world.

Despite the strict security with which the rebels guarded the city gates, citizens still managed to escape and seek refuge with the Romans. This gave the Romans an accurate picture of what was happening within the city walls.

Since suffering his attack Rapha had lost all his confidence. He only ventured outside when absolutely necessary. And inside his house he used all his time and effort to turn his home into a fortress. Well, he tried to anyway. He started to build a wall behind his front door to repel burglars but had to break it down again when he realised that it also stopped him from getting out.

He dragged all sorts of materials around in his house and went from room to room to barricade the doors and windows, only to break them down again if he needed to get to something. He was driven by panic and fear that the attack he had suffered would repeat itself. He had neither rest nor peace and he constantly talked to himself.

"I told them nothing… haha… And they thought they could make me talk!… But even if they beat me to death, I won't talk… Haha, then I really can't tell them anything anymore. If you're dead you can't talk… And they know it… Don't they?... No, they know nothing! Because I did not tell them anything… Nothing at all! They will keep their hands off my money. Tsk tsk, they would want to have it, wouldn't they? In Emmaus … In Emmaus!... Let them search for it there… That was very clever of me, hahaha, yes that was clever…"

He had a terrible fright when one day Kish appeared on his doorstep. At first he wasn't going to let him in. Why should he? There was nothing to buy from him anymore, was there? He had said so himself. No there was nothing to trade with Simpleton any more…

He could sell his goods himself.

He didn't need anyone else for that…

What would Simpleton want now…?

Maybe he wanted payment for the assistance he had given? He could forget it! Nothing of the sort! Even if he hadn't found him, he would have stayed alive anyway. You could count on that. A human being doesn't die so easily. He, Rapha, most certainly wouldn't die so easily. He could handle being roughed up. As long as they did not get hold of his money…

However, Kish inquired about his health and asked if there was anything he could do for him. And although he didn't quite trust him, Rapha eventually let him in because he was worried that others might notice them whispering at his front door. So they again sat opposite each other in the room where he had received Kish the first time.

He looks terrible, Kish thought.

I won't give him anything, Rapha thought. Not even a bowl of water. After all, I didn't ask him to come here! He was already regretting that he had let him in.

"I wanted to have a word with you," Kish began, and Rapha felt even more regretful.

"Talk?" Rapha hissed nervously. "Why? What about? What do we have to talk about?"

"About the situation in the city… and about you," Kish replied. "I'm not sure you'll understand Rapha, but I'm worried about you. You were near death, and all because of your miserable money. Had I not found you in the nick of time and had Gedor and Tirza not lovingly cared for you, then… yes where would you have been?"

Rapha flinched and at that moment, he hated himself for being so stupid as to let Simpleton come inside. He should have known better! They wanted payment for the small service they had done for him!

"You quietly slipped away without so much as a thank you. And I know why you did that Rapha. Simply out of fear that other people would want some of your money."

"I'm not giving you anything!" hissed Rapha.

"Rapha, you are sick," Kish said in a firm tone. "I'm not at all interested in your money… You are sick in the head. You simply cannot accept that other people do things for their fellow human beings without expecting payment in return.

I saw you lying here in the entry hall, close to death and felt deeply sorry for you. You are losing your soul Rapha, and that's what I wanted to talk to you about. Even if a man gathers enormous treasures here on earth, your life is not one of your belongings… Stop and consider what you are busying yourself with… Jerusalem is doomed to destruction. Many people are dying already because of lack of food. And all you worry about is your money."

"I don't have money!" Rapha screeched.

"No, money has you," said Kish. "Everyone knows that you are filthy rich, Rapha! What they don't know is where you hide it, or else they would have taken it from you already! Surely you've noticed that by now. The city is full of robbers and thieves."

"I'm not saying anything!" Rapha yelled. He was beside himself with rage.

"You don't need to tell me anything because I already know where you keep your treasures," said Kish.

Rapha thought he would choke. He gasped for air and his eyes nearly popped out of their sockets.

"Yes," Kish repeated, "I know where you hide your treasure…! Over there!"

He bent down toward him and tapped a finger onto his scrawny chest. "Money, money, money… in your heart! It's so full of money that there's no room left for any normal human feelings… If you do not repent you will be lost Rapha! Have you ever thought about that?"

Rapha managed to draw breath again.

"I'm not telling you anything," he sniggered.

"Rapha," Kish said in a soft voice, "in this very street where you live, children are dying from hunger. You won't be able to save all the children in Jerusalem, but you could save some of them… You can still make up for things. God asks of you that you show mercy and do anything in your power to help people.

You can do a lot of good with that barley and those figs which I bought for you. You wanted to give it away to the poor people, remember? Now is the time to do just that…

You thought you could spin me a yarn, I'm aware of that. But right now people are in desperate need, while you have a big stash of food in your house. It would be a great sin if you let children die so that later on you can make obscene profits. Help those people around you Rapha! It won't bring you a lot of money, but you will have treasure in heaven…

Those who hunger will bless you and bring your name before the Eternal One… You can still right some of the wrongs Rapha. The Lord our God is merciful and gracious. You will find a safe shelter with Him if you confess your sins."

"Sins? You are mad! Totally mad!" Rapha shouted.

"If you continue on this path you will suffer eternally," Kish answered. "If someone knows the right thing to do, but refuses to do it, that is sin, Rapha. Don't you ever think about that? Those who will die because of your greed, will one day testify against you. Then there will no longer be any room for regret and repentance."

"Just leave," Rapha hissed.

"At least give me some barley to take along," Kish tried one more time. "I will help the hungry on your behalf."

"Simpleton!" yelled Rapha, "do you think I am crazy?"

"Yes, as a matter of fact, I do," said Kish in defeat. "Stark raving mad about your money… Listen! There outside the prophet is calling… Do you hear it…

Woe… Woe… Don't you take that to heart Rapha?"

"Get out of here, out! I will never let you in again!" Rapha raged.

CHAPTER 25

"I FEEL I DON'T HAVE much longer to live, Gedor. It saddens me that my life will come to an end under such sad circumstances. The city under siege… And the temple…? What will become of it…? I'm afraid you will be right. Israel will be defeated… Our poor people… Gedor, that Saviour whom you worship… I thought He was a gentle Person?"

"Yes indeed, gentle and lowly in heart. He also mourned for Jerusalem, Pagiel. He takes no pleasure in punishment. He invited us to come to Him. But we didn't want to. We did not notice that the Eternal One visited us, Pagiel. Not only did we think that was an absurd idea, but we even considered it to be blasphemous and we rejected Him."

"I'm able to contemplate that now Gedor, without getting angry… But I still have many questions…

God, who wants to become a man, in order to save us from our iniquities? Who came and walked this earth among us in order to suffer and die in our place…?

I have to admit that He is able to do that… Of course, the Almighty can do that… But who on earth would have thought that He would really do that…"

"Who else could have done it, Pagiel? I couldn't have borne the punishment for my own sins, let alone the sins of others."

"When I look back on my life, I've become convinced that I cannot be saved by anyone else but that kind of Saviour, however…"

"He Himself tells us that outside of Him there is no salvation. In whom else should we put our hope and trust Pagiel? If the

Messiah would be no more than a human being like you and me, even if He was a most pious man and a great prophet, how would He be able to justify us before God? For He Himself would need forgiveness of sins! Solomon also testifies that there is no one who can do good without sin. Our Messiah would therefore have to be a very special Person."

"I am starting to see it too, Gedor…"

"Our Messiah is the Son of God, Pagiel! He can be no less."

"The more I think about it, the more miserable I feel. It shocks me when I hear you say these things. My world is turned upside down… Has Israel been blind? Have my eyes also been shut all that time? Or was my heart hardened? Perhaps it was because of my character, my uncontrolled anger…

My conscience torments me, Gedor. I suffer because of what I have done in the past and I'm unable to undo it. At the same time more and more Bible texts come to mind that testify of these things. The Lord is holy and we are unholy. I've always known these things but only recently have I come to feel the weight of that burden. The distance between holy God and sinful man is too great for me to bridge, you are right… I realise that only He can do it…"

"And He has done it, Pagiel!"

"But how can you know if that Man from Nazareth was truly the Messiah, Gedor? You know as well as I do that we've been deceived many times in that respect. Even now there are men walking around calling themselves Messiah. Every time again they prove to be deceivers, or simply liars out for personal gain. How can you know that He was the true Messiah, Gedor?"

"Everything He said was true Pagiel. We compared everything with the Scriptures! There was no lie in his mouth. It's true that what He said was rejected and opposed, but no one has been able to accuse Him of a lie. Do you know anyone of whom that can be said…? Those who believed Him on His word were never put to shame… Isn't that already very special Pagiel? I've already spoken to you about these things. Jesus had told His disciples beforehand what would happen to Him, His suffering and death and the reason why He did all that. He also foretold that they would all abandon Him in His suffering and would only believe in Him once they had seen everything. That is: later, after His resurrection from the dead… He bore our sins and conquered death!"

"Only the Almighty can do that, Gedor."

"And that's why we finally discovered that He is the One. Someone from Capernaum came to Him when He was in Cana in Galilee. He had come to ask if Jesus would come to his home to heal his son who was dying. The Lord told him that unless people could see signs and wonders, they would not believe.

But the man insisted and said, 'Lord, please come down before he dies.' And the Lord said to him, 'Go, your son lives.' And that man believed Him on His word and went home. On the way back his servants met up with him and told him that his son was alive and healed. After making further enquiries, he worked out the time of the healing, and it was the exact moment when the Lord had said, 'Your son lives.'

These things took place while the crowd was jostling around Him. At times there were over a thousand eyewitnesses to His miracles. He did things which God alone can do. He healed the blind and deaf and raised people from the dead. He drove out evil spirits. Surrounded by many people He raised a dead man who had already lain in the grave for four days. Yet He accused the crowds of following Him because of the miracles, and that they failed to understand their meaning! They were signs to show them Who He was. The works He did were the works of God…

I could go on for hours Pagiel.

He didn't proclaim Himself to be God wherever He went, but He did continually state things which would have been blasphemous if He had not been God! You be the judge!

He said, 'I am the Way, the Truth and the Life; No one comes to the Father except through Me.' That means, it's impossible to know God in His essence, except through Him!

'I and the Father are one,' He said. 'He who has seen Me has seen the Father'!

He said that He had come to save sinners and that everyone who would believe in Him would have eternal life. And also, that

He would be judging the world! He commanded His disciples to pray to God in His name.

I say again: If He was not God, Who would He have been? The works which He did could never have been performed by a human being! Even the mightiest of angels could not have spoken as He did!

Still, we delivered Him into the hands of the heathens to be crucified. But again, that was not an accident, Pagiel! It was all in accordance with His will! Do you remember what Isaiah said? The punishment which brought us peace, was upon Him. Countless prophecies were fulfilled in His suffering and death! Just read the Psalms and you're confronted with the Messiah in His suffering on the cross!

'For dogs have surrounded Me; the congregation of the wicked has enclosed Me. They pierced My hands and My feet; I can count all My bones. They look and stare at Me. They divide My garments among them, And for My clothing they cast lots.'

That's what the soldiers did who crucified Him.

Isaiah prophesied that He would be with the rich in His death and indeed, a rich man made a new tomb available for Him to be buried in."

"Something like that could have been arranged beforehand," Pagiel suggested.

"It could have been," Gedor admitted, "but then there were a lot of other details that would have required meticulous attention. For example, if the Lord had not died on exactly the right moment, His legs would have been broken. And that would have been contrary to what David prophesied about the Messiah in his Psalm, that not one of His bones would be broken!

And just imagine that Pilate had refused permission when asked if they could take him down from the cross and bury Him. His grave would not have been with the rich! Then no heavy stone would have been rolled in front of the tomb's entrance, nor would it have been sealed up! He would have been treated like a common criminal and perhaps thrown into a mass grave…

The Romans made doubly sure that He was dead by stabbing a spear into His side. Zechariah said that Israel will one day see Him whom they pierced!

No Pagiel, in all these events so many prophecies had to be fulfilled that any hint of clever deception is impossible. He proved to be the Son of God by fulfilling all righteousness and by rising again from the grave. Death could have no hold on Him because He has indestructible life within Himself."

"According to the Sanhedrin His disciples came and stole away His body and then started the rumour that He had risen."

"Those who want to deny the facts must invent a lie, Pagiel. What else could they do? But just think it through for a minute. If it was indeed true that they stole His body and started a false rumour, the disciples must have firmly believed their own lies," said Gedor. "Because they willingly sacrificed their own lives and most of them gladly died a martyr's death. A man wouldn't easily do that for something he knows is a lie, Pagiel.

Besides, we know very well where that story of the stolen body came from. Not all the men of the Sanhedrin were against Jesus! The soldiers received a great deal of hush money so they wouldn't reveal what had taken place on that third day at the grave site. But in the end that plot was leaked anyway and besides, there were other witnesses who met the risen Saviour near the grave. Hundreds saw Him in the flesh and spoke to Him after His resurrection. There were even five hundred together at one time. For forty days He appeared to His followers and spoke to them about the Kingdom to come... Until He was taken up into heaven. Several of the people here in our congregation in Jerusalem, were eyewitnesses of that event. I've met with them and spoken to them. And Pagiel, I can tell you, something like that leaves a deep impression…!

We confess that the blood of Jesus Christ, God's Son, cleanses us from all our sins."

For a while Gedor quietly observed his brother, who was deeply lost in thought.

"That's what I believe Pagiel… and your daughter… and Thomas… and so many others… Our lives belong to Him… And despite persecution and opposition, this faith is spreading all over the world…

I'm glad we've had time to talk about these things together.

We are not heretics. We still believe in the same God! We have simply come to know Him better. In Christ, He has come so very close to us and showed us even more clearly Who and What He is! In Christ He has reconciled us to Himself… So that whoever believes in Him will not be lost but have eternal life…

I hope you will think about it some more."

Pagiel nodded. "I certainly will," he promised. "I should have listened to you much earlier Gedor."

"It's not too late yet Pagiel."

CHAPTER 26

FEAR AND HATRED COMPETED for dominance. Rapha was racking his brains to figure out what he ought to do. The encounter with Kish had frayed his nerves and now he felt threatened. He was convinced that Kish was after his money. Of course he had denied it but Rapha had not fallen for that ruse. Kish had first tried to tell him that he wasn't interested in money and then played on his conscience to talk him out of a few bags of barley! Haha, did he really think he was that stupid?

Hadn't that fool told him that children were dying from hunger? What a simpleton! Anyone would realise that now you could ask a fortune for a bag of barley.

And someone who was even a bit cunning, like Rapha himself, would not be silly enough to start lugging a big bag of barley around. Perhaps a handful, so people could see how scarce it had become.

You could ask any price you liked. No one had to know that he had his cellars full. Nobody was *allowed to* know that because… He broke out in a sweat again when he thought back of those fellows who had tried to steal his money. He would rather die than reveal his secret. They could think what they liked, but he had no money… Neither did he have barley… Only now and then a handful which he would sell at a high price…

But Simpleton knew about his secret!

He had clearly said that he knew Rapha was very rich. Of course he'd never told Kish but having bought so much barley and figs for him, it must have been obvious. And Kish also knew that he had a lot of food stashed away in his house! All in all, this was very dangerous.

That Simpleton was not so simple after all. He must have realised that he hadn't handed it out to the poor…

Rapha felt driven into a corner.

That last talk with Simpleton had done him no good.

That miserable fellow with his preaching about judgement and repentance. Rubbish, all of it! Scare tactics, that was all! Sure, he would like that, wouldn't he, that scoundrel, scaring him into handing him over a bag of barley. That oaf would have been instantly rich!

Guaranteed he would have immediately sold it for a pile of money… And then he would come again to ask for another bag of barley… and then again and again… Rapha could see his stockpile dwindling away…

Simpleton was the only one who knew…

Suddenly it occurred to him!

If Simpleton was the only one, there was but one solution to his problem. Kish would have to go! Just disappear, from the city… far away. No, even further away, otherwise he could still come back again… Rapha clapped his hand to his mouth!

"Dead!" Rapha hissed between his fingers. Yes, that was it! He would not have peace till that Simpleton had been cleared out of the way… But how was he going to do that?

The cleanest option would be if he simply perished by the hand of a Roman arrow or stone… But then he would never hear of it because these days so many people died, all the time.

No, that was no good. He had to know for sure… He hardly dared to think it, but he could ask some of the bandits to kill Simpleton for him. It wouldn't be difficult for them, but of course they would want money. Most likely a lot of money… Rapha didn't even want to consider it. He also understood that he himself would be running a great risk. If they saw he had money after all… they would realise immediately that he kept it in his house since he couldn't have gone to Emmaus to get it, could he?

He trembled…

No, he could not rely on others. That was too risky and would only cost him money. He would have to do it himself!

Fighting hand-to-hand combat with Simpleton was out of the question. Rapha would need to use cunning if he wanted to succeed. However, he didn't even know where he could find Simpleton…

Even though he detested the thought, he would have to wait till Simpleton came and bothered him again. He now regretted having said that he didn't want to see him again…

But that Simpleton was a bit of an odd one. Wait a minute… How had Simpleton managed to get in when he, Rapha, was lying there unconscious? It was an uncomfortable thought but one he might be able to use.

If Simpleton would come again to ask about his well-being, he would hide himself. And if Simpleton still managed to get inside, Rapha would have a trap prepared for him from which there would be no escape… Maybe, a noose or a trapdoor… Or a rope, low to the ground to trip him up. He could have a bad fall and be knocked unconscious and then…

Or a heavy piece of stone which he could rig up to drop on that wretched man when he came into the entry hall…

With evil enjoyment Rapha made preparations.

He was going to get him all right… Asking barley for children, yeah sure. Excuses.

His lovely barley. He wasn't born yesterday… Just now when the value increased so greatly too. No, he was going to wait a little bit longer. The greater the need, the more expensive the bread would be… haha, that sounds so good! He wallowed in the idea.

War wasn't so bad after all, as long as you stayed away from the city walls and didn't venture outside too much… And as long as you had something to sell! It was just this Simpleton he had to be careful with, him and his sob stories. He had to go, to disappear!

Rapha built one trap after another and appeared to enjoy it more and more as he went along. This despite the fact that sweat was running off his face and his scrawny body was shaking feverishly.

Now and then he would break out in loud laughter when he imagined getting the better of Simpleton. At other times he would cringe and groan when he imagined that Simpleton would enter and catch him at what he was doing.

"Oh, I'll get you…" he puffed. "You don't scare me so easily! Filthy blackmailer… Hahaha… you just wait till it's finished, all finished. Then you may come in. Clever hey?"

He stumbled to the secret entrance of his underground rooms. After having closed the passage door behind him, the lamp fell from his shaking fingers. As he attempted to catch it, he lost his balance and tumbled headlong down the stone steps.

CHAPTER 27

"I CAN STILL SEE HIM walking over that wall," said Caleb. "And always crying out … the same message … 'Woe to Jerusalem!' But then he said something I'd never heard from him before. Suddenly he called out, 'Woe to me…!' And immediately he was hit by a stone from a Roman catapult, and he collapsed and died… That made an impression, I can tell you! I can still hear him crying out... They say he prophesied the same message for at least seven years. That's quite something, don't you think?"

"I believe it's a sign," Thomas answered. "I think his task here was finished because the end is near. The Lord in His mercy took him away before the destruction of Jerusalem so that he wouldn't have to experience it."

"I've seen them bring the battering rams and attack towers closer to the wall," said Caleb. "An impressive sight, those high towers clad with metal plating. Did you hear the crying in the city when the battering rams started up?"

"Who could have missed it!" Thomas replied. "Everyone knows what that thumping sound means. The only option left to us now is unconditional surrender. John and Simon are leading the people to their doom."

"They're crooks. Villains! And incompetent as well!" declared Caleb. "If you ask me, they're insane to think they can take on the Romans. Look how those rebels behave themselves on the walls! They insult and taunt the Romans as though they're little boys. The foulest language comes from their mouths. But I have to admit they fight heroically when they break out to try and destroy the war machines. They don't seem to value their own lives. It's like they're on suicide missions. And the Romans treat them with respect. They remain on high alert because they *do* value the lives of their people."

"War is terrible," said Thomas. "I can't imagine why you're so attracted to it."

"I just want to observe it, not participate in it."

"Death and destruction."

"Yes, you're right. I often feel ashamed, but I'm so fascinated by it. For example, how the Romans build a ramp to reach the Antonia fortress. It's extremely clever."

"But in doing so they've cut down every tree and transformed the landscape into a barren wilderness. And when they come into the city, what then Caleb? Then they'll let loose and go mad creating a bloodbath."

"That's indeed to be expected," Caleb admitted. "But aren't we ourselves the cause of it? The Romans weren't sitting around waiting for a rebellion … But you're right, in your position I would also be very worried. It's horrible to know that your fiancée is locked up in this city. You've gained an extra burden Thomas. All I can do is promise that no matter the circumstances, you can count on me."

"For that I'm grateful. But outside those walls are more than twenty thousand Romans who will soon overrun us. And the rebels who were so determined to fight them are not our friends either."

"I know what you mean. But as yet I've been able to escape out of all the besieged cities where I've been. If the Lord wills, I will also get out of this one. And I'm determined not to leave without you, Thomas."

"Having heard all your stories there seems to be little chance to get through their battle lines."

"Yes, that's true. But sad as it may be, when the walls fall and the Romans break through, all their attention will be focussed on the temple. For some reason they have the idea that it's full of gold. And when gold fever hits, everyone tries to get their share. We'll have to exploit an opportunity like that, to get away. It will be very dangerous but in my opinion that will be our chance."

"I wish I could already get Silla to safety."

"I can understand that. But you'll have to wait for an opportune moment. And besides, as long as her father is still alive you won't get her to leave."

"I know that, but I'm still worried about her. The whole situation is worrisome. It's becoming increasingly difficult to get food, too. So many people are starving already, especially those who came from outside the city and are living out in the open without shelter. They are suffering the most."

"Yes, everyone looked for refuge here. I think it wasn't very smart. The city is bursting at the seams."

"And what about you? You came all the way from Galilee, didn't you? That wasn't so smart either was it?"

"Ah, but that was different. I had to flee. And I was looking for relatives here."

"Most of the people who were in Jerusalem for the feast of unleavened bread could no longer get away because when the Romans came, the rebels wouldn't let them leave. I wonder how many there were."

"Was that at the start of the siege? From what I've heard there would be over two million."

"Seriously? That many?"

"I heard that, according to the priests, the figure is accurate. They did a count and kept a tally."

"No wonder that there's a shortage of food!"

"Does Silla's family still have food?"

"She reckons they do. And in their circumstances, it's probably true. But they must be starting to see the bottom of the barrel. That's another thing that worries me. Silla will deny herself food to give it to her father."

"That's not a bad thing, is it?"

"You're right, it's not a bad thing. But I love to see her healthy and well too."

"Of course, and you understand, that's not what I meant ...

Hey Thomas, when you see the Romans work like slaves on that embankment, that ramp they're making for their war machinery to get to Antonia, you can't help but be impressed. It's an enormous task of baffling proportions. Even without interference, it would be a massive job, but now they're constantly being harassed while they're busy. From the walls they are being bombarded with rocks and continually shot at with arrows and at the same time they need to keep watch for possible raids by the rebels. I've already seen that happen a few times."

"You'd better be careful."

"Oh, but I am. I don't take unnecessary risks. But it might still come in handy to know exactly where they are positioned. Don't you think?"

"You keep talking as if it concerns a celebration, Caleb. You should realise that they are fighting against us. They've now brought their weapons up close to the city. I can't see that it's something to celebrate."

"Is that what I'm doing?"

"It sounds like it sometimes."

"That's not my intention at all. I'm sorry Thomas... Yes I saw they relocated the catapults. They have whole batteries of that light artillery. Well, it depends if you can call them 'light'. They call them scorpions. They have a very accurate aim…

But you're right. Perhaps I should focus more on the awful consequences of those things."

Thomas looked at him and sighed.

"You're incorrigible Caleb… Our God is not a God of war but of peace."

"You wouldn't say that of David, yet he was still a man after God's own heart."

"Yes, he was indeed. Not because he was such a great warrior but because he believed!"

"That's what you say."

"No, that's how it is! He always went to the Lord to confess his sins. If you read the book of Psalms, you'll notice he was deeply aware that he was a sinner. But also that he could find shelter with the One Eternal God. He lived by grace… But he had much blood on his hands. That's why he was not allowed to build the temple."

"I know that. It was the privilege preserved for the king of peace. For Solomon! I also know my history, you see… And yet Thomas, we're at war again. The waiting is for the Messiah."

"He has come already. Jesus Christ, the Prince of Peace."

"I forgot about that, you're a Christian. You believe in that Nazarene, just like Kish."

"Kish?" Thomas asked surprised. "How do you know Kish?"

"I met him once. And now we're trying to stay in contact."

"But did you say that he's a Christian?"

"I had that impression."

"Do you know his nickname?"

"Yes, Simpleton. But he's definitely not simple!"

CHAPTER 28

"**M**ARIUS!" BELLOWED GAIUS.

A frightened soldier poked his head around the corner of the tent.

"Did you want something centurion?"

"Is Marius close by? Go and call him."

"Did you take the splint off your leg?"

"Yes, as you can see. I can kick and stomp on things again if I have to! But Marius thought that it could only heal by resting. Go and get him, so he can see for himself."

A few moments later Marius walked into the tent, smiling broadly.

"What do you reckon?" asked Gaius. Looking at Marius triumphantly, he spun around on his toes and bent down through his knees several times. "What do you think? It's looking as good as new again, don't you reckon?"

"Terrific, but I can't say it's pretty. I'd rather look at the graceful legs of a dancer than at those hairy calves of yours."

"Watch out who you're talking to, mate! What was all that waffle of yours about resting? I would say we've been working very hard indeed, and I didn't have much rest at all. But look, and you'll see that I can walk like before."

"I'm very happy for you."

"I would think so. A crippled commander on the front lines is not a good show. And all that time I felt almost written off while actually I haven't even rested long enough."

"Do you still feel it? I mean, does it still hurt?"

"Not at all. You can hardly even see that it was broken. It looks a bit paler and skinnier but that's all."

"That's because it was bandaged for so long. It will soon regain a healthy colour… And all thanks to that Jew. Must have been someone who knew what he was doing."

"Whatever the case may be, he did a very good job."

"Shall I clean up the mess?" asked Marius as he pointed to the splints and bandages on the ground.

"No, I won't get rid of it just yet. I'll keep it as a kind of souvenir."

"A reminder of the Jew or of your accident?"

"Both," Gaius grinned. "Maybe it will prevent me from doing something so stupid again. It also reminds me that not every person will kill another so easily. He could just have killed me there in the bushes. No one would have blinked an eye."

"Well, knowing you, I doubt that very much."

"There's nothing I could have done. You would understand if you'd been in my place. I couldn't even stand up. With a heavy branch he could have wacked me over the head and finished me off. I could only try to bluff him."

"That worked really well for you then?"

"No, not at all. That Jew was in total control of the situation. And he knew it too. It really bothers me that he's now holed up in the city. You'll probably think it's ridiculous but all the time I have the feeling that we're shooting at him."

"How many people do you think there are, crammed together between those walls?" Marius laughed. "It would be a great coincidence if we manage to pick him out in the crowd. No, that wouldn't cause me to lie awake at night. War is war and you even warned him, didn't you? Then the rest is his own responsibility."

"You don't get it do you."

"Oh yes, I do. That fellow saved your life."

"And splinted my broken leg and cared for me!"

"All very nice of that man! He even bandaged your sprained foot. I understand full well you don't easily forget something like that. But to be afraid with every shot we make that you would target that particular Jew… I'd say you're overthinking it."

"It just happens, those thoughts just pop up in my mind… Actually, he did much more than just let me live. Putting me on his own donkey, he brought me to safety. I would not have taken such risks, I can tell you that!"

"It's about time they call on you to do some heavy work. Now that you can use your leg again, they'll probably send for you. The legions are working hard. The ramp to the fortress is nearly completed. Hopefully they will direct us there and you can go back to your work. A few days of constant thumping will be good for your head. It will get rid of all those sentimental ideas. And you can enjoy your fight with the giant stones."

"It's a good thing for you that you ended up under my command," said Gaius. "With that disrespectful talk of yours, you wouldn't have lasted a day with another commander. He would have sent you to the Jews to deliver a message, never to return."

"I wouldn't like to fall into their hands," Marius said in a serious tone. "You can say what you like but they are fierce fighters. Just look at the damage they caused to our defences! For a moment I thought we were goners. It was a very close shave. If it hadn't been for Titus who kept a cool head, it could have been very different…"

"Reckless Jewish courage," Gaius stated. "They have the element of surprise working in their favour. And they don't seem to care how many men they lose. But they don't plan carefully and there's no strategy to their attacks. They know nothing about discipline. They're a rabble, a band of robbers. If we didn't keep them occupied, they would no doubt be at each other's throats again."

"They're a peculiar people. I don't get what drives them. With this war they've invited a lot of trouble for themselves. I heard that Titus would like to spare the city as much as possible but those inside won't consider surrender."

"Somewhere I can understand it," said Gaius. "Those rebel leaders have apparently been so brutal among their own citizens, they could expect nothing less than the death penalty. It looks like they'll fight to the last."

"Starvation might make them change their minds."

"We'll see, Marius. In any case I am fully fit for duty again."

"Thanks to that remarkable Jew. I wonder if he's fighting with them."

"Who knows," Gaius grumbled, "but I don't think so. However, I do get the feeling that he'd be a good commander for them."

"You're a sensitive guy," mocked Marius. "Even toward stones… But at a critical moment you're tough as nails."

"You better get going," said Gaius. "You know about my leg now. When we have a bit of time, I'll challenge you for a run. I want to see if you can run as fast as you can talk."

CHAPTER 29

KISH KNEW ALL THE nooks and crannies of Jerusalem. Even on a dark night, when thick clouds covered the moon and stars, he would find his way flawlessly through the labyrinth of streets. And so, on a night in which you couldn't see your hand in front of your face, finding Rapha's house was not a problem for him.

On his way, he was however confronted with the terrible suffering of his people. Jerusalem had become a ghost town. The obstacles he encountered were primarily the bodies of dead people. Occasionally, moaning could be heard from one of the houses. The cry of a desperate human being. Hunger… It was hard to think of something worse. Especially the suffering of little children cut him to his soul. The hollow faces and the lack of comprehension in the questioning eyes. The children in Jerusalem were going to die. If it wasn't from starvation, then before long it would be the victorious enemy who according to custom would kill all the children, sick and elderly.

Kish couldn't save them but perhaps he could try to lighten the suffering of some of them. The frenzy of the rebels had plunged the whole city into the misery of hunger. By their infighting, the vast food supplies held within the city walls, which could have provided even for the increased numbers, had been destroyed. As an offering to the king of darkness those supplies had gone up in flames. This fact had even upset the pagan Romans who saw it as a curse which had come over the city.

It was the great suffering of the children which moved Kish to make another attempt to soften the heart of Rapha. He had prayed to God to make this successful. For the sake of the soul of the miser and for the compassion in his own heart for his fellow citizens.

Kish was also driven by guilt. He had helped the miser to stockpile food while he knew very well that Rapha's intentions were not honourable. He had strung the man along, teased him and scared him, albeit with the intent to prick his conscience. Now that, at their last encounter, it had become clear that he couldn't count on Rapha's sympathy, and now that the situation was so desperate, he could no longer suffer seeing children starve to death while he was aware of a secret stash of food that could save them from starvation. He knew that if he ever survived the siege this would always testify against him. He would be burdened with the guilt of doing nothing… Once more he would try to persuade Rapha to cooperate.

Although Pagiel wasn't bothered by the food shortages, it didn't escape his attention that in Jerusalem the people suffered terrible hunger. He noticed it on the people who cared for him. He himself didn't have much appetite and ate very little but even so, he could understand that it became increasingly hard to provide a regular meal for him. From overhearing snippets of conversations and seeing the appearance of those around him, he understood that food was scarce. The supplies in his own house were nearly exhausted. He noticed that to provide food for him, others denied themselves. It touched him deeply that the people from whom he had least expected it, showed him such dedication. At the same time, it bothered him. He had noticed for some time already that Silla looked tired.

"Silla, I don't want you to go hungry because of me," he began.

When she tried to protest, he motioned her to be silent.

"I'm grateful for what you've all done for me, my child. But I don't want to see my daughter starve before my eyes. I don't need a lot, but it seems it's still too much. I want you to eat Silla. It's bad enough that you suffer this siege because of me. Please tell me honestly what provisions are left. It can't be much. I know roughly how much was in store before I became ill. And I understand you don't want me to worry but that's no longer possible. I can see you are withering away. How much is left?"

"How would it help you to know that?"

"Perhaps I could call more fervently on the Name of Him who supplied out forefathers with manna from heaven. Is there anything left Silla? Please be honest?"

"No more than just for today… It's been like that for some weeks now. Thomas and Caleb provide me daily with whatever they can scrounge up, but that's getting less all the time. It's already a miracle that we've been able to keep going this long. There are rich people out there who spend a fortune on a handful of barley."

"When is the last time you had something to eat Silla?" asked Pagiel with dread in his voice.

She evaded the question by answering, "I don't need much."

"In any case you need more than you're getting!" said Pagiel. "Silla my daughter, I have pleaded with the Lord to forgive me for being the cause of your suffering in these terrible circumstances."

She again wanted to object but he motioned to her that she shouldn't.

"Please allow me to say something Silla. My life is rapidly coming to an end… I hope for your sake that it's fast enough… No, don't cry and don't be sad… Last night I dreamt… Or perhaps it was a vision… I felt crushed under God's hand because of my sins, but at the same time made alive by the same hands. And wonderfully comforted by a flood of grace that washed over me. And then I heard a Name called out over me… Silla my child, I heard a Name…! The Name which I have cursed and which I rejected and did not want to hear in my house…"

Pagiel wept…

"Father!" Silla cried as she embraced him tearfully.

Together they cried until Pagiel regained his composure and could continue to speak.

"He has opened my eyes Silla. I thought I would die but He has made me alive! How I would love to put my whole life into His service… now that my earthly life is nearly over… It's taken so much to bring me this far. Silla I've brought you so much misery."

"It's the Lord Who guides all things Father," said Silla. "For those who believe in Him, all things are turned to their benefit. If this may be the fruit of our decision to stay with you in Jerusalem, it exceeds all expectations. Great is the Lord and greatly to be praised! He doesn't deal with us according to our iniquities but offers us forgiveness because of Christ. I'm overjoyed that the Lord has opened your heart and worked mightily in you."

"I owe you and uncle Gedor a great debt of gratitude Silla."

"The Lord alone can make someone be born again," Silla fended him off.

"I'm aware of that," said Pagiel, "but faith comes through hearing, my darling daughter, and you both have been good witnesses. I can't claim that for myself. I was blind… Blind as a bat!"

"But now you can see!"

"Yes," Pagiel agreed, "now I can see… And how ashamed I am… Oh, how I wish I could start all over again."

"You will," Silla comforted her father.

"Yes, you're right… But here on earth things are coming to an end for me Silla… There is something else I wanted to tell you… The last few months I've experienced great turmoil. The things I heard from you… the things the Lord Jesus Christ worked in my heart… and everything that's happened in Jerusalem and the dreadful stories which filtered through to me about the sins of my people, have really shaken me up. I'm starting to make sense of it, but I've had a very difficult time. I asked myself if the Almighty was abandoning His people. Would He Who cannot lie, break His covenant with Israel after all? Was His covenant with Abraham not an everlasting covenant? Would He reject us today after being so longsuffering with previous generations?

I couldn't believe, didn't want to believe that Jerusalem would be destroyed. But Gedor pointed to something which I actually already knew, namely, this has happened before. Then the temple which Solomon built was also destroyed. Now indeed I believe that the words of the Lord Jesus will soon be fulfilled. Jerusalem will fall and be trampled underfoot by the heathens. We deserve it. Israel has brought this judgement upon herself.

I struggled with that idea, prayed it wouldn't happen and cried about it at night. It caused me such grief… But whether it was in the dream, or that the words came to me when I woke up, I can't say. But I was greatly consoled by the words of Jeremiah who prophesied about a distant future when the Lord would make a new covenant with the house of Israel and the house of Judah. Not one like the covenant He had made with our fathers when He led them out of Egypt; the covenant we broke time and again while the Lord remained faithful, 'But this is the covenant that I will make with the house of Israel after those days, says the Lord: I will put My law in their minds, and write it on their hearts; and I will be their God, and they shall be My people. No more shall every man teach his neighbour, and every man his brother, saying, "Know the Lord", for they all shall know Me, from the least of them to the greatest of them, says the Lord. For I will forgive their iniquity, and their sin I will remember no more.'

What He has done for me, He will do for all of Israel in the future. I do not know how, but I do believe it will happen because He has said so… Wasn't it you who told me that the Saviour had said that Jerusalem shall be trampled underfoot by the Gentiles until the times of the Gentiles are fulfilled? Whatever that last part may mean, I think we may at least conclude that there will, one day, come an end to the suffering of our people. As David said: 'The Saviour shall come from Zion and will turn away the godlessness from Jacob'. Our sins prevailed over us, but Christ has come to save us. Through Christ, the Eternal One was busy reconciling the world to Himself. Yes Silla, my dear child, I believe that Jesus Christ is the Son of God."

"How wonderful that now we can freely talk about these things together," said Silla and she kissed her father. Her eyes were aglow and for a moment their miserable circumstances were forgotten. Her heart rejoiced.

"Merciful and gracious is the Lord, longsuffering and full of lovingkindness," Pagiel quoted from one of David's songs of praise. "Silla, even as a child I wanted to serve the Lord. As far as I know, your uncle and I have done our best to faithfully keep His commandments. With great joy we celebrated the temple feasts. We praised and glorified His great Name amidst the gathering throngs of the tribes of Israel…

But when He fulfilled the prophecy, my brother recognised Him, but I despised Him. It leaves me feeling very uncomfortable.

All my life I've believed in the one true God and only now I've come to know Him. He has shown mercy to me. On this earth I cannot become any happier, Silla. The only thing that overshadows my joy is that I must leave you behind in this city which is doomed to destruction. Yet even in that the Lord shows mercy by allowing me to entrust you to Thomas. It is my dearest wish that you and he will have much joy in life…

He Who worked such a mighty wonder in me is also powerful to keep you safe. Even to allow you to escape from Jerusalem. That's what I pray for. I must trust that He will do so because I won't witness it. My hope is in God."

"Praised be the Lord!" Gedor exclaimed joyfully when he heard from Silla what had happened to her father. Thomas and Tirza too, were ecstatic and praised God for what He had done in the heart of Pagiel and that in the midst of much misery, their prayers for Pagiel had been heard.

"The Lord is good," said Thomas.

"Hallelujah," Gedor added.

"I see this as the Lord's confirmation that you made the right decision by staying in Jerusalem, Silla," said Tirza with joy. "Whatever happens, we'll never have to doubt that this was the path for us."

From that day onward, the hours spent together with Pagiel, were joyous times, allowing the gnawing hunger pains to be temporarily forgotten. It seemed as if they tried to make up for lost time. Through the working of the Holy Spirit, his vast knowledge of Scripture became a treasure trove from which he could draw, to his heart's content. For the others it was a joy to hear him and Gedor be busy with the Gospel. He wanted to know everything that the Gospel could tell him about the Lord and His apostles.

"It's always like this," Gedor explained. "We've seen it happen so often. When the Lord opens someone's heart, there's no end of wonderful images for the future."

"The future is far more beautiful than I had ever dared dream," Pagiel agreed. "The Name which I wanted to ban from my house and life, has become for me the most wonderful of names. It is the miraculous work of the Almighty. How can I ever thank Him enough for that…? And that He in His mercy wanted to use you for it, after all the injustices I had inflicted on you… Now I may know Him as my Saviour and Redeemer, Jesus Christ, my Lord and my God… I will glory in Him…

Oh, how I rebelled against the thought that the Almighty would humble Himself to the point where He was born as a human baby from the line of David. That He was the Child of which Isaiah spoke. The Son of the Holy One, who would be King over the house of Jacob and sit on the throne of David. A Kingdom of peace which shall have no end. A Light to the Gentiles and to the glory of Israel!"

Pagiel's sickbed became the best time of his life. The others took courage from it. He in turn was a blessing to them.

His health deteriorated rapidly but there was an intense joy in his heart. His voice became weaker but his songs of praise more powerful. He radiated joy while confessing God's eternal faithfulness with words of the Psalm:

"'Praise the Lord, O my soul! While I live I will praise the Lord; I will sing praises to my God while I have my being... Happy is he who has the God of Jacob for his help, whose hope is in the Lord his God, Who made heaven and earth, the sea, and all that is in them; Who keeps truth forever... The Lord shall reign forever - Your God, O Zion, to all generations. Praise the Lord!'

O my children, I would give all that I have if only Israel would acknowledge this salvation. If they would only recognise our Lord Jesus Christ as their Messiah. But seeing, they were blind and hearing, they were deaf. How long will it remain hidden? But one day, according to the words of Zechariah, the Spirit of mercy and prayers will be poured out upon us. Then they shall see the Lord Whom they have pierced. May that day come soon!"

He asked Gedor to tell him honestly about the situation in Jerusalem and her inhabitants and then cried when he heard the details, confessing his sins and the sins of the people. He was convinced that in this way, God was judging them. He suffered especially because he realised how he had cooperated in rejecting and refuting the salvation which Jesus had offered. But despite the depth of his grief and remorse, it couldn't prevent his elation over the mercy shown to him, from lifting him up again.

"It is undeserved Gedor, and now I say with Job, 'I have heard of You by the hearing of the ear, but now my eye sees You.'"

CHAPTER 30

MEANWHILE, THE BATTLE CONTINUED. The Romans had built ramps which allowed them to bring their war machinery closer to the city. The Jews fought with death-defying zeal which astonished their opponents and, in some instances, engendered a fear of defeat. John and his helpers had secretly dug tunnels which extended to beneath the Roman ramps. They then brought in flammable material which when lit, sent everything above it into flames causing whole structures to collapse into the tunnels below. At the same time the Jews sent out raiding parties seeking to destroy the Roman war machinery. Battering rams and attack towers were set alight. Many fell in these bloody fights. The Romans were not inclined to give up easily and attacked them in return, but the Jews would not retreat because they knew how much was at stake. They forced the Romans to withdraw to their own positions and the dismay of the besiegers was obvious when they realised that the work which had cost them days of arduous labour would have to be surrendered to destruction. Even battle-hardened soldiers find it hard to fight against desperate people. As the Romans attempted to pull the burning battle towers out of the flames, the Jews in most cases managed to prevent them from doing so. Titus himself, with his elite troops, had to intervene and force the death-despising rebels back into their walled city.

Caleb could not resist reporting to Thomas all the details of the fights that he observed. Also about the rest-breaks Titus granted his men, during which he would distribute wages to the soldiers. Receiving their pay was a happy event, and it was done with a display of much pomp and ceremony which at the same time was intended to discourage the Jews. He obviously wanted to demonstrate that the Romans could afford to pay their soldiers and were sure of their eventual victory.

Soldiers who had shown exceptional courage received distinctions or were promoted in rank. The whole ceremony was a display of strength and composure, which greatly impressed Caleb. He observed it with a sense of awe. He was also impressed by the new reinforcements the Romans built, for which their soldiers had brought in materials from afar because very little useful material was left around Jerusalem.

Thomas patiently listened to all the stories. He had become used to Caleb's method of reporting on the battle, as though he was merely an impartial spectator.

The story about John digging the tunnels made him wonder if that might be a way for them to escape the lockdown of the Romans. At the same time, he realised that many more citizens in Jerusalem would be contemplating the same thing, and many might even make the attempt. It was also clear to him that digging a tunnel would require much manpower and very good equipment and since he had neither at his disposal, he had better forget about that possibility. Thomas had no desire to observe the battle and tried as much as possible to stay away from the city walls but from Caleb he learned that it had become virtually impossible for escapees to avoid the attention of the Romans. He wondered about Caleb when all this didn't seem to bother him, and it even irritated him at times. Part of that was due to his increased concerns about Silla.

The hunger in the city had become so widespread and intense that it defied description. The most harrowing stories were circulating. Stories so terrible, that even the Romans who heard them, shuddered. Their conviction that judgement had come upon the city increased when they heard how the rival bands kept at each other's throats. Despite hardships and the fight against a common enemy, civil war between the factions continued.

Until now, Thomas and Caleb had managed to provide Silla and her family with some food, little as it may have been. But the situation was becoming desperate. To his shame, Thomas found himself hoping that Pagiel would soon pass away, so they could make an attempt to flee the city. Although the chances of escaping were small, anything was preferable to starvation. It broke his heart to see the suffering children who cried out in vain for food, and the desperate mothers who denied themselves the last piece of bread to be able to give it to their children.

What was the use? He had seen how men fought bitterly for a piece of an old sandal, which at least gave them something to chew on. There was very little compassion among people. Pity for others only sealed one's own death. All of life's lustre had gone. Men, women and children, fought for sheer existence.

"Jerusalem is about to go down, Caleb."

"Without a doubt," replied Caleb. "But you wouldn't say so when you hear the rebels fighting each other and shouting from the walls. How they dare I'll never understand. While they taunt the Romans and call for the Almighty's wrath over them it's abundantly clear that it's coming over *us*. They seriously still believe a miracle will happen, shouting that at the last moment the Messiah will appear to destroy the heathens. They don't realise that through their deeds they are more deserving of God's judgements than the heathens. The destroyers of Jerusalem are no longer in front of the wall but *on* it, Thomas! It's unbelievable that people can be so blind. I truly think they don't realise they're defeated and that they're dragging all of Israel along in their downfall."

"Has it ever been different?" Thomas asked. "Our entire history is one of rebellion. Rebellion against God and against the prophets He sent us. We were led out of the house of slavery by the Lord, but we stubbornly continued to behave as slaves. Just out of the house of bondage and we made a golden calf. We've always been quick to adopt our own ways over those of the Lord's. Who has heeded the prophet who walked here in the city for more than seven years? The things happening to us were foretold by the Lord Jesus Christ, Caleb. It's happening exactly as He said, even as it did with all the Lord's prophecies. The city will be conquered by the heathens and destroyed by them. Not one stone will be left upon another, and Israel will be scattered among the nations."

"And after that? What is there left to hope for?" asked Caleb.

"The hope, the expectation, the longing… Looking forward to His return. The day when the Lord will gather us to Himself from east and west, from south and north and Israel will repent."

"Is that what you believe?"

"Yes, and if you would only believe the prophets, you would also believe it. One day Israel will see Who it is that they rejected in our Lord Jesus Christ. Then they will behold Him Whom they have pierced, the God of Abraham, Isaac and Jacob! The Almighty Who has chosen us to be His people."

"That sounds very strange to me," Caleb admitted freely. "If I may say so, it sounds outright blasphemous."

"No one can save us from our sins but God alone," Thomas explained. "And He has done exactly that by going to the cross for us! One day Israel and all the world will see it; that He is the One Who revealed himself in Jesus Christ."

"A man who wanted to make himself equal with God," said Caleb.

"And Who did mighty works, which only the Creator can do?" asked Thomas. "No Caleb, think about it, that's not possible, is it…? We haven't rejected a man who claimed to be God, but the Almighty Who became man to save us…! Israel's history would have developed very differently if she would have understood this incredible offer and accepted it… But those who reject it are under judgement."

"But then you also fall under it," was Caleb's quick reply. "You've stayed in the city and are subjected to the same misery."

"True, we are experiencing the same suffering," Thomas admitted, "and I don't know what else is coming, but for us there will be no condemnation."

"That goes over my head," said Caleb.

"The Lord Jesus Christ has said that he who hears His words and believes Him Who sent Him, has eternal life and won't suffer condemnation. Such a person has now already crossed over from death to life."

"So He was an ordinary person after all?" Caleb responded. "A man lets himself be sent, the Almighty does not!"

"Jesus said: 'He who sees Me, sees the One Who sent Me,'" said Thomas.

"That means He would have sent Himself!" Caleb remarked.

"Yes indeed," said Thomas, "God from God."

"Half man, half… That's not possible, is it?"

"Not half a man," corrected Thomas, "but true God and true man."

"That's impossible!" Caleb reckoned.

"With the Lord it is not!" Thomas insisted. "With Him nothing is impossible. That's our confession: Jesus Christ, Son of God, our Saviour and Redeemer. His blood cleanses us from all our sins."

"I'm not sure what to think," Caleb sighed. "My head is spinning. You're telling me things that upset me, and I think that I should be raising objections. But on the other hand… I need some more time to think about it."

"And learn more about it too," Thomas advised. "Spend less time watching the Romans and more time being busy with these things. And especially pray that the Lord God will enlighten you. He wants to lead you in the truth. Our eternal salvation is at stake, Caleb!"

"You're not the only one telling me that."

"Who else does?"

"Silla and her father, when I drop in there … And then of course Gedor and his wife…. And I shouldn't forget Kish."

"Kish?" asked Thomas. "You've mentioned him to me before. What do you know about him?"

"Not much really. I don't even know where he lives. But I do know that he's a decent fellow… And yes, now and then he talks just like you. We've had some discussions about these things. I don't see things clearly yet, but I am busy with it, Thomas… Perhaps that's one of the positives in these awful circumstances, that we are driven closer together. Under normal circumstances we would never have met. Or if we had, we would not have been in a hurry to talk about these things. Although… You people are so full of it. Out of the abundance of the heart…"

CHAPTER 31

NO MATTER WHAT KISH tried, there was no response. Stubborn Rapha must be faking deafness. But then again… Rapha was not expecting him and besides, Rapha had sworn to never let him inside again. On top of that, it was very likely that the miser had locked himself up in his secret hiding place.

Kish had to knock softly in order not to draw attention to himself. One never knew who or what was hiding in the shadows. The friendly darkness could easily become a brutal foe.

Kish thought for a while, considering his options. It wouldn't be hard for him to gain entry, but circumstances were different from when he still got on reasonably well with Rapha, with the intention to try and save the miser.

If he broke in now, he would probably be treated as a burglar. Although Kish was not afraid of the little miser, he should still be extremely careful.

He wanted to talk to Rapha, one way or another. And he could no longer wait…

Kish managed to open the front door but didn't immediately enter. He felt around the inside of the door frame as well as along the threshold which he had to cross. This cautious approach was rewarded when his hand found a tightly strung rope. Rapha had set a trap for him!

Kish now understood that he had to be prepared for the worst. The wicked man wasn't the type to simply pull a prank. This was intended to kill him!

However, Kish didn't even think about cancelling his mission. He had discovered the trap in time, so the biggest danger had passed, but in order to proceed he would need to light a lamp. Although he knew where he could find the oil lamp, he realised that getting there could be fraught with danger. Rapha was clever enough to have considered that.

Taking out his knife, he cut the tight rope. A dull thud followed. Something heavy must have dropped down behind the door. He paused for a few minutes to see if anyone inside or outside had heard it.

When nothing happened, he opened the door wider and proceeded to carefully feel the floor. There he found a tightly tensioned cord that had been put up about ten centimetres off the floor. He cut it... Nothing happened... He tried to figure out what Rapha would have been thinking. Was the idea that he would trip over it?

After being convinced that there were no further dangers around the door, he ventured inside and pressed himself against the wall next to the door. Carefully he closed the door and listened attentively...

And still there was no reaction...

Nevertheless, Kish counted on the possibility that Rapha could be hiding in the dark, waiting to kill him. He didn't doubt for a moment that the miser would try it if he had half a chance.

With extreme care he inspected the wider area bit by bit, first the wall and then the floor, on the way to the place where he expected to find the lamp.

He found another object which, as far as he could make out in the dark, resembled a clamp but it had failed to work. He also had a fright when his head bumped into a rope that was hanging from the ceiling. He assumed that it was a noose of sorts...

He had now come to the place where the lamp should be! What would Rapha have done with it? Would he have left it in its place? Or would he have anticipated that Kish might evade his traps...? If that was the case, it would have been smart to remove the lamp.

Prepared for anything, Kish was not going to risk his unprotected hand by reaching for the lamp but used his knife instead. He searched … and found it! The lamp was still in the same place and there was nothing suspicious around it!

While reaching for the lamp and lighting it, he was aware that this would be a dangerous moment as he would be an easy target for someone waiting in the darkness… He breathed more easily when he found himself alone in Rapha's hallway.

He could clearly see the traps Rapha had put up for him. Their set-up was so simple and unimaginative that it was surely the work of a madman. The ropes had been strung criss-cross through the available space, alongside all kinds of strange constructions, which only a sick mind could have invented.

Only the heavy rock near the front door could be considered as a serious threat to his life. Kish guessed that if he had been hit on the head, as no doubt the intention was, he would at least have been unconscious. He counted himself lucky that he had been so cautious.

But what now? Where would Rapha be? With all the traps set up near the front door, the miser couldn't have left that way, for then it would have been impossible for him to prepare an intruder's reception.

As far as Kish was aware, there was no other exit from the house. But to make sure that he wouldn't be taken by surprise, he searched the house from top to bottom. He even looked out on the roof to see if there was another way to leave the house. There was a staircase that led along the facade to the roof, but the door to the roof was bolted on the inside.

Despite Rapha's attempt on his life, Kish became increasingly concerned about the man.

The only option was that Rapha had retired to his treasure room. That meant he would now have to go down there…

Kish hesitated, wondering what to do.

It was dangerous to have no rear-guard protection. There was a possibility that Rapha would be waiting to attack him down there. Or someone entering the house while he was down there could cut off his escape. That would put him in a precarious position. So, he would have to close the secret entry door behind him. If something were to happen to him down there, no one would ever find him…

He still took the gamble and in his heart he prayed for Rapha.

He opened the secret door as he had watched the little profiteer do it once before, stepped slowly inside, and closed it behind him.

Carefully he went down … and arriving at the bottom of the stairs, the light of his lamp fell on Rapha who stared at him with a frozen expression on his face!

The wretched soul sat slumped against the wall and didn't stir… He was dead!

The shards of the lamp Rapha had used to light his way down, were scattered all around him. Although he had seen many corpses, Kish was deeply moved when he inspected the dead body. From the injuries he could deduce what must have happened.

"You fool," he whispered and closed Rapha's eyes. "What does it benefit a man if he gains the whole world but loses his soul? May the Eternal One have mercy on you… Rapha, why didn't you listen to me?... Now you can't even buy yourself a tomb… Even if you wanted to give your whole fortune for it. Who will mourn for you? You leave no grateful people behind. Not even those who owe you money and won't need to repay it. They too will die… just like our beloved Jerusalem… And then money no longer counts for anything … Gold and silver… pigs don't even eat it…

You died a miserable man Rapha. Many cursed you while you lived… But I'll try and find a place for you and try to pray for you… Because you are after all a human being… and because I am your neighbour… It is for God alone to judge…

Hear O Israel, the Lord your God is One…"

CHAPTER 32

"DO YOU EVER SLEEP?" whispered a shocked Gedor, while he let Kish in. Then he noticed the serious look on Kish's face. "Has something happened? Are we in danger?"

"Rapha is dead," answered Kish. "I found him dead in his house. He had an accident and died all alone."

"How sad," said Gedor. "But in this city, it no longer shocks you. If the Lord doesn't provide relief soon, we will all starve to death."

Kish took a small bag from beneath his cloak and placed it before Gedor.

"Barley," he said. "You won't be dying of hunger. Not you."

Gedor couldn't believe his eyes.

"Where ... did you ... get that," he stammered.

"How do I get rid of it!" Kish retorted. "The Jews are killing each other for a handful of barley. That's how far we have fallen, Gedor. And now I have a problem... Rapha owned a stockpile of food which he was hoping to sell for a huge profit when food would become scarce."

Deeply shocked Gedor asked, "Surely you didn't murder him to claim it all for yourself?"

"No, I did not," Kish responded calmly. "But thank you for asking. As I said, that's how deep we've already fallen. I don't blame you for thinking it of me. Who knows what I would have done to him if he had continued refusing to help starving people while he was sitting on such a pile of food..."

No, I didn't touch him… He did however intend to kill me, but as you can see, he failed."

Kish related what his intention had been for a visit to Rapha by night, and what he encountered when he got there.

"But I'm not exaggerating when I say that now I have a problem Gedor. And because I highly value your opinion, I immediately came to you to discuss the matter. I want to do what's right before God, and I need you to provide counsel. As far as I'm aware, Rapha left no relatives behind in this world, so I shall take possession of his goods. Not for myself but to keep some people alive… for as long as the supplies will last," he added with a sad smile. "The suffering of the children pains me most. They are almost beyond help already but perhaps we can relieve their suffering by giving them a little food… However, each child that I supply with food will be envied by others.

I purchased this barley for Rapha at the time when it was still used as fodder for horses. Now such a bag is worth a fortune… I knew what kind of person he was but took pleasure in playing the fool with him. I honestly never anticipated that the war would bring us into such a hopeless situation. When that did happen, I went to him and tried to soften his heart. But I found no way to appeal to his conscience. You would almost think that he no longer had one. Although I played his game, I also truly felt sorry for him… Only the Lord Jesus Christ would be able to soften his heart Gedor."

"Do you believe in the Lord Jesus Christ, Kish?"

"Yes, I do," Kish replied. "I believe that He is the Messiah, the Son of God… I have heard the gospel. And have seen it in action too… with you and others … how it functions in your daily lives… It has slowly grown on me… I would love to talk more about it but not now. I first need your advice. In the current circumstances I think I would be allowed to distribute Rapha's possessions. What do you think Gedor?"

"I think it would be a great evil if you didn't. It is Rapha's legacy. He has no family that I know of. If you can save lives, I think you're obliged to do so. Help as many people as you can."

"I'll bring you some food regularly," Kish promised, "but we must be sensible about it. Eat only small portions and don't draw attention to yourself. Everyone is suffering from hunger. It will look suspicious if you appear strong and well fed and you'd even put yourself in danger. If the rebels suspect anything they will kill you for a bite to eat. I particularly want to try getting food to some of the children. But it must be done in great secrecy and as inconspicuously as possible."

"Where is the food?" asked Gedor. "Where do you keep it?"

Looking him in the eyes Kish replied, "I won't tell you Gedor. For your safety and for mine. Please forgive me. I trust you completely, but the fewer people who know about this secret the better."

"But if you're the only person who knows about it and something happens to you," said Gedor, "have you considered that?"

"Yes, I have," Kish assured him. "I will confide in Thomas and Caleb. I know I can count on them. They're young and strong and that's what I need in this situation."

"You're right," said Gedor. "I'm an old man and not very suited to these adventures… But if you're stuck you can count on me."

"I know that and I'm grateful. But don't even tell your wife where the barley comes from. Honestly, it will be safer for all of us. There shouldn't even be a whisper about it. I'll take it upon myself to distribute the barley in very small portions, without revealing to anyone where it comes from. Let them think it's a sort of manna from heaven. And in a way it is. It's harsh, but I'll try to restrict myself to children… That weighs on me, Gedor."

"You're handling it wisely, Kish."

"I had not anticipated that possessing food could be such a great problem," said Kish. "And that also counts for distributing it fairly."

"And that there's so much danger attached to it," Gedor added. "By the way, the question just occurred to me Kish, what have you done with Rapha's body?"

"Nothing yet… I simply can't bring myself to lay his body in the street. Then the best outcome would be that his body is thrown over the city wall into the ravine… But then everyone who sees him, will know that his house is empty…"

"What are you planning to do then?"

"I will try and bury him."

Gedor looked at him in admiration.

"You are a man full of secrets, brother," he said. "Let's pray together…"

Perhaps Thomas and Caleb were less surprised than Gedor had been, when Kish visited them by night, but they certainly hadn't expected it. When Thomas heard the whole story, he was overjoyed. When Kish mentioned the food at his disposal his first thought was that at least Silla wouldn't starve to death. She was foremost in his mind.

"Rapha's house has some secret apartments," Kish revealed to them, "and their entrance is particularly well hidden. I would probably never have found it if I hadn't at one time spied on him."

"Ah, so that's what you needed me for," said Caleb.

"Yes. On that occasion, I saw where the entrance was and how he opened it. I wanted to know where he stashed all the food that I was buying for him. I considered that if something happened to him, the food might all go to waste, and I couldn't bear the thought. I was convinced there was a secret hiding place in his house because he never left anything of value lying around. As it turns out, I was right. I haven't told anyone about it, but now I'm going to share it with you.

I've also consulted Gedor but didn't want to burden him with these details because it comes with grave danger. However, I did tell him that I would be confiding in you. Remember that this secret stays with the three of us! It's dangerous information. If the wrong people get wind of it and one of us is captured, there's a big chance that the secret will be discovered… If that happens everything is lost. We would not only lose the food but also our lives. You're not allowed to confide in anyone…

If I could find out Rapha's secret, others may also try with us. We must be extremely careful, take no risks and strictly adhere to our agreement."

"You can count on us," said Thomas.

"Of course," Caleb agreed.

"Well then, first I'd like you to promise that if something were to happen to me, you speak with Gedor and let him take my place, so that there's always three people involved. I think that's necessary and the safest way of operating. I also ask for your trust, that for the time being, I'm the only one who goes down into the hiding place while you two stand watch, one inside and one outside the house. Oh, and something else, never show yourselves in the vicinity of Rapha's house during the day. Whatever needs doing must be done at night."

The others nodded in agreement.

"Then I'll show you all you need to know... Come with me!"

Although stress and anxiety had become part of everyday life for Caleb and Thomas, they nevertheless felt a strange tension as they approached Rapha's house. "Caleb," Kish whispered, "you stay here and keep watch... I'll first show Thomas how it all works and then you can swap around."

After he had made his two friends familiar with the secret of the hidden entrance, he had Thomas stand guard outside and Caleb inside while he himself descended into the underground storerooms. He was soon back with Rapha's corpse in his arms, and he locked the entrance behind him. The young men carried the dead man while Kish led them through the dark city. Coming to a section of ruins, Kish stopped and asked them to lay the body behind the remains of a partially collapsed wall. It was still completely dark and neither of the young men knew where they were but without hesitation Kish led them safely back to Thomas' home. On the way none of them spoke a word but Thomas and Caleb both tried their best to move forward as silently as Kish did. It had become clear to them that in many respects he was their superior.

"Shalom," Kish whispered as he took his leave and disappeared as a shadow in the night. Only then did they notice the handful of barley he had left behind for each of them.

"There's always something mysterious about him," Caleb said when they were alone again.

"He certainly knows what he wants," replied Thomas. "He's a peculiar chap… He doesn't explain more than the bare essentials. Do you understand why we had to lug Rapha's body around? And why did he want the body right there?"

"I think he's going to bury him," Caleb answered.

"What makes you think that? Why would he do that?"

Caleb just shrugged his shoulders.

"I don't know. It's just what I think. It seems to be something typical for Kish to do… By the way, did you see all those strange contraptions in that entry hall?"

"In Rapha's house? A bit of a mess there… Ropes across the floor and other things…"

"I had a closer look and I think that Rapha did some strange things before he died. Did you see that the ropes had been cut in several places?"

"No, I hadn't noticed."

"And those battens and pieces of wood. And what about the steel pins? And that heavy rock near the front door?"

"That's typical of you to notice all those things. But what's behind it all?"

"I wouldn't be surprised if Rapha had set up traps to protect himself from intruders."

"Kish never mentioned any of that."

"That's what he's like. He doesn't tell you everything…"

"He did say that Rapha had an accident."

"That's true, no doubt. He must have fallen down the stairs."

"Just like Kish suspected."

"Yes… But if you ask me, something happened beforehand… I believe Rapha tried to kill him."

"Kish never mentioned a word of it."

"Perhaps he mentioned it to Gedor. In any case, I've seen enough," Caleb maintained. "We may count ourselves fortunate that Kish managed to survive."

"And now out of gratitude, he goes to bury him?" asked Thomas a little mockingly.

"No, of course not... But perhaps out of compassion... He really did feel for him."

With the dead Rapha in his arms, Kish navigated his way through the underground tunnels. He had picked up the body from the ruins and disappeared behind some dense shrubs hiding a narrow shaft. Through the shaft he descended into the underground spaces which lay below Jerusalem. From the way he moved through the tunnels it was obvious that he knew his way around the derelict and forgotten structures below the city. At a certain point he halted and felt the surface of the wall. Putting down his load he moved some heavy stones, exposing an opening. He crawled through it on all fours...

All this took place by touch because it was pitch dark.

He had arrived in a room and lit an oil lamp. There was just enough light to make out the walls. They appeared to have recesses dug into them. Although far below ground, the air in the room was fresh.

Crouching down near the opening, Kish dragged Rapha's body inside. He brought it to one of the recesses and straightened it out.

"I can do no more for you Rapha," he whispered softly. "Of course it's also self-interest... While you were alive, people hardly saw you on the streets... Now that you're dead they should certainly not see you. Perhaps someone would enter your house and start searching... for your money, for which you lived... and which caused your death...

I would pray for you, but I cannot find the words ...

When you were alive you didn't want to listen...

May God be merciful to you..."

Kish extinguished the lamp and left...

CHAPTER 33

WITH A QUICK GESTURE Hassub wiped the sweat from his eyes. The battle was in full swing. The thumping sound of siege machinery battering the city wall, was deafening. Everything shook and vibrated. Loud screaming filled the air. Together with other fighters he threw large blocks of stone from the wall, hoping to stop the battering rams or at least slow them down. Although the Jews prided themselves in the strength of the walls and the invincibility of the Antonia fortress, they did everything in their power to make it impossible for the Romans to operate the battering rams. Any available object which suited the purpose was thrown down at the weary soldiers who laboured there at great risk to their lives. On the wall loud rejoicing was heard whenever a projectile hit its target, usually involving death or injury to a soldier. However, the Romans knew how to retaliate. Stone throwers and bowmen ensured that a position on the wall was most unpleasant.

Partaking in the battle, Hassub vented his rage on the Romans who so ruthlessly ravaged the holy city of God. Setting aside any doubts about the validity of the uprising, he fought as fanatically as the fiercest Zealot. Hassub was aware that neither he, nor any other fighters could expect mercy from the Romans, unless they would surrender unconditionally. Deep in his heart he had long despaired of a good outcome of the war, but he couldn't bear the thought that Jerusalem would fall into heathen hands. So he fought as bravely as the others although he no longer shared their conviction that the Almighty would eventually turn the war in their favour and allow Israel to be victorious. He knew that so far they had faced only a small section of the Roman forces. There simply wasn't enough room for all their legions to engage in battle at the same time. He had heard that Titus had proposed to John, the Jewish leader, to have their armies oppose each other outside the city walls and continue the war there, thus sparing the civil population and the temple. But the tyrant had scorned the proposal and rejected it. Jerusalem was the city of God and would never be taken, was his reply. The horrendous suffering of the citizens didn't seem to affect John. Also toward the fighters who dared to disagree with him, he showed excessive cruelty. And Simon, the other leader, was no better. Fear and terror reigned among the defenders of Jerusalem. How could anything good come of it all? These were questions that lived in many hearts but could only be expressed in the company of very trusted people. And then, only in a whisper.

Hassub had seen and heard enough to realise that he had to keep his mouth shut if he wanted to stay alive among his fellow fighters. Distrust seemed to have killed off any comradeship among them.

He pulled frantically at a rock which proved to be too heavy for him to lift. He received help from a young Jew fighting beside him. Together they lifted the block of stone and cast it down below. As arrows rained down on them, one struck the young man in the chest. Mortally wounded he sank to the ground. This was nothing unusual since fighters perished in great numbers, yes even in the hundreds, and the men around them didn't pay him any attention. But Hassub could suddenly no longer accept that the dying were trodden underfoot by the defenders of the temple of the Gracious One. He began to drag the boy away from the battleground but in doing so, he hindered some of the other fighters. Almost tripping over the body they furiously lashed out at Hassub.

"Lunatic! What do you think you're doing?"

Before Hassub could regain his composure, the others had picked up the body and cast it over the wall. He had witnessed such actions before, but it had never touched him as it did now.

"He was still alive!" he shouted in disgust.

"Not any longer," was the cruel answer.

"Are we no longer brothers?" Hassub screamed in desperation. His feelings had been suppressed so long he could barely contain his fury.

"This is war, man!" they responded.

"Who is that guy?" he heard someone ask.

"Hassub, a son of Pagiel… His brothers have already disappeared."

"Away from the wall!" Gaius bellowed. He appeared to pop up everywhere at the same time. The old soldier was in his element. Not that things were going particularly easy for him. Marius had frowned deeply when inspecting the foundations of the Antonia.

"If you can move this massive mountain, Titus will make you a tribune and I will personally salute you," he had said.

Together with their division they had been ordered to move from the mount of Olives to take up position opposite the Antonia, the place where Gaius had long desired to be.

He could walk again as though his leg had never suffered any injury, and whenever possible, he told those willing to listen that it was all thanks to one of the Jews up there in Jerusalem.

Yes, the Ram was in his element and felt honoured to have been given the task of making a breach in the mighty fortress. He had activated his heaviest battering rams, thereby acknowledging that the comments of his friend Marius had not been an exaggeration. The Antonia was built on a rock which would never yield to even a thousand rams. And even the wall was amazingly solid and strong.

Enduring fierce opposition from the Jews, Gaius had managed to take up his position and put the machinery in order.

Being so close to the wall, the soldiers who were working on the battering rams were naturally in constant danger. All their attention was needed for the heavy work, and they were therefore protected from attacks by their comrades who covered them with a screen of shields. Meanwhile other divisions, at a somewhat safer distance, guarded against surprise raids by the Jews. At times, hundreds of Jews would storm out in a desperate attempt to destroy the siege machinery.

"Don't try to play the hero," Gaius bellowed when his men took far too many risks for his liking. "You can only show off medals if you're alive!"

His men knew that he himself would shirk from nothing. The most dangerous jobs he often did himself. Oh sure, he would do so while complaining that "you can't leave anything to those dummies," but the soldiers admired him for it. They would go through fire for him. Although he appeared to be tough, he showed great care for his men.

Gaius was a battle-hardened soldier but even he was disgusted when he saw how the Jews sought death and how mercilessly the rebels often dealt with their own people.

"Those men must be possessed," he said to Marius. "They act like heathens."

"That's a bit strong coming from you!" his friend mocked.

"Are you able to reach that section of the wall I pointed out to you?"

"I just came from there… Under cover of the shields, we were able to dig under the wall a bit and with the leverage beams we tried to undermine it…"

"And? Was there any movement in it?"

"We loosened a few stones… I think we'll manage to get three, maybe four of them out of there today."

"That would be great… If we can make a hole… Those fellows inside will have a big surprise… But Marius… no funny business hey?"

"Would you perhaps prescribe some rest for me?"

"Not exactly," grinned Gaius, "but one sunny day I would like to march into Rome together with you and all the others. You understand?"

That night, with thundering noise, the section of the wall which had been rammed, and where the soldiers had partially undermined it, came crashing down. It turned out to be a place where earlier on, the rebel leader John had commanded a tunnel to be dug, from where to attack the Roman defences.

There was great consternation among the Jews, but when they saw that the Antonia had remained standing, they regained their courage.

To their annoyance the Romans discovered that behind the first wall, a second wall had been erected on John's command. The ruins of the first one however made it a lot easier to tackle the second wall.

The battle was far from over.

CHAPTER 34

"S ILLA…"

She looked up in surprise. She had not heard anyone coming. Kish was standing in the doorway holding a child in his arms. It was a boy of about seven years old and it looked as though he was at death's door.

"I found him among the ruins with his sister in his arms. She was about three or four years old. The girl must have been dead for several days. He was busy shooing the flies away from her… just as Rizpah the daughter of Aiah did to the ravens in order to protect the carcasses of her sons … It cut me to the heart… I couldn't leave him there like that Silla… Will you please help me?"

When he walked up to her and showed her the child, she noticed tears running down his cheeks. The child seemed to have no interest in his surroundings. The big dark eyes in his shrunken face stared at her without reaction. It filled her with compassion.

"He is near death Silla, but there's still some life left in him," Kish whispered. "He is like our dying city… Israel is going down… But the Lord is mighty and able to raise the dead…"

"What do you want me to do?" Silla asked. "How can I help you?"

Kish looked around helplessly. Suddenly he appeared to be Simpleton again.

"I don't know his name yet," he said… "He's too far gone to respond to my questions. But it somehow feels as if I'm carrying all of Israel in my arms. I would dearly love to help him… Silla, with God's help, I want to drag this child out of this hell hole…

Why this child, while there are thousands of others dying? I don't know... I found him among the ruins... And his touching care for his dead sister just broke my heart. Let him be a symbol, a sign of hope... like a firebrand plucked from the fire... If the Lord wills... In this child I saw the love of Christ for dead sinners...

I would dearly love to see this young boy stay alive, Silla... Please try to make him eat... He won't know how to anymore... Take care of him, for me... That's what I came to ask you."

Carefully she took the child from him.

"I will do what I can," she promised, "with God's help."

"With His help," agreed Kish. "If the Lord allows us to escape from Jerusalem, we'll take this little one with us."

Kish left.

Silla took good care of the child. With her endless patience, but perhaps more due to her warm heart surrounding him with love and prayers, she was able to arouse in him an interest in life. She cried for joy when he let her feed him the food she had prepared. As reality set in, his big dark eyes began to register the upheaval and sorrow retained in his memories. Yet his thankfulness for all the good care increased. She had gained his trust.

When she managed to get him talking again, she asked for his name and learned that it was Joseph.

"Love is still stronger than death, Silla," said Pagiel when he heard about it.

"By the grace of God, you were allowed to work the same things in me. Faith, hope and love... But the greatest of these is love, for it remains unto eternity."

Pagiel's condition worsened rapidly. At times he became rather restless.

"I'm keeping you hostage here and that burdens me greatly," he said. "I know that the Lord guides all things, and everything is in His hands. But I'm increasingly aware that it's my fault that you're all trapped here."

"The Lord Jesus once said that we should never worry," Silla told him. "He said that we cannot add one cubit to our stature. All we need to do is trust in Him… believe in a childlike manner… We are His in life and in death."

"I know it, my dear child," Pagiel answered. "I can wholeheartedly say amen to all of that. But once you've been a stubborn, hard-headed man like me for so many years it's so hard to be childlike again. I thought I knew it all so well, but meanwhile I did so much wrong… And even now I'm not doing much better…

Yes indeed, when I consider what He has done to save me from eternal damnation, my heart rejoices. For now I know that I'm saved by grace.

But when I'm plagued with thoughts of how I'm leaving you in this hopeless situation, I feel as though I'm suffocating. It's so difficult to hand things over to God."

"But also in these things we rely on God's grace, Father."

"We can't provide rest for ourselves," said Gedor. "We like to have things organised as we think they should go. But only the Lord can give a solution. We can make plans as much as we like but more often than not they don't succeed.

You know that I'm just like you, Pagiel. You're not an exception. Each time I need to repeat the Messiah's words to myself and then I still fall into the same trap. We are incorrigible people. It's so difficult for us to rest in Him. Yet it's the only way. We must believe that He speaks the truth. When He says that we need not fear, then we need not be afraid. 'Trust in the Lord with all your heart and lean not on your own understanding,' Solomon tells us."

"A man can't discover anything about his own future," Tirza added, "but the Lord is unchangeable. He will bring us safely into His heavenly Kingdom."

"I want to trust that He will care for you all," said Pagiel. "I feel so privileged to have you all here together with me… I'm so grateful that the Lord opened my eyes to see the salvation He has revealed in Jesus Christ… Wasn't I furious, Gedor, when you reminded me of the torn temple curtain … I feel ashamed thinking about it.

But you were right. I can see that now. It had everything to do with the dying of our Lord Jesus Christ… By His blood we gained access to the throne of mercy…! What a miracle. What a wonderful reality…

Tell the boys that too, if you ever see them again… Tell them their father got to know the Messiah even when everything seemed lost… I hope so very much that God will work the same miracle in their hearts as He did for me."

Pagiel fell silent for a moment and looked around the room.

"Thomas, I would love to be at your wedding feast. Take good care of my Silla, please… of course I know that you will. I pray that the Lord will make it possible for you to escape Jerusalem and that you may find happiness together."

Then, reaching out with his healthy hand to stroke young Joseph's black curly hair, he said to the boy, "Joseph, my little lamb, listen carefully when aunty Silla tells you about the Lord Jesus. She can do that so well. He is the good Shepherd…"

And turning to Tirza he said, "You always saw right through me, and I was so often annoyed by that. Now I want to thank you for everything. Forgive me for my harsh words. I didn't know any better even though I should have known…

To be surrounded by the people whom I love so much, is a real privilege…

I don't forget about you Caleb. Thanks to you I learned more about the situation in and around the city than others thought was good for me… You admire the heathen Romans. Not so long ago I would have cursed you for it. But now I might even go a step further than you, when I pray that God will allow them to come to the Light which He has brought into this world. Salvation is also for the Gentiles…

Yes Gedor, your teaching has not been wasted on me. I was allowed to learn so much from all of you. I thank you all from the bottom of my heart. The Almighty has seen fit to bless it all. Praised be His Name."

"Are you not tiring yourself out too much?" asked a concerned Tirza.

"Why should I spare myself?" Pagiel asked with a smile. "I am going home."

"Father!" Silla pleaded.

"Don't feel sorry for me, my darling," Pagiel comforted her and squeezed her hand. "I should be envied."

"I recall from the preaching of Eliphelet that the Lord spoke about that," said Gedor.

"About what?"

"About our Father's house."

"Please tell me more," Pagiel begged him. "I can't get enough of it."

"Well, the Lord said that in His Father's house there are many mansions, and that He would go to heaven to prepare a place for us. And after He would have left and prepared a place, He would come again to take all His own, to Himself. 'So that they too may be where I am,' He said. 'And where I go you know and the way you know.' But Thomas, His disciple denied that, saying that they didn't know at all where Jesus was going, and asked how they could know the way. The Lord Jesus then spoke those well-known words which I've mentioned to you before. He said: 'I am the way, the truth, and the life. No one comes to the Father except through Me.… If you had known Me, you would have known My Father also; and from now on you know Him and have seen Him.' But they did not understand at all what He was saying to them.

Philip asked Him to show them the Father. Then Jesus said to them: 'Have I been with you so long, and yet you have not known Me, Philip? He who has seen Me has seen the Father.'"

Gedor paused.

"Those words have been etched into your heart," said Pagiel.

"Indeed they are," Gedor confirmed. "As are the words of Eliphelet's preaching in which he told us about the prayer of the Messiah at the Passover feast, shortly before He gave Himself up to be nailed to the cross. At the time I wrote down those words and then read them over and over again. He prayed: 'Father, the hour has come. Glorify Your Son, that Your Son also may glorify You, as You have given Him authority over all flesh, that He should give eternal life to as many as You have given Him. And this is eternal life, that they may know You, the only true God, and Jesus Christ whom You have sent.'"

Pagiel glowed.

"At first I thought," Gedor continued, "those words applied to the first disciples... Because who could assure me that those words applied to me? Yet I longed for it so much... Then I heard Eliphelet say that in the same prayer the Lord had said: 'I do not pray for these alone, but also for those who will believe in Me through their word.' Then I knew: It also applies to me! Because I yearned to know Him! And I believed His Word. And that's only possible because He has worked that in my heart. Of myself there was nothing that reached out to Him. Don't the Scriptures teach us that there's not one person who earnestly searches out God? Believing in true faith can only come from God. Christ has believed in our place even unto death. The Messiah did for us, what we couldn't do ourselves, Pagiel... believe! believe that God listens to sinners and is willing to forgive them! Burdened with our sins, Jesus called out to His Father in our place, and was heard by Him. In that way He has shown us Who God is. His love is so awesome that we can't contain it with our minds. 'For God so loved the world that He gave His only begotten Son, that whoever believes in Him should not perish but have everlasting life.'"

"Yes, I believe Lord, come to my aid!" Pagiel prayed. "My soul longs for you."

"Our longing for Him can be great but His longing for us is infinitely greater," Gedor assured his brother. "The Lord Jesus has prayed for you: 'Father, I desire that they also whom You gave Me may be with Me where I am, that they may behold My glory which You have given Me.'"

During these holy moments they forgot about the world around them. It was as if they existed under an open heaven. Completely according to the Saviour's words: 'For where two or three are gathered together in My name, I am there in the midst of them.'

CHAPTER 35

F ROM HIS WELL-HIDDEN POSITION, unseen by friend or foe, Caleb had observed the attempts of the Romans to capture the Antonia fortress. Initially that had proved to be a difficult undertaking. The rebellious Jews offered stubborn resistance and managed to hold their position for a long time.

That was until a small group of about twenty Roman soldiers of the watch, had ventured to attack by night. Under the cloak of darkness, they crawled through the breaches and surprised the guards, killing them in their sleep. Next they occupied the wall, after which their trumpeter sounded a signal, which caused everyone to awaken in fright.

The Jews were totally taken by surprise and presumed that an overwhelming enemy force was upon them.

As soon as Titus heard the signal, he called up his army and together with his commanding officers he led the way to the top of the wall, ahead of a select troop. The Jews panicked and fled into the temple and the Romans pursued them through the tunnel which John had dug. An intense battle ensued with soldiers fighting man to man. Neither bow nor spear could be used as the combatants were so densely pressed together.

The Jews realised full well that if the Romans managed to occupy the temple, the rest of the city would inevitably follow. With a massive effort, fuelled by desperation, they threw themselves into the battle and managed to halt the advance of the Romans who, in spite of their better fighting skills, didn't have sufficient men to force a breakthrough.

The breaches in the wall were too small to allow the legions to climb the fortress and take part in the fighting. Titus was therefore satisfied for the time being to occupy the Antonia and ordered the army to make their way up to join him. When he heard that the Jews had to cancel the daily offerings, he repeated his offer to John to take the fighting outside of the city and to spare the citizens and city further hardship. The prisoner Josephus was given instructions by Titus to relay the proposal to John.

Caleb observed how Josephus selected a safe position for this purpose which protected him as much as possible from an unexpected attack from his fellow countrymen, many of whom saw him as a traitor and would be only too pleased to kill him.

But in choosing his position he also seemed to have in mind, or perhaps this was an order, to not only address the tyrant John, but also the general population. He delivered the message from Titus in the Hebrew language and added to it his own earnest plea to spare Jerusalem and the temple. Both had already been terribly desecrated. John and his cohorts had even resorted to setting fire to part of the temple colonnades in order to impede the progress of the Romans. Titus's offer would allow the existing fires to be extinguished and the daily sacrifices to resume as the Lord had commanded them.

Although the citizens were impressed by the address, John didn't take any notice but declared with great scorn, that this was the city of God and it would therefore be impossible for the heathens to conquer it.

No matter how much Josephus pleaded and begged, the rebels would not be persuaded.

They cursed him instead because of his friendship with the Romans.

However, their situation was hopeless, and the Romans found it impossible to comprehend their behaviour.

The judgement over Jerusalem seemed to be sealed.

"Their God has turned against them!" Caleb heard the Romans call out in indignation.

No! Caleb said to himself, that's not the cause. Israel has turned itself against God, and that is totally different…

Pagiel had passed away peacefully.

"The Lord be praised," said Gedor, "He provides rest for those whom He loves. Pagiel loved Jerusalem so much. Isn't it a mercy that he doesn't have to witness the downfall of the city? And the temple where he used to spend his days? It would have caused him great sorrow to see the events unfolding there right now…

The Lord is good! He knows those who seek refuge with Him. We can be glad that the Lord has called him home."

Pagiel's death affected Silla the most. She was indeed glad that she had seen her father come to believe in the Lord Jesus Christ, but now she sorely missed him. For a long time she had cared for his daily needs, and they had spent much time talking about the Gospel together. She had benefited from his vast knowledge of the Scriptures and her own insights had deepened.

"God's Word is inexhaustible," he had said. "The deeper you dig, the more you will come across things which you never even realised. And that never ends Silla. Even in eternity, we'll never come to a point that we can claim to know it all. No, for God will always be greater! I never realised that the whole of Scripture is one witness of Jesus Christ. I was spiritually blind. Now that the Almighty has opened my eyes, I see Him everywhere. All Scripture testifies of Him. Just fetch me the book of Isaiah and I'll tell you what we'll read today."

Those hours she spent with her father had been so enriching. She would never forget it. Their study of the Bible always became a song of praise to God, during which Pagiel extolled the glory of his Saviour.

Those precious memories softened her sorrow.

Pagiel's death presented them with a problem which they had already anticipated. The streets of Jerusalem were filled with unburied corpses and the very thought that this would also become the fate of Pagiel, was unbearable.

"If Kish was able to find a final resting place for Rapha, he would surely have a solution for your father," Thomas tried to reassure Silla.

"Of course, it's not possible to have a funeral like we are used to. But in case Kish is unable to help us, I'll make sure your father has a proper resting place. I promise you."

However, Kish immediately indicated that he was prepared to help.

"You will understand that it must all be done at night and in a place that I need to keep secret. And later it may prove to be totally inaccessible for you," he told Silla. "If you agree to that, I can provide a good resting place for your father… You'll have to say your farewells here in this house and say your prayers here. That goes for all the family… Thomas and Caleb will give me a hand."

And that's how it went. Gedor conducted the funeral service and thanked God that words of comfort could be expressed.

Later that evening, when the city was shrouded in darkness, three men left the house with the body of Pagiel on a simple stretcher.

This time Kish took both his friends down with him into the underground tunnels. Under different circumstances that might have been rather taxing on their nerves, but this time Thomas and Caleb needed all their concentration to manoeuvre the stretcher through the narrow, pitch-dark tunnels. Needing all their agility to avoid tripping on the uneven ground, they simply didn't have time to let the eerie surrounds affect them. It was so dark that all they could do was to trust Kish completely. On his instruction they halted and put down the stretcher. They heard Kish move stones and after a few moments they saw a weak light coming through the opening and shining onto the floor. Kish told them to carefully slide the body of Pagiel into the opening after which he requested them to come in as well.

"I want you to see where we are laying him," he said to Thomas. "Perhaps Silla will ask about it later and then you can explain it to her.

We'll lay him there in that recess… It's perhaps different from what we're used to, but it's an honourable burial and he's in a safe place… Thomas, will you please finish with a prayer?"

Thomas and Caleb had experienced much over the last years and were not easily impressed anymore. But this underground funeral deeply affected them and they found it hard to control their emotions. Above ground again they heaved a sigh of relief even though the stench of the dying city was far less pleasant than the air they breathed below.

Kish accompanied them back home.

"We'll have to consider what to do next," he said. "Now that Pagiel is gone there's no longer a reason for you to stay in Jerusalem."

"You say that as though we could simply walk out of the city," said Thomas. "All the gates are guarded, and the Romans have barricaded the roads outside the city. We've also seen what they do with prisoners of war. Didn't they crucify hundreds of them within view of the city walls?"

"A horrifying spectacle to witness," Caleb chipped in. "They know how to instil fear."

"I'm aware of that," said Kish. "However, every day it's also becoming more dangerous to remain in the city and that's why we must consider every possibility of getting out. We don't even have to contemplate defecting to the Romans, I agree with you there. I've even heard of Arabic and Syrian soldiers cutting open escapees if they suspected they ingested something precious to smuggle out of the city."

"It seems that the commanders have dealt with that quite severely," said Caleb.

"That may be so, but for the victims involved, that came too late," Kish replied. "It does however show what kind of dangers we're confronted with."

"Getting out of the city will be hard enough," Thomas agreed.

"I can see a way to get out," Kish said. "But that's only the beginning. We have to cut through the Roman lines and that won't be easy. It wouldn't be such a problem if I went with only the two of you, but there are others to consider. We need to take care of Silla and Joseph. When it comes to speed or possibly to a fight, they'll make us a lot more vulnerable. On top of that we have Gedor and

Tirza. They're not so agile anymore. We'll need to take the way of least resistance."

"Does that even exist?" Thomas asked.

"We'll have to look for it."

"Would there be a possibility to avoid the enemy lines all together?" asked Thomas.

"In any case we'll have to evade the sentries," said Kish.

"It will be difficult," answered Caleb. "The Romans have totally locked us in. I can sketch it out for you. Have a look…"

He took his knife and drew a rough outline of Jerusalem on the floor.

"Here is the temple where they have fully concentrated their attack… And then the encampments of the legions… The tenth legion here on the Mount of Olives… And opposite that, on the other side of the city, the fifth legion… Then over here the main camp of Titus on the north side. See? And the battle ramparts which they have built run here approximately, from one encampment to another."

"When I see what you've drawn it looks like everything is sealed shut," Thomas commented.

"But it can't really be like that," Kish suggested. "Some parts of the ramparts will hardly need to be guarded. Here for example," and he pointed to a place in the sketch Caleb had drawn. "Here their rampart runs through a ravine. If you ask me, they wouldn't need to expect a raid from there. Titus has focussed his attack on Antonia and the temple because his greatest opponent is located there. John has turned that whole area into a battle ground. He has as it were, drawn the Romans to the temple… Their whole attention is focussed here on the temple area."

"If they get the temple, they'll have the city too," said Caleb.

"And then Jerusalem is lost," Kish agreed. "But unfortunately, she already is. The city will be destroyed."

"Would John and Simon really let it come to that? Would they eventually not face reality and surrender?"

"The Lord has said so," Kish answered. "And everything we've witnessed over the last number of years testifies to it. We invited this judgement upon ourselves by not listening to the Lord but rather instigating this war. Even the Romans are filled with abhorrence about today's events, and that's saying something...

And as for those tyrants you just referred to, they have nothing to gain from a surrender. They know they can't count on any mercy from the Romans. I think they'd rather see both temple and city go up in flames."

"How terrible," sighed Caleb. "I hope you're proved wrong."

"I'm convinced of it," Kish replied. "I agree that it's terrible, but it's likely to be the best moment to escape the city."

"I see what you mean," said Thomas, "Caleb has mentioned something like that before. If it indeed comes to the point that the Romans storm the temple, they won't have attention for anything else."

"Exactly. Titus won't leave the ramparts unguarded, don't think that for a moment. But it will be a huge challenge for him and his commanders to keep the soldiers in check once they've broken through. They've encountered so much resistance and at times, such great losses, they'll be highly agitated."

"Besides, they've got it in their heads that there's gold piled up in the temple."

"So that's the plan as far as the Romans are concerned," said Kish. "But the rebels too, will only be thinking about the battle. If you ask me, they'll keep defending themselves to the bitter end."

"It will turn into a bloodbath," Caleb said mournfully. "I've witnessed it several times, but I fear this will be far worse ... Think of all the citizens."

"Those of the starving residents who are still mobile will head for the centre of the action," Kish predicted. "Curiosity is a strange thing. People start to panic, they're scared to death, yet they want to see what's going on even if it costs them their lives. It's a bit like a mass hysteria. It's good for us to realise it ahead of time, because before we know it, we may be drawn in as well. It sounds egotistic but if it happens as I'm suggesting, don't be tempted to go and see what's happening. It will be gruesome...

Especially you Caleb! Think about it! It would most definitely be the last you'll ever see of Roman warfare. Resist the urge and make sure we can count on you. We'll need you."

"Although they've taken the Antonia fortress, I think they're still trying to ram a hole in the temple wall," said Caleb. "I saw them make preparations. They're pulling out their heaviest equipment."

"As far as that goes you always seem to have the latest news," smiled Kish. "But I plead with you to leave that last battle scene for what it is. I want you to promise me that, so we can be sure of you. We must make committed decisions. The Romans still have a big job ahead of them, but our time of waiting will soon be over and then we must have our plans ready. When that time comes, we must each know exactly what to do. Naturally we also should instruct the others."

"Assuming that we manage to get away safely, where would you go?" asked Thomas. "I would very much like to go with Silla to Perea. My parents are there, and many of the Christians who left Jerusalem earlier on have gone there."

"If that road is open, I don't have objections against going there," answered Kish. "But it will depend on the circumstances. Perhaps for safety reasons, we'll first need to go in a different direction. The most important issue is to get out alive and to avoid being caught."

"We also have to be clear on what things we can take with us," said Caleb.

"As little as possible," Thomas answered. "Everything that's not strictly necessary for the escape, must be left behind."

"Easy enough for me," said Caleb. "I'll wear the clothes I have on, and I'll take nothing else except some food for the journey."

"It's rather special to be able to say that," said Kish earnestly. "Among all the suffering people in the city, we are very privileged to be able to feed ourselves from Rapha's stockpiles. However also in this respect, we won't take away more food than is strictly necessary for the journey. It will have to be an estimate of course."

"I assume you'll take care of that?" Thomas asked. "It's best if everyone carries his own portion of food. It should be hidden in a safe place, ready to grab at a moments' notice. You know good hiding places Kish. We've experienced that again with Pagiel's burial."

"Yes, I'll take care of it," Kish agreed, "and I'll tell you where it can be found, in case something happens to me…

Let's pray together and ask the Lord for wisdom."

CHAPTER 36

THOSE WHO HAVE NEVER experienced hunger, cannot begin to imagine the suffering into which the people of Jerusalem were plunged in the year 70 A.D.

The besieged population was desperate. Whatever they could chew on and swallow, was eaten.

People ate rotten straw.

The fighters cut pieces of leather from their shields and attempted to still their raging hunger with it.

Even if they simply suspected that something edible was hidden somewhere, they would set out to steal it and nothing could stop them. Their hunger had become so intense that everyone became a target.

Friends and family members spied on each other, crazed with envy. No edible morsel was shared with another, no matter the size of the portion.

In great dismay, Kish received the terrible news which filled all those in and outside of Jerusalem with horror - a mother had in desperation killed her own child and eaten it. She had offered the remains to those bullies who had come looking for food.

She was a rich lady of noble blood who had sought refuge in Jerusalem but was forced to endure the siege when the Romans encircled the city. Time and again the food for her child had been stolen until totally distraught she had taken this insane course of action.

Friend and foe were equally upset.

Such a thing had not been thought possible. Loud crying ascended to the heavens and God's wrath would undoubtedly come.

"Woe to Jerusalem… Woe to the temple… Woe to the entire nation…"

Those frightening words spoken by the prophet would have echoed in many ears.

Tirza burst into tears when she heard of it.

"I've seen much unrighteousness in this city, Gedor, but this exceeds everything," said Kish. "The curse is inescapable. The robbers came to steal her food and she offered them the remains. Even those crooks fled away trembling. The earth can longer bear this, Gedor! Such horrors are unheard of."

"Oh, but it's happened before," Gedor answered sadly. "Tirza and I read it just recently. The prophet Jeremiah speaks of it in Lamentations. It happened in those equally terrible days when Nebuchadnezzar destroyed Jerusalem and made the temple go up in flames. Wait a moment, I'll get the book and read it to you."

They read it together.

The Lamentations of the man of God.

With sorrowful hearts they read the description of the horrors, which they themselves were suffering almost 700 years later. History repeated itself…

'But the daughter of my people is cruel, like ostriches in the wilderness. The tongue of the infant clings to the roof of its mouth for thirst; The young children ask for bread, but no one breaks it for them. Those who ate delicacies are desolate in the streets; those who were brought up in scarlet, embrace ash heaps. The punishment of the iniquity of the daughter of my people is greater than the punishment of the sin of Sodom, which was overthrown in a moment, with no hand to help her!

Her Nazirites were brighter than snow and whiter than milk; they were more ruddy in body than rubies, like sapphire in their appearance. Now their appearance is blacker than soot; they go unrecognised in the streets; Their skin clings to their bones, it has become as dry as wood.

Those slain by the sword are better off than those who die of hunger; For these pine away, stricken for lack of the fruits of the field. The hands of the compassionate women have cooked their own children; They became food for them in the destruction of the daughter of my people.'

"You see Kish, that besides describing the events in the days of Jeremiah, these words have prophetic meaning for our time."

"It's really too gruesome," said Kish.

"But there's a reason for it. The Lord didn't pour out His wrath and the fire of His anger on His people for nothing! Let's read on! 'The kings of the earth, and all inhabitants of the world, would not have believed that the adversary and the enemy could enter the gates of Jerusalem— because of the sins of her prophets and the iniquities of her priests, who shed in her midst, the blood of the just.' It's because of the sins of the prophets and the misdeeds of the priests, who spilt the blood of the righteous."

"Israel did not recognise the Messiah," said Kish.

"Because it was hidden from us," Gedor agreed. "We were blind because of our sins. In that state we don't understand the works of the Lord. We couldn't believe that the Lord would reveal Himself in the form of the suffering Servant."

"So how come we believe it now? We were blind too, weren't we?" Kish asked.

"The answer to that question is hidden with God," Gedor replied. "No one can see the kingdom of God unless the Lord opens his eyes to it. Just as in the days of the prophet Elijah, the Almighty has made sure a remnant would remain today. We believe that the Lord Jesus Christ is our God. That's not something we earned but it is the electing grace of God."

"And what about all the others?" Kish asked.

"I believe that the Lord won't allow anyone to be lost who can be saved. You may say: He can do anything, so why doesn't He save everyone? But that's not how the Lord works. Our Lord reproached Jerusalem for not wanting to turn to Him. A person can resist his Creator and be lost, Kish. Think of Judas, who betrayed Him... The Lord invites us but does not force us. He said that all who labour and are heavy laden should come to Him and He will give them rest… I hold on to the words of Ezekiel where the Lord speaks: 'As I live,' says the Lord God, 'I have no pleasure in the death of the wicked, but that the wicked turn from his way and live. Turn, turn from your evil ways! For why should you die, O house of Israel?'"

"The streets of the city are full of death," said Kish. "Israel is already dying, Gedor! When I see the suffering of the children, I feel so helpless…"

"My heart grieves as well," said Gedor, "and I'm appalled at how far Israel has fallen."

Thomas tried to hide the terrible news from Silla. But that proved impossible. With eyes filled with terror and disgust, she came to Thomas with the news.

"I've heard it already, that terrible news," he said. "The woman must have been mad. It's too terrible to even talk about it. That something like this could happen in Israel. Who would have thought it?"

"It makes me feel so guilty," said Silla, crying.

Thomas held her in his arms.

"How can you be guilty? You've taken such good care of your father… You've cared for Joseph. You've done all you could to help others."

"But we have food Thomas… Even if we keep it minimal and sober, we do have food to eat… Every time I eat something, I feel guilty. And then to think that others have nothing left at all."

"I heard she was a rich lady and that she managed to buy some food now and then, but each time it was stolen from her," Thomas said, trying to reassure her. Nevertheless, his heart went out to her because he had also felt guilty toward those starving in the city. Then he would try to soothe his conscience with the thought that Kish would provide where the need was greatest.

He shared these thoughts with Silla in an effort to try and soothe her conscience too. But she, like Thomas, realised that it was merely a desperate excuse to make themselves feel better. The anguished fight for food by so many hundreds of thousands of people, could not be overcome with a handful of barley.

"I also feel miserable when I have something to eat," he admitted. "But it wouldn't benefit anyone if we didn't eat. We were also in a dire situation and in need of food. It was only that Kish suddenly had access to Rapha's stockpile, otherwise who knows what would have happened to us. The Lord has protected us from a worse fate, Silla."

"That poor woman would have been greatly helped by a handful of barley. Had she been given some, she may never have resorted to such a terrible deed."

"Kish would definitely have brought her some if we'd known about it. But it's unlikely that she would have had opportunity to give it to her child. Every time again they stole it from her, Silla! That's what drove her mad…

It's a miracle that you've never been raided by people in search of food and that they took no interest in your father's home. That surely is by the grace of the Lord.

Come now Silla. I've heard it said that he who saves one person, saves the whole world… See Joseph standing there? That he is alive, is only thanks to you and Kish… As long as there are people like you, there's hope for Israel!"

CHAPTER 37

FROM A DISTANCE THEY observed the work done by the massive battering ram.

"We have nothing bigger or better than this," said Gaius, "but I'm having doubts about it, Marius." He pensively rubbed his chin. "Yes, you're probably surprised to hear me say that."

"I am indeed. I can't recall you ever saying that before. I thought you could move mountains!"

"To tell you the truth, I'm a little scared about this one. I could handle the fortress of Antonia. Even though we didn't reduce it to rubble, we managed to get inside. That was a worthy challenge … But to take it up against the temple walls … Perhaps I'm a little superstitious but from the start I've felt uncomfortable about it. I would have rather kept my hands off it."

"Orders are orders," said Marius.

"Tell me about it!" Gaius snorted angrily. "Are you pretending to play the good boy? Just cut the nonsense!"

"It's just a reminder," Marius grinned. "It was a command from Titus, wasn't it?"

"You know as well as I do, that he would also rather leave the temple alone! However, we're compelled to dirty our hands on it because those scoundrels have made it their stronghold. It's become their hiding place."

"Then they're forcing us, aren't they?" said Marius. "You don't have to take the blame. If you ask me, we've tried to be reasonable with the Jews! Just remember all the propositions made by Titus to avoid this situation. I admire his patience. Mine would have run out a long time ago."

"I'm coming to believe more and more that there's a curse hanging over this people," said Gaius soberly.

"Then it's the work of the gods," Marius responded light-heartedly. "And we're just doing our duty."

"You don't get it do you?" Gaius said impatiently. "If there's a curse, it would be from their God. They say that the temple is His house, that temple there, inside. They speak of the holy of holies. That's the meeting place. Only their high priest is allowed to enter once a year. No one else!"

"And then the high priest sees God?"

"No, their God is invisible…"

"That's strange!"

"What's so strange about it?" snapped Gaius. He was not in a good mood. "Have you ever seen a visible god?"

"Mars, Jupiter, Isis, Mithras," Marius named just a few. "At least we have images of them. Don't they have that?"

"They're not allowed to make any."

"Says who?"

"Says their God."

"How do you know that?"

"You've been here so long; how come you don't know these things?" Gaius asked in return. "If you want to understand people, you should know something about their lives and habits… Their God has forbidden them to make an image of Him. And they're not allowed to have any other gods besides Him."

"You know a lot about it," Marius admitted, "where did you get all that wisdom?"

"Simply by listening," answered Gaius. "And to tell you the truth, I learned a lot from that rabbi we had to guard."

"You've been a good student for him… So, if I understand it correctly, that Jewish temple is basically empty? I've heard stories that it's supposed to be stacked full of gold."

"No doubt you'll find some precious things there," Gaius agreed, "but the most important thing for them is the inner sanctum, that dark room."

"The lads think the walls are overlaid with gold."

"None of us can have seen that. Only Jews are allowed in there. If others try to enter, they'll be killed. There are warning signs everywhere."

"Did you learn all this from that rabbi?"

"Yes. I've never been here before. Neither have you."

"I'm still curious to see it though. But first we have to make a hole in the wall to crawl through."

"This time we won't be successful," Gaius said sombrely. "We've been hammering it for two days without interruption."

"You're not losing heart, are you?" Marius asked.

"I can't lose it if I never had my heart in it in the first place."

"You're not having a good day," Marius quipped. "And then you start to doubt yourself. Tomorrow everything will look much better. I'm sure we'll get inside that temple."

"Not this way in any case," Gaius maintained. "I can even hear it on the sound... It bounces... The ram ricochets on the hard stone. There's no movement in it... Mark my words, that wall can't be broken like this."

"Shall I go and tell the workers?" Marius asked. "That will greatly encourage them. They're breaking their backs on it!"

Gaius looked as though he could tear him apart.

Gaius couldn't get to sleep. It was stuffy in the tent. He got up and went outside. It had been a hot day. The night brought no relief either. The stench of the city hung like a dark cloud over the surrounding region.

He walked toward the wall on which they had wasted their energy for several days, with no results. Wandering around aimlessly, he was stirred by a strange restlessness. This had slowly developed since the command had come to break through the temple wall. He felt annoyed that it affected him so much.

This country, this people, this war…

Deep in his heart however he knew that it was especially since meeting that one particular Jew…

He was proud of his reputation to be a tough fellow and yet a reliable comrade. Marius and all the others in his division, knew that as their commander he would go through fire for them.

What that simpleton of a Jew had done however, had gotten under his skin in a peculiar way.

For a mate you'd risk your own life, but not for the enemy; you'd knock his brains out.

This simple reasoning was the rule under which Gaius operated. But ever since he owed his life to someone who despite being an enemy, had acted as a friend, his soldier's perspective had become a lot more complicated. He was well aware that without the encounter with Kish he would never have made it to Jerusalem.

Perhaps if the man had really been a simpleton, he wouldn't be so bothered by it, but Gaius realised full well that he'd been dealing with an intelligent person. Someone who thought very clearly. A man who was well able to judge the military situation and understood the consequences of his actions.

In a brazen and proud manner, he had told Kish what he was going to do in Jerusalem. Only in hindsight did he realise how that must have cut him to the heart. It would have been so easy for Kish to change his mind and end Gaius' life.

Gaius had racked his brains to find something that would indicate Kish acted out of self-interest. But he was unsuccessful.

In his heart he knew that Kish's actions had something to do with his faith. While Gaius was not what you'd call a pious man and didn't exactly lead an exemplary godly life, like a good Roman he kept to the traditions which he'd been taught. Over the years, he had heard of legionnaires who had been punished or even executed because they had become Christians, and therefore no longer wanted to carry the Roman standard and refused to participate in the Roman sacrificial festivals. On those occasions he may have questioned the stupidity of such persons who put their lives at risk for such a reason. But now it seemed that he was more or less forced to think about these issues…

A guard called out and Gaius identified himself.

"Have you seen or heard anything more?" he inquired.

"Nothing to report… Are you passing through?"

"No, it's too dark to see anything near the battering rams. I'm returning to my tent… I hope the night goes well for you."

Gaius walked back, deep in thought. But even if he'd been on high alert and actively observing his surroundings, he wouldn't have spotted the silent shadow that followed him from a distance…

Having arrived in his tent, he drank a bowl of water and had just stretched himself out to try catch some sleep when a figure appeared in the tent opening. Gaius shot up immediately.

"Marius?" he asked. "Is there something to report?"

"It is I, Kish," a reply came softly, "Marius will be asleep."

"Kish!" Gaius gasped, startled. He couldn't believe his ears. "How come you're here? Who let you in?"

"I didn't ask anyone. That seemed safest to me," answered Kish. "I just wanted to have a word with you, Gaius."

"What a stupid thing to do!" Gaius whispered. "We're in the middle of a war here, Kish! Make yourself scarce if you value your life! Quick…! Before they discover you!"

"Even if they do, you wouldn't be to blame. I came here of my own volition," said Kish calmly. "Remember I asked how I could find you if it proved to be necessary. It certainly hasn't been very difficult… Thanks to the guard and your night wanderings…"

"Don't tell me …" Gaius dropped his voice… "That would be too crazy! Surely you didn't get it in your head to…"

"Oh yes I did," said Kish.

"You're mad," Gaius whispered, "completely insane…!"

"That's not how I regard myself," Kish replied calmly. "I even think you would have done the same… If you could just have a look in our city… You may normally be hard as nails, Gaius, but if it was your people, you would be crying … just as I did."

Gaius forced himself to stay calm.

"If you're discovered here, my rank is not so high that I could give you the protection you'll need," he said.

"Let's stop talking about it," said Kish. "I'm not asking for your protection anyway. Besides I'm not here for myself but for others. Had I been on my own, I would without great difficulty, have managed to get through the blockades. However, I have a small group of friends whom I wish to get to safety. That's why I come to you for help.

It's become very dangerous for us, both inside as well as outside the city walls. We don't participate in the uprising and that makes us loathsome to the rebels. And when you Romans capture the city before long, the soldiers won't make a distinction between guilty and innocent people."

"What do you think I can do for you?" asked Gaius. "Do you want to defect? I wouldn't recommend it. You know that the rules of war apply. You can no longer set conditions. The only option is unconditional surrender."

"We know that, but we're not considering that either. We want to get out of here. Out of Jerusalem and out of this region."

"I told you beforehand not to go to Jerusalem," Gaius reminded him.

"And I answered you at the time that my friends were here, and I didn't want to abandon them," Kish replied. "Their motivation to stay was not wilful stubbornness... Although these people believed that you would besiege and conquer the city, they braved the dangers because of loyalty and love for their sick father. They stayed in Jerusalem to care for him… But now he's passed away and they're locked up in the city."

"Well then, again I ask what you think I can do for you?" asked Gaius.

"Write me a note of safe conduct."

"A what?" Gaius mouth dropped open in amazement. "Who do you think I am? I'm not a general Kish. I'm only a lowly centurion."

"But you're well known," said Kish. "Besides, I can hardly go to Titus and ask him for it, can I?"

"But what good is a document in my name?"

"Perhaps more useful than you think. First of all, there's no one else in your camp whom I can trust. You know me a little. I ask no more than to write me a commendation for favourable treatment. It's just in case we would be stopped by Romans somewhere. For the rest we can only pray that we'll meet with people who are sensitive to such a request. It's an honest request Gaius and you're not committing treason by writing it."

Gaius looked at him thoughtfully.

"You're a peculiar person Kish," he said. "You would endanger your life for a note from me."

"Why?" asked Kish. "I'm doing this for friends aren't I? Our Messiah gave His own life for His enemies. That's another thing altogether!"

"Your Messiah…"

"Jesus of Nazareth, the Son of God. He is our Saviour and Lord."

"Do you believe that Kish?"

"With all my heart!"

Gaius retrieved his stationery and wrote his letter.

"I hope you won't be needing this," he said, handing it to Kish… "But if that is the case, I hope it may be of some help… I owe you a great debt, mate. I wish I could do more for you. I'll certainly never forget you."

"Many thanks," said Kish. "May the Lord bless you."

"For ramming His temple?" Gaius growled.

"That's not your fault. Not one stone will remain on top of another."

"Says who?" asked Gaius.

"He said it Himself," answered Kish, "Jesus our Lord… Shalom Gaius."

The Roman looked at him with sorrowful eyes.

"Farewell Kish… I hope you make it out alive."

After the strongest battering ram had in vain rammed the temple wall for six consecutive days, the Romans gave up, and decided to try a different way. They raised up ladders against the colonnades and attempted to climb up. Naturally the Jews tried to prevent them, and the ensuing battles inflicted high casualties on the Romans. Some of the ladders, loaded with soldiers, were knocked down by the Jews. Soldiers who managed to get onto the wall were usually struck down before they could raise their shields. Others were thrown backwards off the walls into the depths below. The Jews even managed to conquer some of the banners which the Romans brought onto the wall. Losing the banners constituted an insurmountable disgrace for the attackers.

When Titus realised that in trying to protect the temple surrounds, he would suffer great loss of manpower, he ordered that the temple gates be set on fire and entry be forced that way.

Whereas the Jews had previously warded off the Romans by setting fire to the colonnades near the Antonia, they were horrified to see how quickly the fire spread out from the gates, and also set the galleries on fire.

And still it did not enter their minds to surrender. The thought that even the holy dwelling would eventually go up in flames, only seemed to increase their hatred and fury towards the Romans.

Titus gave the order for some of his men to douse the fire in the galleries and to construct a path along the gates by which the legions could march up.

He consulted with his commanders what to do with the temple. He wanted to spare the holy building but some of his generals were of the opinion that if the Jews kept defending themselves from within the temple, it could no longer be regarded as a holy place but rather a stronghold which must be attacked and destroyed by fire. The Jews themselves would have to bear the blame, not the Romans.

The most prominent generals however sided with Titus in saying that the beautiful building would be like a precious adornment for the Roman empire and that therefore everything possible had to be done to save it. They agreed with Titus that vengeance was to fall on the rebels and not on lifeless buildings. The temple had to be spared for the greater glory of the invincible Roman empire.

And so the Romans decided.

The Lord God however had planned differently.

At the building of the first temple of Solomon, the Lord had warned that the holiness of the temple was not derived from the beautiful and glorious architecture, but from His presence. And if Israel were to reject Him, He would also reject the temple which He had hallowed by His Name and would cause it to become a pile of ruins.

In the days of Zedekiah, the king of Babylon had to execute the same judgement because the people of the Lord had become unfaithful.

The beautifully renewed and richly adorned second temple, built by King Herod, was about to suffer the same fate. Israel as a nation had wandered away from the Lord and had failed to recognise the time of the Lord visiting His people. He came in the appearance of a servant and was not known by His own. He came into the temple and found that they had turned His house of prayer into a den of thieves. He chased out the merchants and spoke to His people about the Kingdom of God. About the need to repent and to be born again, about heaven and hell, about the only way to God and about the judgement on all those who refused to go that way. He spoke about the cross and resurrection and eternal life.

People listened but did not understand.

As Isaiah in his day was allowed to issue the invitation: 'Ho! Everyone who thirsts, come to the waters; And you who have no money, come, buy and eat. Yes, come, buy wine and milk without money and without price,' so eventually the Lord came to walk among His people and could invite them personally on the great day of the Feast of Tabernacles when He said with emphasis, 'Everyone who thirsts, come to Me and drink.'

The people listened to every word He spoke.

But no one had come to drink.

No one could believe that God in Christ, had come into the world to seek and save the lost.

Woe to you Jerusalem… city of the great King!

CHAPTER 38

HOW MUCH LONGER COULD he hope for the miracle? And on what grounds was he even allowed to hope? Had he not seen with his own eyes how his fellow fighters had desecrated the temple? How they had polluted the whole area and turned it into a battle ground? Had he not seen how they had set the galleries on fire? What else would need to happen to convince him that he'd been completely blind to the facts and deaf to good advice, by staying involved in the revolt?

Yes, he had let himself be misled.

Hassub knew that he could blame no one but himself.

He had lied to himself. He could have known that it was impossible to defeat evil by doing evil. It should have been obvious to him from the outset that this rebellion was not from God. The course of events had only confirmed it.

The temple would be lost. The city was doomed. What would happen to the people? What profit was there from the rivers of blood that had flowed?

Especially in the short breaks, when the battle allowed it, these thoughts terrified him.

Numerous times he had been at the point of following the example of his brothers and withdrawing himself from the battle. Now that it had become clear that the battle was lost and the decisive strike would soon come, Hassub at last made up his mind.

Seeing that the temple was being used as a stronghold, Hassub could no longer fool himself. The words of his uncle Gedor rang in his ears: the ruler of darkness would lead this rebellion. After witnessing so much cruelty and wickedness, Hassub was finally inclined to believe those words. He had abused his own conscience and he regretted that deeply. Only now when it was too late.

But was it too late? Perhaps too late to expect mercy. But not too late to stop participating in this evil. Whatever the consequences, he would no longer cooperate. This time Hassub didn't hesitate and that very night he took the opportunity to escape the temple precincts. He didn't contemplate defecting to the Romans. Even considering the danger that it would entail, he still regarded it as treason...

It had been a long time since he had visited Gedor.

His priority was now to find out the situation of his family and then he would consider what to do next.

The misery he encountered on the way to his parental home, made him shudder. How would his father be? What would he find when he got home?

He understood that for a long time he had lived in a kind of stupor. He had repeatedly supressed the horrific reality by fanatically throwing himself into the battle. He had wanted to silence his conscience.

It hadn't worked.

Despite the remorse that plagued him, he was also grateful for that failure.

When he arrived, it was a relief to see the house of Pagiel in one piece. As far as he could make out in the darkness, it didn't appear to have been plundered.

He had to knock repeatedly and was about to conclude it was deserted when a voice behind the locked door enquired who was outside.

After identifying himself he was quickly admitted. Inside he encountered people he hadn't expected to see. Caleb, Thomas, Gedor and little Joseph.

He wanted to ask about his father but before he could do so, there was a loud hammering on the front door. The others looked at him, startled.

"Is there anyone else with you?" Thomas whispered.

Hassub shook his head.

"Were you being followed?" asked Gedor.

Hassub gestured that he didn't know.

"We'll keep quiet," said Thomas. "Under no circumstances will we open the door."

Again there was a forceful pounding, and they heard Hassub's name being called.

"They're after me," Hassub whispered. "I fled the battle and thought no one noticed but apparently I was followed." He drew his sword. "I can't expect any mercy," he said grimly.

Thomas fetched his iron rod and positioned himself beside the door, ready to strike.

Caleb picked up a small table to use as a defensive shield as well as a weapon.

"Go to the room behind here," Hassub advised his uncle. But Gedor refused and stationed himself opposite the doorway.

The men outside took action and kicked in the door. They didn't immediately storm inside but hesitated in the porch.

"Show yourself, Hassub!" they yelled out.

Gedor saw that there were four of them and signalled it to the others with his fingers.

"Is that the custom in Israel these days?" he asked. "Has the brotherhood completely vanished?"

"Don't talk rubbish!" one of the rebels snarled. "We're here for the deserter. We know he's inside. Show yourself Hassub! Or we'll come and get you!"

"What are we waiting for?" shouted another, who apparently thought they had waited long enough. He leaped into the room with drawn sword but was immediately struck down by Thomas with a blow to the neck. The next man stumbled over the body and crashed to the floor where Caleb knocked him out of action with a well-directed blow. Number three was confronted by Hassub and Thomas who cornered him and struck the sword from his hand. Thinking that the danger had been averted, they saw to their horror that the fourth attacker had grabbed little Joseph. He had taken the boy by the neck and held a knife to his throat!

"Back off, or else I'll slit his throat," he said loudly. There was no doubt that he meant it...!

They all froze.

"Lord, be merciful to us," whispered Gedor.

"How low must a man sink before he abuses a child?" Thomas asked. "Is that your dedication to God? His wrath will be upon you!"

"Not one more word!" the rebel warned.

With a grin he observed their powerlessness.

"Take your sword and finish them off," he said to the man who had been disarmed by Thomas and Hassub. "At the first sign of resistance the boy will cop it... Go for Hassub first. After all, that's who we came for."

"If that's true," said Hassub, "take me with you and let the child go... Don't increase your guilt before the Almighty with a senseless murdering spree."

"Such noble behaviour," the man taunted him, "but the reception we received here must be punished as well... You seem to care rather a lot for your family, Hassub. All right, let's start with them then! Keep the traitor for last, he deserves it," he instructed his companion.

During all that time, Joseph had not uttered a sound. He had followed the events and conversations in dismay. As young lad he had already experienced the need to fight for survival. He felt the unbearable tension in the people he loved and understood that it was unlikely his life would be spared even though they sacrificed their lives for him. For these rebels a life meant nothing. Not even that of a child. He felt it more than he could express it in words. The terrible experiences of the war gave him insight beyond his years. The moment he realised that of all those doomed to death, he was the only one able to do something, he yelled out at the top of his lungs so that he could be heard streets away, "Father Kish!"

His cruel assailant pressed the knife a bit harder and swore at him to stop. "Be quiet!" he growled, "or I'll kill you!"

"You'll die at the same moment!" Thomas promised. His brain was working feverishly. He recognised the opportunity. A terribly small chance that might still be given them, to escape this nightmare. The help would need to come from outside. But it had to be quick!

He hoped that Joseph understood some of it and he prayed that the child would keep on screaming!

The boy showed no intention of stopping. Though his voice was breaking with emotion, he kept on screaming, "Father Kish!... Help! Father Kish!"

"Go on and strike them down man!" the rebel yelled, appearing to lose all his self-control. "And you stop that screaming or..."

Thud!

A muffled smack and the assailant let go of the boy. The knife fell from his hand. He clawed about desperately and then collapsed.

Caleb leapt upon the remaining rebel and knocked him to the ground with the small table. He was the only one who knew instantaneously what had happened. He had kept his eyes trained on the doorway, the only place from which to expect help. And he had seen the barely noticeable shadow appear.

"Father Kish!"

Joseph threw himself into the arms of the man appearing in the doorway. As they saw how lovingly Kish comforted the child, they sensed what many others had previously experienced, and how he had received his nickname. But the image of Simpleton had totally disappeared when he handed Joseph over to Gedor, asking him if he could take the boy to another room.

"We can no longer stay here," he said to the others, "and neither can they," pointing to the slain men.

"I deserted and came here," said Hassub. "I shouldn't have done it. They followed me to punish me. It nearly cost all your lives. I realise it's all my fault."

"Fault..." Kish sighed. He bent over the man whom he had killed by throwing his knife into his back.

"The others are still alive," Caleb noted. "What shall we do with them?"

"Tie them up and take them to a place where they can be found by others?" Thomas suggested.

"Isn't that too risky?" asked Hassub.

"I think so too," said Kish. "We would need to be extra careful if we allowed them to walk around freely again. It seems better to keep them captive till we leave the city."

"And then what?"

"Then we leave them behind. But in such a way that they can't bother us and will need to put in a considerable effort to escape their prison. What else can we do? I assume no one suggests that we kill them?"

"They'll die of starvation anyway," Hassub presumed.

"No, we'll give them some food," said Kish.

"Food?" Hassub asked in disbelief.

Hunger was written all over his face. Suddenly the others noticed that he looked far worse than any of them.

"Plain food," said Kish, "but sufficient to keep them alive… Here, you should eat some too…" He dug into his pouch and produced a small quantity of roasted barley which he held out to Hassub.

The starving man could not believe his eyes. He asked no questions however but quickly gobbled down the food.

Meanwhile they informed him of the passing away of Pagiel and the relationship that had developed between Thomas and Silla.

Kish, together with Caleb had gagged the three rebels and tied up their hands and feet. He had wrapped the dead man in a blanket. After that he told Gedor that Joseph could come in again.

"We can't afford to be seen around here anymore," he said. "You'll have to say your last farewell to your home, Gedor. If there's something you absolutely need to take, get it now. We won't return here. Tirza and Silla must also come now. We'll go to a safer place to await the time of our departure. And you Hassub? Now you must make a choice."

"You saved my life," Hassub responded. "I would be glad to accompany you."

CHAPTER 39

K ISH HAD BROUGHT HIS friends to a fairly spacious room. No one knew exactly where they were, other than somewhere under Jerusalem. Although water and food were available, they had to adjust to primitive living circumstances. Nevertheless, their life below ground was comfortable compared to life in the severely ravaged city above.

A small corner section had been partitioned off for Silla and Tirza, where they could enjoy some privacy when needed.

Joseph adapted to these dark confines as if he had never known anything else. He was not at all afraid. Not during the rather scary nocturnal trip through Jerusalem, nor during the descent into the pitch-black tunnels in which only Kish knew his way.

Hassub had come to respect the man whom he had previously known only by his name and nickname. Initially it had surprised him that the others accepted Kish's leadership as a matter of course. But his amazement had soon turned to admiration. As time went on, he found himself feeling much safer when Kish was around. Simpleton was someone to be respected.

During their forced period of waiting, Gedor wanted to make good use of the time and he kept busy teaching them the Word of God. One of the only things he had taken from his and Pagiel's possessions was the Holy Scriptures.

"After all, only this has lasting value," Gedor said, "the Word of God. It's the anchor for our soul. We must leave behind everything that we've been attached to. The city which we love, where most of us were born and raised… We will abandon it all…

Letting go is something we all will be confronted with, at the end of our lives… It's a good lesson to learn early on.

Nothing will remain but only the Word of God.

As long as the good seed has fallen into good soil, into a heart which the Almighty has prepared for it, we need nothing else for all eternity.

Everything begins with the Word…

The Lord our God is a God Who speaks! He has proclaimed the Word to us. It's a miracle we must be deeply aware of. Even after our fall into sin, He kept speaking to us. Not only to punish and admonish, but especially to draw us near! The Lord is holy and righteous, but also merciful and gracious… In Christ, He came to reconcile the world to Himself…

He has commanded us, believers, to pass on that message to one and all…

Everything was created through the Word…

The Word was with God and the Word is God. The Word is the Life and Light of mankind.

I am reminded of the words of the apostle John: 'And the Word became flesh and dwelt among us, and we beheld His glory, the glory as of the only begotten of the Father, full of grace and truth.'"

For Caleb it was no longer strange to hear someone preach about Jesus Christ being the Son of God, but Hassub had great difficulty with it. It had shocked him to hear that at the end of his life, his father had accepted this teaching as the truth. For him it was unthinkable to confess that the prophecies concerning the Messiah were fulfilled in Jesus Christ. His only memory of Pagiel was as a fanatical opponent to that doctrine.

But Hassub didn't react as in earlier days, when he would become furious and deliberately block his ears. He was considerate of his current companions of whom most were Christians. After all, hadn't they saved his life?

Besides, he couldn't isolate himself from them, since they shared the same living quarters.

Through the circumstances he was more or less forced to listen to his uncle. But it wasn't a punishment because Gedor was a fascinating storyteller.

On top of that, Hassub heard things which made him think.

Jesus of Nazareth had foretold the downfall of Jerusalem and the destruction of the temple and that's exactly what was happening.

Hassub had not wanted, nor been able to believe that God would ever allow it, but the facts were hard to deny as he had personally experienced. Hassub was a defeated man.

He felt deeply disappointed in his rebel comrades whom he had regarded as sacred warriors for the good cause. But he was mostly disappointed in himself, that he had been so blindly carried away. He felt deeply ashamed that he'd tolerated all the injustices for such a long time, carried out in the name of 'fighting for freedom'. For wasn't he also partly to blame?

'Come to Me, all you who labour and are heavy laden, and I will give you rest. Take My yoke upon you and learn from Me, for I am gentle and lowly in heart, and you will find rest for your souls. For My yoke is easy and My burden is light.'

Those are the words which he heard Gedor recite, explaining that they were the words Jesus had spoken.

Rest for his tired and heavy-laden soul… Hassub had to admit that he craved for it...

But when he heard the prayers of his companions, his heart rebelled within him!

It had surprised and touched him that they didn't just pray to the Lord for themselves but also implored the Lord's mercy for the people in general and even for the rebels with whom they had such fundamental differences of opinion, and from whom they could expect nothing but evil…

Yet he was appalled when he heard them pray even for the enemy!

With great difficulty he suppressed his anger but eventually he simply had to ask Thomas about it, who responded that the Lord Jesus had commanded it, saying, 'But I say to you, love your enemies, bless those who curse you, do good to those who hate you, and pray for those who spitefully use you and persecute you.'

"But that is utter nonsense!" Hassub lashed out. "Pray for the Romans? Let them be cursed, those heathens…! I admit that much wrong has been committed on our side, but when I hear you pray like this, my blood begins to boil! It sounds like treason to me!"

He intended to add that he wasn't surprised to hear that this foolishness came from the Nazarene, but he just managed to control himself.

"It's certainly difficult, but not nonsense," said Thomas.

"Oh really? And what would be the sense of it?" Hassub wanted to know.

"That we behave as children of our heavenly Father," Thomas answered.

"How do you mean?"

"Because the Lord sought us while we were still His enemies. He prayed for those who cursed and crucified Him."

"Well, I wasn't part of that! How am I to blame for that?"

"He died for our sins. While we were His enemies."

"I didn't even know Him!" Hassub scoffed.

"That doesn't take away from the fact that you hated Him!" Thomas replied. "Silla told me how scornfully you always spoke about 'that carpenter of Nazareth'. Hassub, if the Lord wants to forgive your and my sins, is He not justified in commanding us in turn to pray for our enemies? What others have done to us can't begin to compare with what we've done to the Most High God!"

"You're talking about the crucifixion…?"

"No, the cause of it… That which made the suffering and death of our Messiah necessary to save us from eternal death. Otherwise we would have been lost for eternity, Hassub!"

For a moment it seemed as if Hassub would lose his temper, but he seemed to reconsider.

"Let's stop talking about this," he responded with a sigh.

"As you wish," was Thomas' friendly reply. He understood that for now his future brother-in-law had enough to think about.

Although Joseph was only 7 years old, he was no longer a child. His young eyes had already witnessed more misery than many an elderly person. The psychological damage he had suffered, ran deep. Through the harsh lessons of life, he had learned to be careful and withdrawn. He wouldn't easily crawl onto someone's lap.

At least, that's how it had been when Kish had brought him to Silla as a wounded bird. The care for his little sister had kept him alive, but when she died, all connection with life seemed lost. He was near to death when Silla received him into her care.

Since then, he didn't freely and openly trust people anymore, but he would gladly sit with Silla.

She told him about the good Shepherd Who searched for the lost lamb till He found it and joyfully carried it on His shoulders back to the flock. Of the Messiah Who hardly ever got angry, except perhaps when people wanted to keep children away from Him. The disciples had once done that, and He had not been happy with them. For He wanted the children to come to Him…

Joseph could spend hours listening to her.

He would drift off with a gleam in his eyes, as children do when they hear and see things that only children understand…

"The Lord wants us to believe in Him as little children," Gedor taught the adults. "He even said that if we refused to be changed and become as little children, we would by no means enter the Kingdom of heaven."

Apart from listening, Joseph could also rattle off a hundred and one questions about the things Silla had told him.

"More questions than a thousand wise rabbis could ever answer," she declared smiling.

His trust in her seemed boundless. Whatever Silla said was the truth. Even Kish couldn't change it, even though the boy was strongly attached to him. Aunt Silla and father Kish were his favourites.

"One could easily become jealous of that devotion," said Tirza.

"When I see how the little boy loves you, I do become jealous," Thomas whispered to Silla as he stroked the curls which escaped from her headscarf and kissed her forehead.

Silla smiled and stroked his cheek.

Their circumstances didn't give much opportunity for a couple in love to show endearment. Nor for uttering words intended only for each other's ears.

But hand in hand, they dreamed of a future of uninterrupted joy, of a peaceful land, a place to live where they could be on their own and have time just for one another…

The relationship between Joseph and Silla, which everyone enjoyed, also made Thomas long to start his own family. He could already imagine Silla with their children… And he prayed that soon they would be allowed to experience it.

"You don't need to be jealous," Silla whispered in his ear. Her beautiful eyes shone. "I'll always be yours."

"We must have a serious talk," Kish said.

Expectantly Joseph turned to him, straightening his back to indicate that he would take it like a man.

"It won't be long before we're on our way, Joseph. We'll leave the city by night, and we'll have to walk very far and very long. I know that you're a strong lad and that you'll do your best. But we must cross difficult terrain and at times I'll have to carry you."

"But I'm able to walk," said Joseph.

"I thought you would say that," said Kish. "That's why I wanted to talk to you now… You're a brave boy Joseph, but we take longer strides than you and at times that will be very important. You would be a tremendous help if you simply do as I tell you without asking why. For we not only need to hurry; we must also keep really quiet. If somebody hears us, we can be in great danger. Do you understand that?"

Joseph nodded, "As long as you stay with me."

"You can count on that!" said Kish and held out his hand.

The boy, full of trust, laid his little hand in his.

"I shall miss Jerusalem," said Thomas. "We've lived here for generations, and we've all been potters. My father and his father, my grandfather and great-grandfather and his father… I would have to ask my father how many generations back that goes because he would know it exactly."

"All potters?" asked Caleb.

"All potters," repeated Thomas. "And all in Jerusalem… It's a beautiful craft… But it didn't appeal to my younger brother Joseph."

"So he wasn't keen?"

"No, but he also lacked the skills, I think. He'll probably become a salesman. That seems to suit him better… We'll surely miss Jerusalem. If you're born here, nothing compares to it, Caleb… When I would wake up in the morning, I'd listen to the sounds of the city… I always took a few moments to listen…

Cocks began to crow… There was the squeak of a door… that was the neighbour who came outside to take his donkey from the stable. Every day he'd set off very early… and then he would chatter to that animal…big, long stories…

And every morning I'd hear the rumbling of the enormous bronze doors of the holy place, when the Levites opened them… It would take twenty men to do that…!

Those sounds were all so familiar… I would hear my dad downstairs, saying his prayers… And all those noises would swell to become the sounds of the day.

But all that is gone. Now there are different noises.

Then there was the voice of life… now the sounds of death…"

"Titus wants to spare Jerusalem," Caleb commented.

"Says who?"

"That's what I heard," said Caleb. "It's just one of those rumours, but it could be true."

"He won't succeed," said Thomas. "When I hear from Hassub what the rebels did to the temple… They made it into a stronghold. But you witnessed it all anyway, didn't you? No, the Romans won't manage to take the temple undamaged, I don't believe it for a moment. And how can you spare Jerusalem if the temple is destroyed...? What is Jerusalem without a temple...? The words of the Lord are being fulfilled."

"Yes, it certainly looks that way," Caleb admitted.

Kish was the only one who went out each day to stay informed about the situation in the city. He didn't take any risks and stayed off the streets, but he observed the surroundings from a higher vantage point until he considered that the time had come for him to need more detailed information.

"Caleb, I remind you of what I said previously, that you can't afford to be swept away by the attraction of the moment, but I would appreciate it if you could go and assess the situation at the temple. You are very skilled at that. It's not that I don't dare to do it but if something would happen to me it becomes much more difficult for you all to get out of the city."

"You don't have to make excuses," Caleb answered. "Nobody here doubts your courage. You are absolutely right. Especially now, you must stay safe. But I would also like to get out of here alive and I assure you that I won't take any unnecessary risks. I will assess the situation and return to report immediately."

He left when darkness had fallen and returned late at night. As usual, he had lots of information.

"The Romans have been unable to break through the temple wall," he reported. "They tried to get over the wall with ladders but that also failed and cost too many lives. After that Titus laid fire to the gates and that got out of hand, because the galleries caught alight. But Titus ordered his soldiers to quench those fires. That's what they're busy with now."

"What do you make of the current situation?" asked Kish.

"It's extremely critical," Caleb replied. "John certainly won't vacate the temple so it must eventually result in a frontal assault. Perhaps one, maybe two more days and then the final blow will fall."

"We had better expect it to happen at any moment," said Kish. "From now on we'll post a watch. Thomas, you, Hassub and I will take that upon us. When the temple falls, we'll notice it and that's the moment for us to try and escape."

CHAPTER 40

T HE SOLDIERS WHO HAD been ordered by Titus to
extinguish the fires worked like slaves.

Sweating, bedraggled and tormented by the heat of the
smouldering remains of the galleries, they endeavoured to execute
the orders of their commander.

It was a far from pleasant task and their hatred for the enemy
grew by the hour. When the rebels suddenly appeared and attacked
the labouring soldiers, they were so violently repelled that they had
to fall back and beat a hasty retreat.

However, by that time the Romans had reached boiling point
and determinedly chased them not only to the temple gates but
even beyond and into the building!

Then, in the heat of the battle, that most terrible thing happened
which later would be considered as a judgement of God.

One of the Romans, a burning piece of wood in his hand, was
lifted up high by his mates and managed to fling the burning wood
through the small golden gate which gave access to the rooms in the
northern parts of the temple.

By this action, he unwittingly made world history.

Flames immediately shot up and spread. It was the beginning
of a chaos which defies any description.

Fire in the temple!

Loudly screaming Jews came running from everywhere to put
out the fire.

Titus, alerted by the soldiers, rushed to the disaster area and gave orders for the fire to be extinguished immediately. It would still have been possible if it hadn't been for the tumult and chaos that caused no one to take notice of him. All his commands were lost in the terrible noise. His gestures were not understood, or simply ignored. It became impossible for him to prevent the legions who came charging in, from avenging themselves on the enemy. When he understood that the temple could not be saved, he had to satisfy himself and his generals with a quick visit to the holy sanctuary, to glance at those things which were forbidden for anyone but the high priest to look upon.

Everything would go up in flames.

No matter how hard he tried, Titus couldn't save anything from the holy place.

The soldiers destroyed everything they came across.

In the passages people were trampled underfoot.

In their frenzied state the Romans no longer differentiated between rebels and citizens. Anyone crossing their path was struck down.

Loud wailing mingled with deafening war cries. Human blood flowed down the steps of the altar.

The flames rose higher and higher.

The temple was being consumed by fire.

Soldiers plundered whatever they could, often at the risk of their own lives. Not surprisingly, many perished in the attempts. The lust for murder and plunder, knew no bounds. All the surrounding buildings and what remained of the galleries, everything was being destroyed and set alight.

Woe to Jerusalem!

It was the 5th of August in the year 70. Centuries earlier, on the same day, the first temple which Solomon had built was destroyed by fire by the king of Babylon.

"The temple is on fire!"

It seemed as if that terrible cry had woken up the dead. All of Jerusalem stirred!

Anyone who could still find the strength to get up, arose. The streets were filled with people badly scarred by the terrible hardships which they had already suffered for so long.

The news went from house to house, from mouth to mouth, "The temple is burning!"

The people flocked to the temple, shaking, crying, upset and angry.

For the moment they seemed to have forgotten their fears. The danger no longer seemed important. All attention was focussed on the temple where fierce fighting still took place, where thick smoke arose, and flames leapt high.

The fire found plenty to devour.

Beautifully carved woodwork was greedily consumed. The terrible heat caused the heavy stones to crack and burst with loud snapping sounds. Streams of molten gold drizzled into nooks and crannies.

The whole temple mount seemed ablaze.

The gathering crowds could only stand and behold it in dismay. Cries addressed to heaven were mingled with curses directed at the heathens who had caused the fires. Hatred grew stronger. The throngs surged!

The Romans however no longer showed any mercy and unleashed a storm of arrows into the crowds to drive them away.

Hassub was keeping guard when the first signs of fire became visible. He saw smoke ascending and heard the swelling of lamentation which had broken out in the city. And suddenly in the distance, there were the rising flames, reaching to heaven. The noise in the city became a voice: "The temple is on fire!"

Hassub rushed inside to tell the others.

"Let's not all go outside," said Kish. "Try to remain calm… Thomas, Caleb and I will go with Hassub to ascertain what is going on… From here it's not easy to determine if the holy sanctuary is actually burning, or only the surroundings. We'll have a look."

He hurried outside with the others to the vantage point.

Even though they were prepared for it, the sight of the huge fire burning in the distance struck them with dismay.

"God has abandoned us!" Hassub shouted in despair. Tears streamed down his cheeks. He fell on his knees, tore his clothes and sprinkled dust on his head.

"No," said Thomas, "I don't believe that for a moment! 'With many woes the wicked are afflicted'. There in the distance we see the truth of that. 'But those who trust in God are well protected.'"

"Shall I try and get closer so that we can find out exactly what is going on?" asked Caleb.

"As long as you're extremely careful," Kish agreed. "We need solid confirmation that this is the right moment for us to leave."

Caleb went to investigate while the others returned to the shelter. Kish decided a guard was no longer necessary as they anxiously waited for Caleb's return.

He came back in the late afternoon, dirty and sweaty and his clothes smelling of fire. His face expressed great sorrow.

"It is indeed the temple," he related. "Nothing can be done any more. No one is even trying to save it any longer. There's only insane fighting and plundering going on.

Amidst the chaos, soldiers are walking around with all kinds of precious items. Some have draped themselves with gold and jewellery which they've stolen from the temple… It looks like they've gone mad. They're shooting at the crowds gathered there, but people won't disperse despite many dropping dead around them. No sooner are they driven apart than they flock together again…

It's terrible to witness but they are simply drawn to the spectacle. As if they're bewitched… More and more people are gathering. Everyone wants to have a look.

John and his men are defending themselves as though possessed…

If they get a chance, they'll most likely flee into the city to continue fighting. There's nothing to be gained and nothing to lose, yet they just keep going."

When Caleb had finished, Kish spoke decisively, "As soon as darkness falls, we leave. All the attention is now focussed on the temple area. Keep close at hand those things we need to take along. We'll stick to the plan and get ready to leave."

Together Kish and Thomas went to their prisoners.

The three men lay tied up on the ground, in the dark.

"Listen," said Kish, placing the small oil lamp on the floor next to them. "Here's a little food for you."

He took it from his pocket and put it next to the lamp.

"We're going to leave you… On one of you I'll loosen the ropes a little around the wrists, so that with some effort he can free his hands. He can then free the others. Even though you were out to do us harm, we don't want you to die a terrible death. That's why we've given you food, more and better than you're used to.

The love of Christ prevents us from taking revenge. You'd be wise to give that some thought. It's up to Him to repay you for the evil you've done if you do not repent…

Pay attention now and remember what I'm going to tell you because your life depends on it. You'll have to get by in the dark because I'm taking the lamp with me. But if you do exactly as I tell you, you'll be free within an hour.

When your hands are loosed, follow us in the direction we're leaving and go to the end of the passage. Turn right and keep going. It's a long passage which ends up in a small shaft that leads upward and ends in a pit. Work your way up from there, and you'll be in the open air again. You'll easily find your way back to your comrades because the temple is on fire and it's clearly visible. The Romans are busy plundering it."

It was obvious that especially the last news shocked them terribly.

Kish did as he had said and adjusted the wristbands on one of the men so that he would be able to undo them with some considerable effort.

"Aren't you scared that they'll try and find us?" Thomas whispered while they made their way out.

"I wouldn't recommend it," Kish answered. "If they don't follow my instructions, they'll get hopelessly lost and will perish down there. I'm sure they're smarter than that."

"And if they look for us when they're out?"

"I'm not scared of that either. It should be dark by then, so we'll be hard to find. And the way we are going is so well hidden that even in daylight it would be hard to find. Besides, I'm convinced that the fire will grab all their attention. And by then we'll be long gone."

Everyone was ready to go.

Hassub had recovered again although sorrow was written on his face. "We fought against that heathen rabble with knives, stones and sticks," he said. "We resisted them for four years. That's at least something to be proud of."

"And for what benefit?" asked Gedor. "I fear this will mean the end of our Jewish nation, Hassub. So what is there to be proud of? I once overheard one of the rebels saying that it was all in defence of the Torah. What has become of it? At the moment, holy documents are going up in flames and drifting as ashes over the city… The Torah doesn't need to be defended by the sword Hassub. The Torah has no need of that.

A life dedicated to God would have been a much better guarantee for our national existence. The Lord promised David to confirm his kingship if he and those after him would walk in His ways…

To obey is better than sacrifice… The fault lies with us, Hassub, not the Romans. We failed to recognise the time of God's visitation upon His people. Towards the end of his life your father came to understand that. We did not recognise the Messiah because we were looking for someone who would drive out the Romans with a sword. But He came as the Lamb of God to let Himself be slaughtered for our sins.

The temple and Jerusalem are lost to us, and Israel will be scattered like lost sheep among the nations. Read the prophecies – they have foretold it."

Hassub did not say a word. Not that he simply agreed with what Gedor had said, but he felt too downhearted to start a discussion.

"We're going on a journey," Kish told them. "It will be an exodus. But not from the slavery of Egypt. Whereas our forefathers were allowed to travel to the promised land, we must leave the promised land. Only the Lord knows where and for how long."

"Till the time of the heathens are fulfilled," said Gedor. "The Lord has said so. He will show pity and gather Israel and Judah once again. From the east and the west, from the south and the north; from the four ends of the earth. He will gather them to Himself and will pour out over them the Spirit of grace and supplication… Not because we have deserved anything, but the Lord will do it because He is merciful and gracious. He will redeem Israel from all their iniquities, but He says to us through Ezekiel, "'Not for your sake do I do this," says the Lord God, "let it be known to you. Be ashamed and confounded for your own ways, O house of Israel!'"

Thanks be to God there is hope, my children! Jerusalem is the city of the great King.

Would we ever forget Jerusalem? The Lord will certainly never forget…!

Let's pray."

"Yes, let's ask the Lord for His blessing," said Kish.

They all knelt down. Joseph laid his head on Silla's lap and folded his hands…

"Yea, though I walk through the valley of the shadow of death, I will fear no evil; For You are with me…" Gedor began, and a wonderful peace came over them while he prayed.

CHAPTER 41

"**T**HE WAR ISN'T OVER yet, Marius. I don't know what has come over those people, but I fear they won't be satisfied till no stone is left on another. Isn't it sad to see everything go up in flames? And even our own people have gone totally mad. You can be sure that they're making a terrible mess of the place. A lot of people die of gold fever, Marius."

"And of poverty," Marius answered tersely. "To be honest, I wouldn't mind rescuing a handful of something or other from the fire. Who knows what's being lost in the blaze."

"Mostly people," Gaius said sombrely. "As far as that goes, it suits me fine that we've been ordered to keep watch over the gear. I don't feel the need to go up there for a look."

Suddenly he laid his hand on Marius' shoulder.

"I've been thinking a lot about that fellow Kish I told you about…Marius, I want to ask you something… I don't want to order you but I'm asking as a friend. Kish didn't tell me from where he planned to leave the city, but I've been trying to figure out what I would do if I were he."

"Perhaps he's already long gone," Marius commented.

"I don't think so," Gaius answered. "I'm convinced that he'll risk it tonight. If you ask me there won't be a better opportunity. All the attention is focussed on the temple area and it's likely to stay like that for a while. If I were Kish, I would take my chances right now and take a route which we are least likely to monitor. A difficult path most likely. That won't be easy for the people he's taking along."

"You've come to think highly of that man, haven't you?" said Marius. "You're seriously worried about him… I don't think you need to be. From what you've told me about him, he's very capable of looking after himself."

"If he were on his own, I wouldn't worry," growled Gaius. "But that's just it. He isn't alone. He's proven that he can easily get out of the city. But then what? Those friends of his are just ordinary citizens, a group of vulnerable people. They could easily be discovered by a patrol…"

"But you gave them a letter, didn't you?"

"Yes, but I'm not sure it will help when it comes down to it…"

"What do you want from me Gaius?"

"To ask you if you would be willing to go on patrol to make sure Kish and his group get safely past our lines."

"I had an inkling you would say that!… What sort of risk do we take by doing it?"

"No risk at all," answered Gaius. "You just select a bunch of suitable fellows to take along on patrol. If you come across armed refugees, you arrest them and turn them over to a guard post…. But if you come across Kish and his people and they've run into trouble…"

"He will of course show that letter…"

"Perhaps you can then lend him a hand…"

"Gaius, you are so lucky that I can actually read your handwriting!" grinned Marius.

It had become a difficult journey through narrow passages. Kish walked ahead, carrying a small oil lamp to see the way forward. The sparse, flickering light allowed them to avoid tripping on the uneven floors and bumping into sharp rocks protruding from walls and ceilings.

Joseph followed Kish closely, holding onto the hem of his coat and bravely keeping pace.

No one spoke a word. Kish had told them to keep as quiet as possible even while travelling through the underground tunnels.

At last he halted and lifted the lamp to see if anyone had fallen behind. When he was convinced they were all there, he extinguished the light. In total darkness they heard him shift some stones and immediately felt movement in the air around them. The cool breeze indicated that they had reached the open air.

One by one they crawled out through the opening and found themselves in an overgrown pit.

After Kish had closed off the opening he went ahead of them again.

They went down a hillside. As it was a moonless night, they only had the dim light of the stars to guide them on their way.

Although the descent seemed endless Kish didn't appear to be troubled by it and the certainty with which he led the way, inspired the others with confidence. Apart from him, no one knew where they were.

It seemed they were following a path but certainly not a path that was frequently travelled.

Once their eyes were accustomed to the darkness, they saw they were in a ravine. If Joseph had not needed all his attention to see where he was going, the vague shadows on the rock walls around them might have filled him with fear. But Kish was near him, keeping him upright on the occasions when he lost his footing where rocky ground gave way to slippery mud, and Silla followed right behind him. He felt secure in their care.

When at last they reached the bottom of the ravine, Kish stopped to allow for a short rest and to let everyone catch their breath.

"We're not there yet," whispered Joseph.

"No," replied Kish softly, "but you did very well. If you get tired you must tell me, and I will carry you."

"I can still walk a long way by myself," Joseph assured him bravely.

They continued walking throughout the night.

For a long time, whenever they looked back towards Jerusalem, they could see the red glow of the burning temple lighting up the sky.

They made a few more brief stops to rest.

Once, when he thought there was danger ahead, Kish commanded them to hide in the bushes. He had not been mistaken as it turned out to be a night patrol…

It was a tense moment but fortunately the danger passed them by…

When Joseph started showing signs of tiredness, the young men took turns to carry him.

Thomas walked beside Silla with the sleeping boy on his shoulders and a prayer in his heart every step of the way.

Fatigue started to kick in. Kish had warned them that by staying away from the main roads they wouldn't be taking the easiest path.

When dawn started to break Thomas knew that the worst was behind them.

Under the protection of dense shrubbery, Kish ordered them to stop.

"We've made it through," he said simply.

He felt for the letter from Gaius which he had kept under his belt. As yet they had not needed it. Hopefully they wouldn't need it at all.

Had his visit to Gaius been unnecessary?

He consoled himself with the thought that many years ago, David had selected five smooth stones from a creek whereas it turned out that he needed only one…

"So far the Lord has helped us," said Kish. "We'll thank Him and then rest a little while… And let's eat and drink something before we continue."

"Praise the Lord," said Gedor and he kissed Tirza.

"Only a few more days Silla," whispered Thomas, "and we will see our loved ones again, the Lord willing."

He put his arm around her.

"Look up there," Joseph said, pointing up to where the sky displayed a brilliance of colours.

The sun rose brightly in the sky, full of promise for the new day.